Book Cover by Rena Violet

Chapter Illustrations by Marta, Interior Art by Hailey Jane, Spread by K. Jaspersen Designs

1st edition 2026

Also by Brittnay J. Sears

The Left Hand

House of Sin

The Oily Cat Series
Book One

Brittnay J. Sears

Dear Reader,

First and foremost, thank you for choosing to embark on this journey with me. Your support and curiosity mean the world to me, and I hope you find both intrigue and enjoyment within this smutty thriller.

I feel it is essential to address the presence of certain themes and content that may be unsettling. In crafting this story, I have strived to explore complex and sometimes unsettling subjects that reflect the darker shades of the human experience. While my intention is to engage and entertain, I recognize that some passages may provoke discomfort or elicit strong emotional responses.

With this in mind, I have provided a list of trigger warnings on the following page. These themes are integral to the story's development and it's characters.

Your emotional well-being is important to me, and I want you to feel empowered to engage with the text in a way that feels safe and comfortable. If anything becomes overwhelming, take the space you need.

I hope these pages captivate you, break your heart when they must, and seduce you with the beauty I intended to create.

With all my love and wickedness,

Brittnay J. Sears

Trigger Warnings:

Explicit sexual content, including but not limited to:

- Bondage & restraints
- Power dynamics & dominance/submission
- Anal play
- Threesomes and group sexual encounters
- Aggressive/rough sex
- Choking/asphyxiation
- Spanking/impact play
- Humiliation/degradation (verbal & physical)
- Voyeurism/Exhibitionism (the joy of watching)
- Dubious or non-consensual encounters
- Sex in violent context (including murder during sex)

Violence and gore, including but not limited to:

- Dismemberment
- Burning alive
- Torture and other detailed, violent murder scenes
- Graphic descriptions of death and gore
- Physical violence and murder

Other themes include:

- Sexual assault/rape
- Grooming and manipulation
- Child abuse (non graphic)
- Abuse and exploitation of sex workers
- Brothel/sex work setting
- Abuse by clergy
- Blasphemy and sacrilegious imagery
- Crude and graphic language
- Death and Grief (loss of a child, loss of a spouse)
- Racism and discriminatory language

I have done my best to list all possible triggers and sensitive content in this story. However, this list may not cover everything, and readers may still encounter material that is distressing. Please take care and read with caution.

For those who were made to feel unlovable. You were never the problem.

"But I ain't never crossed a man that didn't deserve it"
—Coolio (Gangsters Paradise)

Scan the QR code below to listen to the offical playlist of The Oily Cat Series

"The finest souls are those
who gulped pain and
avoided making others
taste it."
-Nizar Qabbani
AMERICAN
CRAFT BEER

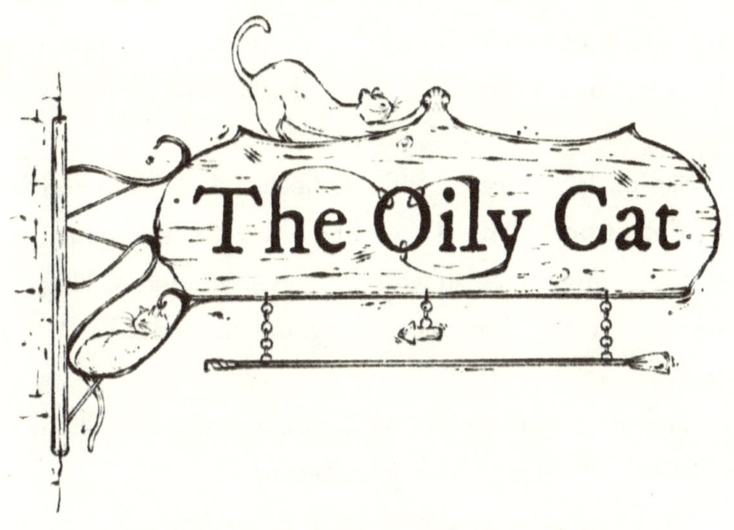

THERE ARE NO HAPPY ENDINGS HERE, ONLY PAID ONES

PROLOGUE

The world ended in fire, though not all at once, and not in any way that made sense when I tried to piece it back together afterward. It came apart slowly, cracking beneath pressure, until everything I knew had split open and left me wandering through what remained, unsure how to live inside it. After the mine collapsed, time lost its shape. Days blurred into one another, and nights stretched on too long, heavy with a silence that settled in after something vital has been taken. I moved through it all as if I didn't quite belong there anymore, like I had been left behind in a life that no longer recognized me.

Before, I had been a wife. A mother. I had known the rhythm of small things. Of warm meals, worn hands, and the steady comfort of a man who came home at dusk smelling of sweat and earth. It hadn't been a grand life, but it had been *mine.*

Then the mountain took him, and everything that followed felt like living in the hollow it left behind.

For a long time, I believed the grief would be the hardest part, that the ache of losing him would be the thing that defined the rest of my life. I didn't yet understand how much worse it could become.

They came in the middle of the night, long after the town had gone quiet. I remember the way the door splintered under their boots. The smell of whiskey. Their cruel laughter. I remember thinking that I should run, but that there was nowhere left to go.

I fought them. I don't think I will ever forget that part, no matter how much I might want to. I screamed until my throat burned, clawed at whatever I could reach, tried to kick until my legs gave out beneath me. But they were bigger, stronger. And the world had already taken everything from me once—what was left to defend?

By the time Emil and Nell found me, I was barely aware of anything at all.

I lay in bed afterward, staring at the ceiling, paralyzed. No matter how hard I scrubbed, how raw I made my skin, I couldn't wash them off. It wasn't just pain; it was a theft. The bruises faded in time, as all bruises do, but what they took was not something that could heal so easily. It settled deeper than that, in a place I could not reach.

There wasn't a dramatic turning point, no sudden clarity or surge of anger that set me on a new path. The change came quietly, almost without my noticing, growing in the empty spaces where everything else had been stripped away. I understood that I could keep drifting as I was, letting what had happened hollow me out until there was nothing left, or I could find some way to shape what remained into something that still belonged to me.

The idea came to me slowly, born out of a need to survive. Butte, Montana, was a mining town, and in every dark corner of it, there were men willing to pay for the things they couldn't find anywhere else. The world of brothels, though hidden, was as old as the town itself. I had never imagined myself stepping into that world. My life before had been far removed from it, sheltered in ways I hadn't fully appreciated until it was gone. But I was no longer that woman.

I started small, the plan in my head taking shape over the course of weeks, although it felt more like years. The old saloon at the edge of town became my starting point. The wood was worn down by years of neglect, the windows clouded with the stale remains of a past life. Still, there was something there I could work with, something I could build from if I was willing to try.

I had no money left, my husband's life insurance hadn't covered much, and my attempts to find work had been met with rejection. So I borrowed what I could, scraping together enough to buy some meager supplies. I bargained in the town square, traded favors, haggled for furniture and linens, anything to make the place livable. I quickly learned how to negotiate, how to smile without meaning it, how to get what I needed from men who thought they were doing me a favor.

Piece by piece, the place began to change. But walls and furniture were not enough to make it what I needed it to be. For that, I needed women.

I found them in the places most people avoided looking, in the corners of the town where hardship had settled. They were not weak, as some liked to believe, but worn down by circumstances that had given them few choices and even fewer chances to reclaim them. What I offered was not perfect, and it was not easy, but it was a kind of control—something many of us had been denied for far too long.

The Oily Cat wasn't a grand name, but it was memorable. There was warmth inside its walls, a sense of intention in every detail, from the heavy curtains to the steady flow of whiskey, to the way the women carried themselves with confidence.

There were rules, too, and they were not suggestions. Respect was not optional, and neither was consent. Payment came before anything else; and any man, or woman, who chose to forget themself was reminded, quickly and without apology, that they did not hold power there.

Over the next several months, my brothel grew in popularity. Men spilled in from the mines every night, half starved for flesh, for comfort, for anything that made them feel bigger than the holes they crawled out of. But no matter how many clients or how much money came in, I couldn't shake the memory of that night, the attack, and the way it had shaped me. The woman I had been before that night was gone forever, buried beneath the ashes of the life I once had.

The Oily Cat was my rebirth, a way to survive in a world that had shown me its darkest side. It wasn't just a business, it was my revenge. My way of taking control when everything had been stolen from me. I thought survival would be the end of the story, but I was wrong.

This is not a story of survival.

This is a story of vengeance.

1

A TRUE GENTLEMAN KNOWS WHEN TO DIE QUIETLY

I rode him until he stopped breathing, the burlap sack stretching beneath my palms each time I tightened my grip. I'd soaked it in aconite the night before and it was still damp, carrying that bitter, metallic scent I'd come to recognize. His wrists and ankles strained against the bindings, the rope biting deeper with every panicked pull, each breath growing more desperate than the last as the poison worked its way through him. Three minutes, that's how long it took. Three long, guttural minutes of my hips rocking in time with the headboard as it thudded against the wall, his gasps wet and uneven, until there was nothing left.

At The Oily Cat, we don't fuss over folks who can't follow the rules. Fussing leads to questions, questions dig up secrets, and secrets get you in trouble.

This place, my place, runs on discretion. But make no mistake: the rules aren't suggestions.

No Glove, No Love.

No Back Talk.

No Dwelling.

No Touching Without Permission.

They're everywhere. Posted in every hallway, every room, carved onto mirrors with lipstick, and framed behind the bar. Ignorance is not an excuse, as they are impossible to miss.

First offense: An introduction to Emil, our bouncer, and a fine equal to your tab.

Second offense: Your body left bruised and broken in the alley.

Third offense: Let's just say that one doesn't make it on the posters.

Lay a hand on my girls without their say, and you'll be gone before dawn. Harm them in any way, and I'll make sure it's the last thing you ever do. So, as I look down at the lifeless man lying before me who had beaten one of my girls until her face was swollen and bloody, I didn't hesitate.

The parlor glows with candlelight, lavender clinging sweetly to the air while sweat, smoke, and desperation fester underneath. The piano rattles out a lively tune, and the room rises to meet it with beer mugs clinking, foam sloshing down arms and onto the floor, and laughter filling the air.

Mr. Cromwell slips in just after sundown, offering the gentleman at the bar a passing word about heading out West. Strangers usually shine too bright in our little brothel, and the moment I see his shoes, I know immediately that he isn't from around here. His coat is tailored, too clean for the miles he claims, and he moves through the doorway without drawing notice from the others. But I catch him the moment he crosses the threshold and there is something about him, something dark. And I don't like it.

He lingers in the center of the room while the others lounge in their chairs, glasses raised in mid-conversation, lost in liquor and laughter. His gaze moves across the parlor, taking in each girl, until it settles on Maeve. I watch him carefully, following the sweep of his eyes as they pass over every detail, noting the way he focuses, and I feel that familiar prickle of unease.

She's wearing a red silk dress edged with black lace, the skirt slit high along her right hip to reveal a matching black lace garter. All my girls are beautiful, but Maeve has an aura that draws attention without effort. Her full lips, almond-shaped green eyes, and copper curls falling softly around her heart-shaped face make her impossible to ignore.

I weave through the crowd, my gaze locked on the new visitor, "Welcome to The Oily Cat," I say, proudly.

He turns, his eyes dark and empty. "Why thank you, Miss . . .?"

"Bernadette," I reply, extending a hand adorned in a sleek ivory silk glove. "But you can call me Birdie."

He takes my hand. "Bridger Cromwell," he says, a grin brushing his lips before he presses a kiss to my knuckles.

"Passing through?"

"Westbound. Just thought I'd treat myself." His chin lifts toward Maeve. "That one of your girls?"

"She is," I confirm.

"She's reeeal pretty," he says, one eyebrow rising as his gaze roams over her.

"They all are. But she's twenty-five for the night, ten more if you want an hour of drinks first, and you buy the round. No exceptions."

He nods, handing over the cash in one fluid motion as I slip it into my bodice and whistle for Maeve.

She takes her time on the stairs, each step measured, her movements smooth, and unhurried.

"This is Mr. Cromwell," I introduce. "He'd like to spend the evening with you."

Maeve's smile is practiced, warm and effortless, captivating in a way that draws people in without question. But she feels the warning in my touch: two quick squeezes at her wrist, our quiet signal here at the brothel, letting her know that this one makes me a bit nervous. She nods, just once, telling me she understands.

I watch their interaction carefully, as there's something in the way he looks at Maeve, a possessiveness that makes my skin crawl. But I can't interfere, not yet. I need him to falter first, to reveal himself, and when he does, I'll be ready.

The upstairs overlooks the lower level, open and exposed. A wooden banister curves along the edge of the second floor, wrapping the space like a frame, with two bedrooms attached to each side.

The rooms upstairs are small and designed for comfort, with heavy curtains framing the windows, offering little light and plenty of privacy. The beds are large, the sheets clean but worn, and the rooms smell faintly of lavender, incense, and the soft lingering scent of the women who have spent countless hours there.

Each room has its own distinct personality, though all share the same dark and intimate atmosphere. Some rooms are draped with satin, the furniture covered in dark lace and velvet cushions. Others are more modest, with only a simple wooden bed and a few chairs. There are small vanity mirrors and dressers, worn down from use, where the girls sit and prepare for their nightly routines, painting their faces with rouge and powder and carefully arranging their hair.

A strange mixture of elegance and grit permeates every corner of The Oily Cat. It is a space where men, and women, can escape the dullness of their lives, a place where they can lose themselves in a world of whispered promises and fleeting pleasures. Yet, beneath the surface of every delicate gesture, there is an edge of danger, a reminder that beneath the silk sheets and velvet curtains, there are consequences for those who step out of line.

Maeve and Mr. Cromwell head into the second door on the far-left side of the building. I take a deep breath and let it out slowly before turning my attention back to the bar and the patrons filling it. *I'll check on Maeve in a little while*, I remind myself while smiling in the direction of Elona, who is leaning up against the piano while the crowd of men beg her to dance a little for them.

Elona is wearing the dress I got her for Christmas, a sage-green velvet dress with lace detailing around the bodice that compliments her tan skin. Her long black hair is in a signature tight braid down her back—"The way my people wear it," she says—and her stunning hazel eyes with flecks of gold in them are outlined with charcoal, giving them the illusion of fire. These features, along with her high cheekbones and sharp chin, make Elona desirable to these men. She's like a goddess, and they treat her as such.

I give her a quick wink, and she returns the favor before I walk over to the rowdy table to my left. A group of men, covered in soot from the mines, is seated at the table, with their attention focused on one young man, hunched over in the corner. I walk up to a pile of money being gathered in the center of the table as the older men lay a few slaps on the young man's back.

"How you gentleman doin' tonight?" I ask in my sweetest voice.

The young man hiding in the corner doesn't look up at me, and I'm instead greeted by one of the older three.

"Just fine ma'am, just fine." He cocks his head in the young man's direction and says, "This here is Timothy. He just started at the mine this week, and we thought we would welcome him by paying for his first whore."

I take my hands off my hips and walk around the table to face young Timothy, who looks so much like my boy that it takes my breath away.

"Pleased to meet you, Timothy," I say, holding my hand out. He takes it and looks up at me with shy eyes, and I crouch down so we are face-to-face.

"You know, you don't have to sleep with anyone if you aren't ready," I whisper, so that the other men can't hear. "You could always just tell them that's what happened," I suggest, quickly tipping my head towards the three men at the table with the pile of cash. This seems to capture his attention, and he gives me the slightest smile before nodding in agreement.

"Good," I say while patting his hand and standing back up. This time when I speak, it's louder so that the entire table hears me.

"I have a real pretty young thing that I'd like to introduce you to." And I whistle for Violet to come over to the table. Violet is the youngest girl at The Oily Cat, with baby blue eyes, blond hair, and innocent features. She resembles a Victorian doll with her youthfulness and perfectly smooth pale skin.

I introduce the two of them, making sure to explain the rules to our newcomer. "Violet, this is Timothy," I say before adding, "he's a little shy and was hoping to spend the evening with you, if that's alright?" I never make my girls go with someone they aren't interested in. It is always their choice. Violet looks at Timothy for a moment before a sweet smile creeps onto her face and she nods in acceptance.

"Timothy, honey, Violet charges fifteen dollars for the night and an extra ten dollars for an hour of talking and getting to know one another at the bar before heading upstairs."

He gives me an eager nod, and the guys at the table grin proudly. They hand Timothy the pile of money that they pooled together, and he hands it over to me. I count it out loud and find that there is an extra five dollars. The men hold their hands out as if expecting me to return it, but instead I tuck it in between my breasts and say, "I'll take this as my finder's fee. Appreciate you gentlemen stepping into The Oily

Cat this evening, and if you should need any other services, you know where to find me." I give them a look that says, *Try me*, before defeat etches itself across their faces and they turn back in their seats toward one another, drinking what remains in their mugs.

I steer Violet and Timothy toward two empty stools at the bar counter and encourage them to get to know one another before excusing myself to check up on Maeve and Mr. Cromwell. Gathering my skirt in my hands, I climb the stairs, pausing just outside the second door on the right, just in time to hear it.

Crack!

A sound that doesn't belong to sex and a whimper that does not come from pleasure. I compose myself, then open the door and step inside.

"Mr. Cromwell! I hope you don't mind that I let myself . . ." I don't even get the full sentence out before I'm paralyzed by the image before me. Maeve is kneeling off to one side of the bed, trying to bring herself to stand, but her eye is swollen shut and I can't tell if the blood that is dripping down her face and onto her breasts is from her nose or her mouth—both of which are bleeding steadily. Her dress is torn, and bruises are already starting to form around her wrists and the bite marks covering her breasts.

"We're just having a little fun," Mr. Cromwell explains, looking from Maeve and back toward me. "Aren't we, sweetheart?" He asks her.

She turns in my direction, but with only one good eye and the other swollen shut, I doubt she sees me clearly. Still, I move to her, burying the fury I feel for Mr. Cromwell. He'll see it soon enough.

I say nothing as I reach her, drape the bed blanket around her trembling shoulders, and press a kiss to her temple.

"I'll take care of this," I whisper.

Then I guide her gently to the door, hand steady on her back, and once she's through, I close it softly behind her.

"Now, I paid good money," Mr. Cromwell snaps. "I expect my full night."

I let out a soft, almost imperceptible huff and turn to face him, schooling my features into something sweet before I offer up a smile. "Of course," I say gently. "Let me make it up to you."

I clasp my hands behind my back, tilt my head just enough to seem playful, and meet his gaze with icy-blue eyes peeking through my lashes. He pretends to be annoyed, like this is all beneath him, but I see the shift. The glint that tells me I have piqued his interest. *Game on, bitch.*

I wait, letting him make the first move, which doesn't take long. He steps toward me slowly, that repulsive grin spreading across his face as he strokes himself, already imagining he's in control. "How do you want me?" I ask, voice soft and laced with practiced shyness, playing the game that will ultimately end his life.

"On your knees," he demands, and I drop down slowly, holding his gaze the entire time.

His hand snakes to the back of my head, fingers tangling in my hair before clenching tight. Then, without warning, he forces himself into my mouth with a brutal thrust that brings tears to my eyes. I close them instinctively, trying to steady my breath. My throat tightens, my body tenses, but I push the reaction down. I will myself not to gag, not to flinch, not to give him the satisfaction of seeing me in pain.

"Open your eyes," he grunts.

Looking up at him, I see his cold eyes watching me, pinning me in place. I wrap my left hand around the back of his thigh, fingers digging into the warmth of his skin, while my right grips him firmly at the base, matching the slow rhythm of my mouth as it moves back and forth, steady and controlled. I want him to feel every inch of my defiance that I've disguised as obedience.

Just before I pull away, I drag a firm flick of my tongue over the tip, watching his expression shift between pleasure and restraint. I keep my hand moving over him, slower now, tracking the subtle changes in his breathing.

"Lay down," I direct, nodding toward the bed. There's a pause as a subtle flicker of resistance flashes in his eyes before he sighs and finally gives in.

I cross the room and kneel before the dresser, easing the bottom drawer open with a soft scrape. Inside, a burlap sack waits exactly where I left it, its rough fibers slightly stained. I keep my silk gloves on, knowing better than to let the poison touch my skin. Carefully, I reach in and pull out four neatly coiled lengths of rope. Behind me, his voice rises with disgusting enthusiasm.

"Think you'll be able to take all of me?"

I force a smile he can't see. "Oh, I'm sure I can manage," I say over my shoulder, just before slamming the drawer shut a little harder than I meant to.

"Whatchu got there, sweet pea?" He asks, eyeing the bag in my hand.

He's sprawled out in the center of the bed while he slowly strokes himself, eager for my return. *Eager to meet his maker*, I think as a devious smile spreads across my face, a smile that he misinterprets entirely.

"I thought we could really have some fun tonight, Mr. Cromwell. Maybe test our limits a bit?" I suggest, reaching down to grab his ankle. With swift, practiced fingers, I tie it to the bedpost using the first rope from the sack. He kicks his feet in excitement, wild and eager, while I quickly mask the wave of revulsion that threatens to spill across my face.

Once his hands and ankles are securely bound to the bedposts, I climb on top of him, pulling the skirt of my dress up as I reach around to guide him into position before sliding down onto him. He lets out a satisfied moan when the entirety of him enters me.

"Pull down your top so I can see your tits," he growls, and I tug the satin string cinching my bodice until it slips free, falling softly to my hips.

He watches my breasts bounce, licking his lips in desperation to bite them. "Do you want these?" I ask while letting him slip in and out of me.

"Please?" He begs, and I lean down in front of him just out of reach so he can feel the soft skin brush against his mouth.

He lets out an annoyed laugh that tells me that my teasing is making him angry. "I said please! You stupid bitch."

I pause my rhythm and look down at him with displeasure on my face. "Tsk, tsk, Mr. Cromwell. That is no way to speak to a lady. Especially one who has you in such a vulnerable position," I scold.

"You are no lady!" He spits. "You're just a whore!"

I nod in agreement. "You're right," I purr, letting the words linger. "Now, how about we make good on our arrangement . . . and have a little fun? I've got a trick I've been dying to try. If you don't like it, I'll untie you—no harm done, full refund. Deal?

He nods, curiosity flashing in his eyes as he runs through every possible way the night could end. But I'm betting there's one possibility he hasn't considered, the one that's about to become reality.

"Good." I keep riding him, even though he's already starting to soften from the lack of stimulation. My hand slides up to his neck, fingers curling around the spot just beneath his jaw—right where the pulse flutters. I press there, not hard enough to hurt, just enough to remind him who's in control. "Do you like that?" My voice is low, almost teasing, but there's steel beneath the softness.

He nods slightly, a small, hesitant motion that only fuels my intent. "The neck's full of pressure points," I murmur, fingers gliding along his throat. "Delicate little switches, tucked beneath skin and bone." I drag my hand lower. "Higher up, it's comfort. Lower . . ." My fingers find the spot. "And it becomes something else entirely." I shrug, casual despite the grip tightening around his neck. My tone flattens, almost clinical. "It's all about where you squeeze and how long you hold. Most men never realize how easy they are to unravel. Just two fingers and a little nerve." I press down harder, letting the full weight of my body settle into my grip, squeezing tight enough to cause his body to twist in panic. "How about now?" I ask, voice cold.

He shakes his head, his eyes clouding with worry. A subtle, but unmistakable, crack in his confidence blooms before me, and to my surprise, it brings me a thrill, a burst of satisfaction that warms the edges of my cold, dark heart. I release him slowly, fingers easing away, giving him just enough space.

Then, I refuse him even the mercy of a glance away as I reach behind me for the burlap sack—its coarse fibers snagging lightly on the fine weave of my silk gloves—right where I left it, nestled at the foot of the bed between his legs.

"Did you happen to notice the rules posted around the brothel?" I ask, my tone almost offhand.

He hesitates, throat working before he mutters a rough, reluctant, "Yeah."

"Good!" I say, voice encouraging. "Just wanted to make sure you knew what was comin'."

I don't give him a chance to scream. I throw the sack over his head, the rough fabric suffocating his words before they can leave his mouth. My palm presses hard under his chin, forcing his teeth to grind into his tongue as the poison begins to work. A faint, blood-tinged foam starts to seep through the fabric as his body jerks in desperation, but it's already too late. I tighten my thighs around his hips and torso, locking him in place beneath me as his breath turns ragged, then shallow, then still.

Finally, the struggle fades, leaving only silence as I exhale and relax my hold, give myself a moment before standing. I survey the room, taking in the all-too-familiar scene before setting to work. With the help of Emil, my bouncer and good friend, Mr. Cromwell is out of The Oily Cat just as quickly as he entered it.

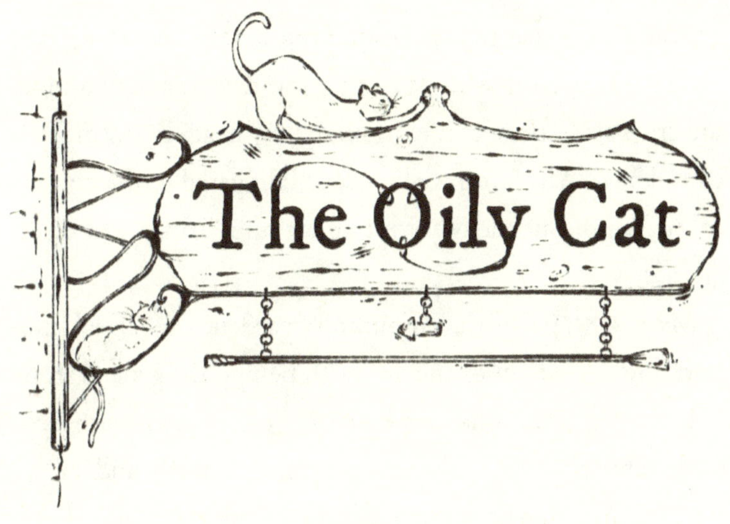

2

FEEDING THE POOR WITH ONE HAND, SLITTING THROATS WITH THE OTHER

The streets were still sleepy, painted gray by the soft wash of early morning. A few miners shuffled toward the mountain with their heads down, while shopkeepers cracked open their doors, sweeping last night's dust out of their thresholds. I moved among them like a shadow, not a part of the morning crowd, but not a stranger either. Just someone with a different kind of work to do.

I pulled my coat tighter around me, a navy-blue thing that had seen too many winters and far too few washings, and let the crisp air settle over me. It cleared my head, or normally it would have. Mr. Cromwell's face still lingered in the corners of my mind, but today wasn't about him. Today was about giving.

My first stop was the community garden, a patch of stubborn life coaxed out of the dry earth behind the general store. It belonged to no one and everyone: old women with bent backs, church ladies with more prayers than teeth, and Tilly, a freckled orphan who thought dandelions were currency. Every week, I brought what I could from The Oily Cat, seeds, tools, money, or just my hands. Most people in town liked to pretend I didn't exist outside of whispered gossip, but Mrs. Barlow, sweet, sturdy, and sharper than anyone gave her credit for, always treated me with kindness.

"Thought you could use a little breakfast, dear," she said, holding out a basket with a still-warm loaf and half a dozen eggs.

"You spoil me." I smiled, taking it with a small curtsy. "But be careful now, you wouldn't want people seeing you being kind to the town whore."

Mrs. Barlow huffed a small laugh, though her eyes softened when she looked at me. "You've done more for this town than most folks ever will. Don't let 'em tell you otherwise."

I nodded, thankful for her kindness. I didn't do what I did for recognition, but coming from her, it landed differently.

We said our goodbyes, and from there I made my way to St. Ann's, the old Catholic church downtown. Inside, it smelled of lemon oil and old parchment, and the wood floors groaned beneath me whenever I walked too fast. I'd spent half my childhood running through these pews, terrorizing nuns, and pestering Father Cyrus with questions no priest should ever have to answer. I spotted him right away, placing hymnals on the benches. He looked almost exactly the same as he had when I was twelve: same gentle eyes, same familiar haircut, though the brown had quietly surrendered to gray.

"Well, well," I said, leaning against a pew with careless ease. "If it isn't the most eligible bachelor in town."

Father Cyrus looked up and grinned. "Bernadette. I assume you're here to pray for forgiveness, or has hell finally frozen over?"

"Oh, Father, you wound me." I clutched my chest dramatically. "Can't a wayward soul just drop in and admire the architecture without being accused of sin?"

He gave me a sideways look, the kind only a man who's known you since you had skinned knees and sticky fingers could give. "With you, I assume sin is already tucked under your arm like a good handbag."

I laughed, delighted by the jab. "You're getting spicy in your old age."

He shrugged, amused. "You're getting predictable in yours."

I smirked, mock offended. "Ouch," I said as I brought a gloved hand to my chest like I'd just been shot, staggering back half a step for theatrical effect.

He chuckled, shaking his head at my drama. Then he set down his stack of books and leaned on the pulpit, watching me with his warm, priestly look that never seemed to demand anything. Just saw straight through people.

"Garden still holding up?" He asked.

"Flourishing," I answered. "The basil's starting to act like it owns the place."

"Must've learned that from you."

I smirked. "It's not easy being queen of both roses and whores, but I manage."

"You always did walk a line no one else dared to draw." There was a moment of silence between us then, comfortable and familiar. "You know," he said gently, "you give more than anyone I know. And still, half this town only sees what they want to."

"Let them," I replied, brushing dust off my skirt. "They can keep their judgment. I've got bread to deliver and bouncers who know how to bury secrets."

Father Cyrus frowned, the corner of his mouth twitching like he couldn't decide whether to scold me or laugh. "You always say things like they are a joke."

I gave him a look, half fond, half daring. "And you always look like you might cry if I don't."

He gave me a knowing smile but didn't press. That's what I loved about Father Cyrus, he knew when to dig and when to leave the dirt where it lay. "I've got more errands," I said, standing. "People to feed, lives to meddle in. You know how it is."

"Of course," he said, still smiling. "You never stop."

I tossed a glance over my shoulder. "Someone's got to keep the world spinning. And I'm not above using a little leverage."

He called out, catching me just as I turned to go. "Bernadette?"

I paused at the doors, hand on the frame.

"You're not fooling me, you know," he said. "I see what you're building, what you're protecting. It matters."

I didn't respond, just offered him a wink and a devilish grin before stepping back into the sunlight.

By midday, I had already fulfilled half a dozen promises. I had given away the last of the garden's produce, a few bags of clothing, and a basket of bread. I had sat with a young girl who was grieving the recent departure of her father, offering her a shoulder to lean on. I'd even met with the constable, slipping him a small sum of money for extra patrols along the town's edge, where the miners sometimes found themselves in trouble.

As I walked back to The Oily Cat, I couldn't help but reflect on how the town viewed me. They saw me as a woman who had fallen from grace, someone to be pitied or scorned. They didn't understand the work I did, the people I helped, the lives I touched, even in my own quiet way. And no matter what they called me—madam, sinner, outcast—I knew what I really was.

A giver.

And, when necessary, a taker.

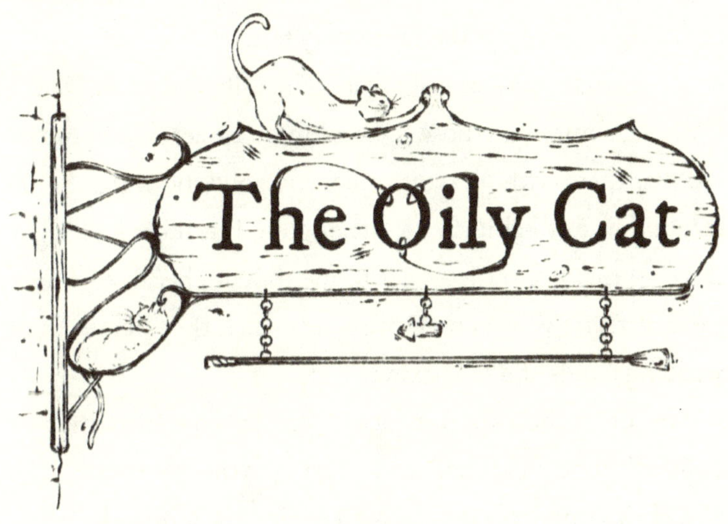

3

...LIKE A WHORE IN CHURCH

On this beautiful Sunday morning I wake early and dress in my finest before heading off to Mass. I run my hand down the front of my cream-colored dress, adorned with a yellow flower pattern throughout, before slipping on my navy coat and pinning a few forget-me-nots onto my breast pocket. My long dark-brown hair is artfully pinned back in a low bun, and my cheeks and lips are dusted with a soft pink, showing off the feminine features of my face. I look like the woman folks used to admire. Now they just look at me sideways.

Status is funny like that. One day you're the belle of the town, the next you're the cautionary tale.

It's an eight-minute walk from The Oily Cat to St. Ann's Catholic Church. In those eight minutes, I greet the townsfolk as I pass them with pleasant smiles and good mornings. Some respond out of habit, some out of guilt, but most look right through me. I don't let it get to me though, because I know their secrets. I've seen their husbands when they pocket their wedding bands and the drawers come off.

The air in the church is dense with incense, the smell of polished wood and candle wax clinging to the stone walls. The pew creaks under my weight as I settle in, smoothing the fabric of my dress, my fingers gently trailing over the forget-me-nots in my pocket. My row is always last to fill, if it fills at all. People would rather stand than sit beside me, and I've made peace with that, but today something's different.

Out of the corner of my eye, I see Emil and his wife, Nell. They shuffle sideways, hands on the wooden bench before them, and nestle up next to me. I offer a surprised yet grateful smile, since I wasn't expecting them to join me today. I continue scanning the room as people deliberately avoid my gaze.

Then it happens.

A ripple moves through the congregation. Whispers rise like steam and I turn to see what has everyone so agape, then I see them: Elona, Violet, and Maeve, walking down the aisle toward me, heads held high. I grip my hands together as a tear betrays me, slipping down my cheek. *Damn them*, I think, *for making me feel so loved in a room full of those who try to shame me*. I'm the only one at the brothel who attends Mass regularly. But today is different, today means something. For them to show up for me makes my heart swell, and a lump of emotion rises in my throat, no matter how hard I try to swallow it down.

Elona blows me a kiss, grinning like a devil in silk. Maeve and Violet smile, radiant despite the hostile location. Maeve's bruises have yellowed, her lip healed, but the shadow of what happened with Mr. Cromwell still hangs between us. Yet her smile, genuine and full, reminds me that we're not just survivors. We're something more . . .we're family. The church stiffens with discomfort. The whores have come to Mass.

With the congregation still in an uproar, Father Cyrus steps up to the pulpit, not waiting for the murmurs to die down. His voice rises above the judgment.

"Jesus sums up the commandments in the Gospel today in two statements," he begins in a commanding voice that I find comforting, like a grandfather sharing advice. "To love God and love our neighbor as ourselves. We have been talking about loving God, and now I want to reflect on loving our neighbor as ourselves." His eyes find mine and the softness there could break a person, if I hadn't already been broken once before. "But sometimes, we almost have a need to be taught by someone in our own time how to love our neighbor as ourselves. I think there is one person in recent years who above all has shown us how to love our neighbor as ourselves, and that person is Mother Katharine Drexel. Again and again, she has spoken about seeing Jesus in others. What we do to others, we do to Jesus. She has helped people in the most awful circumstances."

He pauses and the silence this time feels earned. Nell reaches over and takes my hand, her grip is light and I glance down and notice the gloves, teal linen, with a white dove and tiny pink flowers. I made them for her last Christmas to help cover the burns she hides from the world. The burns she earned because of me. Her touch grounds me, it reminds me that being seen doesn't always mean being judged, sometimes it means being loved.

"Though she grew up in wealth, Katharine always saw her stepmother opening up their home to the poor and distributing food, clothing, and rent assistance to those in need." Father Cyrus continues, pulling me back to the present.

"They would also seek out and visit women who were too afraid to visit their home, to give them charity. After becoming a sister, a suggestion which came directly from the Pope, Katharine gave everything to God, including her entire inheritance, and is spending her life educating and caring for Native and African Americans." Father Cyrus takes a long pause, letting this sink in, before finishing it out.

"Loving like this is finding God hidden in the other person. Loving like this is not judging, but being merciful and trying to understand the other person. Jesus said the Spirit is mightier than the flesh and so with Jesus there is no room for fear, but we can witness the truth with enthusiasm, with love, and humility. So, I encourage you to pray. For to love one another, we must pray much. For prayer gives a clean heart, and a clean heart can see God in our neighbor."

After Father Cyrus finishes his sermon, we take part in the Holy Communion as a way to share in the sacrifice of Christ but also to symbolize and foster unity within our church community. Row by row, the people of Butte file past us. Some mutter, others just stare, their glances razored thin. But Elona, God bless her, meets them with a flick of her tongue and a few scandalous kisses blown into the air. I nearly choke on the wafer trying not to laugh.

Once the church clears out, we gather near the back pews.

"Emil, Nell," I say, taking their hands. "You didn't have to join me today. That must've felt like walking into a furnace."

Nell smiles. "We'd never let you sit through that hell alone."

"Yeah," Violet chimes in. "We're family."

"Supper at my home this evenin'," Maeve announces in her lilting voice. "You won't be spending this day alone." She's talking to me, and I hope she sees how much that means.

Elona wraps me in a hug. "Sorry for antagonizing the hens," she says, referring to her playful blasphemy. "I just won't let them think they're better than you."

I take her face in my hands and press my lips to her forehead. "I love you for it."

Emil quietly places a hand on my shoulder. His eyes stay low, but I feel his grief before I see it. His shoulders tremble.

"Don't you dare, Emil," I whisper, lifting his chin. "Not here. We hold our heads high, just like my boys would've wanted."

He nods. "Yes, ma'am."

Nell wipes the tears from his cheeks, then her own. We stand together a moment longer before they head off, one by one, down the church steps toward home.

I watch them go, letting the hush settle again. "Now to do what I came here to do," I say under my breath. Then I square my shoulders, turn on my heel, and head toward the altar.

Toward Father Cyrus. Toward the place where confession doesn't always mean penance, sometimes it means redemption.

4

FORGIVE ME, FATHER, FOR I'VE KILLED AGAIN

Light stutters against the old confessional walls, as if it too is hesitating to hear what I have to say. I can hear the faint thrum of the church's old pipes, a haunting melody that coils around my words before they're even spoken. Father Cyrus, a steadfast presence, is my anchor to this storm of secrets, sins, and the tangled web of my life.

"Forgive me Father, for I have sinned," I begin, my heart racing with the gravity of my words. "It has been three months since my last confession." I share.

"Jesus, Bernadette!" Father Cyrus sighs loudly, the sound harsh in the hush of the confessional.

Through the dim mesh of the privacy screen, I can just make out the blurred silhouette of his head bowing in exasperation. I don't have to see him clearly to know he's shaking it—his silvery hair catching what little light filters through, gleaming faintly like a halo. Fitting, really, for a true man of the cloth.

"How long do you think you can keep this going?" His tone held genuine concern. "This is Butte, not Babylon, Birdie."

Birdie. He's called me that since I was a girl, running down the aisle for Communion wafers and hiding in the sacristy like it was my own fortress.

"This one had it coming," I say, the bite in my voice sharper than intended. "I couldn't stand by and do nothing. Not after what he did to Maeve."

Silence follows, then the familiar sound of Father Cyrus shifting in his seat. "Did he, now?" He asks gently. "Did he really?"

The question came more as a challenge than judgement.

I lean closer, the scent of old wood and candle wax swirling around me. "He did," I begin, voice low. "He had her cornered, bent by the bed. Her clothes ripped, bite marks covering her chest, already swelling and inflamed. Blood streaked down the front of her body, and I couldn't tell whether it came from her nose or the gashes across her face."

Father Cyrus lets out a slow, ragged breath, that seems to carry a hint of a quiver in it. Whether from sorrow or the fact that this isn't the first time I've confessed something like this, I can't tell. "You do have a knack for finding trouble," he mutters.

"What can I say?" I shrug, exhausted. "Trouble has excellent taste."

"Let me guess . . . you didn't let him walk away."

"Obviously not."

I can almost hear the smile in his voice, despite the seriousness of my confession. "Of course not. What was I expecting? An ordinary confession?"

I chuckle. "Where's the fun in that?"

He sighs. "You've made yourself protector *and* proprietor now, haven't you?"

"I didn't ask for the job," I say, softer now. "But no one else was stepping up."

A pause settles between us, the gravity of our conversation still hanging in the air, until Father Cyrus finally breaks it. "You know, I admire your fire, Birdie, but just once I'd like to hear about you *not* murdering someone to solve a problem."

"It was only *mostly* murder. There was other stuff mixed in there." I grin. "Besides, you love the drama."

A low, rich laugh rumbles from his chest. "You keep the Holy Spirit on its toes, that's for sure. But even you, Bernadette, are not above penance."

"Fine." I sigh dramatically. "Let's do the thing."

I close my eyes and gather the words from memory: "God, I am heartily sorry for having offended you, and I detest all my sins because I dread the loss of Heaven and the pains of Hell; but most of all because they offend You, my God, who are all good and deserving of all my love . . ."

As I finish, I unclasp my hands, blood rushing back into my fingertips while pins and needles crawl across my skin.

"Give thanks to the Lord, for He is good," Father Cyrus adds.

"And His mercy endures forever," I respond, the words rising from my lips like muscle memory, automatic, practiced, and far more comforting than I'd care to admit.

For a moment, there's solace in the cadence, in the familiarity of faith performed. But then Father Cyrus shifts slightly in his seat, a subtle realignment that carries with it a change in atmosphere, and I feel the softness in the room begin to curdle.

"How are you today, Bernadette?" He asks. His voice, barely more than a whisper, is interlaced with a tenderness that feels almost intrusive.

The question, simple and well-meaning, rakes across my skin like sandpaper, and I bristle. "I'm fine," I reply, the words abrupt and precise.

He doesn't challenge the lie, doesn't try to pry it open. Instead, he pivots with the practiced grace of someone used to evasion. "It was lovely to see your friends at Mass today," He offers, his tone softening even further. "That was . . . a beautiful gesture."

A wry smirk curls at the corner of my mouth, uninvited. "Nothing like a gang of whores filling up the pews to really stir the faithful," I say, the sarcasm spilling out before I can tame it.

"They were there for you," He reminds me gently.

"Yeah. They were." I sigh. "And your sermon was beautiful, too. I mean that." I shift uncomfortably in my seat, the wood protesting with a low, splintered creak that seemed louder than it had any right to be and I curse it under my breath.

"I knew you'd like it," he says softly. "If you ever need anything, Birdie . . . I'm always here. Your family—"

"Thank you, Father." The words come too fast and a breath too early. Panic starts to flare up in my chest before I can suppress it, and I know I can't let him finish, not with that pity in his voice that hangs in the air like a noose.

I push myself up from the booth, the old wood groaning under the sudden force of my escape. My body moves before my thoughts can catch up. I take quick, purposeful strides down the center aisle, eyes fixed ahead, refusing to glance left or right, as if acknowledging that the sacred space around me might unravel the last threads of my composure. The church blurs as I pass through it. The polished pews catch glimmers of fading morning light, marble saints watch in mute witness and stained-glass angels cast fractured rainbows across the floor. There is beauty everywhere and yet, none of it touches me.

Then I'm outside.

The door swings shut behind me with a hollow slam that echoes off stone. The sunlight is immediate, warm, blinding; I stand still for a moment, letting it wash over me. My chest heaves once, then again, as I try to remember how to breathe like a person who isn't splintering from the inside.

"Don't let them see you cry, Birdie," I whisper, the sound of my own voice barely audible over the distant rumble of the street. It's tight, threadbare with restraint, but it steadies me just enough.

I close my eyes. Let the warmth of the sun press against my skin. Let the breeze tug at my hair, teasing it loose from the pin that holds it in place. Let the city buzz around me while birds chatter in the trees, leaves skitter along the sidewalk, and a child's laughter rises in the distance.

I inhale. Hold. Exhale. Again. And again.

Get it together, Birdie.

I force a smile and glance around just long enough to be sure no one is watching. Then I take a step forward, then another, back into the living, breathing chaos of Butte. Back into the noise and motion and small-town eyes that always see too much and understand too little.

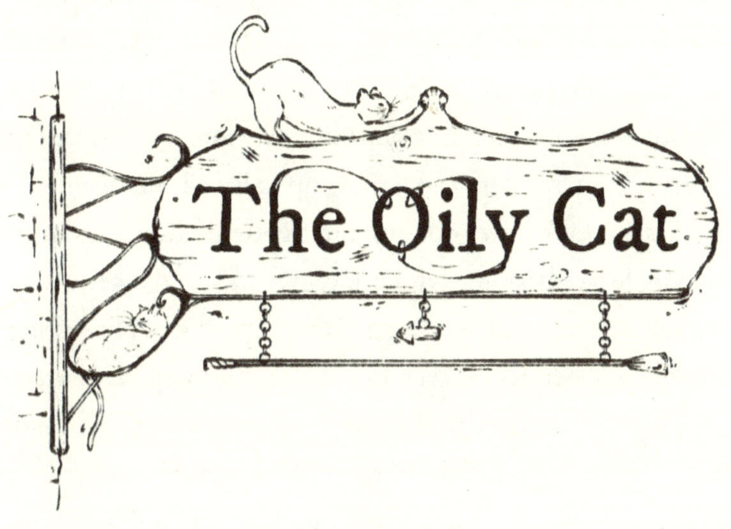

5

THE FAMILY THAT PLAYS TOGETHER...

THEN

"Mama!" The voice called from outside, urgent and full of excitement. I quickly set the dish towel on the counter and headed for the back door.

"What is it, darling?" I asked, walking down the steps into our backyard.

Ray was standing in the grass, glancing over his shoulder with a smile so wide it lit up his whole face. A strand of blond hair fell into his eye, catching the evening light. I'd named him Ray because when he was born, he felt like sunshine, warmth and peace wrapped in a perfect little body. Holding him that first time was like stepping outside after a long winter, feeling the sun kiss your skin, and waking up to life all over again.

"Mama, look how good my aim's gotten!" Ray called out, his whole face beaming with pride, eyes wide and eager.

Half a dozen battered tin cans stood in a crooked line along the old wooden fence, each one dented and weather-beaten, wearing the marks of weeks' worth of ambitious target practice. The fence marked the farthest edge of town, where streets gave way to silence, and the backyard bled into miles of open land—untamed, sun-scorched, and stretching all the way to the horizon.

I knelt beside him, lifting the hem of my skirt out of the dewy grass. Ray pulled his slingshot from his back pocket, his focus fixed, his little body brimming with a kind of determination that seemed far too big for someone so small.

"Watch this," He said, flashing me a sideways grin.

He loaded a yellow-and-white marble into the pouch, squinted with one eye while he adjusted his footing in the grass, and pulled the band back with steady fingers.

I found myself holding my breath alongside him, the whole yard suddenly still, as if even the birds and the breeze had paused to see how this would go.

Thwip.

Ding!

The marble hit dead center, sending the can spinning off the fence with a metallic clatter that rang like victory.

"Did you see that, Mama?!" Ray shouted as he leapt in the air, bursting with pride.

"I sure did," I said, my heart swelling. "That was very impressive, darling."

The slingshot, John's birthday gift to Ray just a few weeks ago, was already well loved. I remembered those quiet nights on the porch, watching John carve the wood, sanding and shaping it while we talked about everything and nothing.

"Daddy did such a good job on that," I said.

Ray nodded, treating the slingshot as though it were more treasure than tool. "Can I try again?" He asked eagerly.

I nodded, settling into the grass beside him. "Remember to breathe," I coached, echoing John's instructions from those nights before.

Ray inhaled deeply, breath caught, his mind honed on the task as he raised the slingshot to eye level. Another marble. Another bullseye.

"Nice shot!" I praised, clapping.

He grinned, then lined up another. I watched as he sent three more marbles flying with the same calm precision, each one knocking the can with a satisfying *clink*.

There was something mesmerizing about it. The way he narrowed his eyes, the flick of his wrist, the little thrill each time the target toppled.

"Alright, mister," I said, glancing at the darkening sky. "Time to get cleaned up and ready for bed. You might not have school tomorrow, but bedtime still stands."

"Awww," he groaned, dragging his feet with exaggerated drama.

I chuckled, unable to help myself. "I know, sweetheart. Being little is no fun at all, is it?"

We stepped through the back door and into the comforting hush of the kitchen, the familiar scent of soap and simmered onions still hanging faintly in the air, when a warm and unmistakable voice met us.

"Who says being little isn't fun?" John called from the base of the stairs, his grin already spreading as he stepped into view.

"Dad!" Ray cried and took off at a sprint, bare feet slapping against the tile.

John dropped into a crouch, arms open wide and ready. Ray launched himself into them, full of momentum and joy.

"I missed you, Daddy!" Ray mumbled against his shoulder.

"I missed you too, buddy."

John stood and reached for me, one arm slipping around my waist as he drew me in close. I leaned in and kissed him, not caring about the fine layer of dust from the mines still clinging to his skin.

He laughed softly, brushing a smudge from my cheek and, in the process, smearing another in its place. "That color suits you," he said, eyes glinting with that same mischief I'd fallen for all those years ago.

I smirked, my eyes twinkling with playfulness as I looked up at him. "Dark like my soul, darling."

"Never," he whispered, voice softening as he stole another kiss, slower this time, more deliberate.

Ray, clearly appalled by this moment of parental affection, let out a theatrical groan. "Gross." He announced, drawing out the word as though it physically pained him.

But the horror didn't last long. With the resilience only kids seem to possess, he immediately launched into a full-speed monologue: "How was it in the mine today? Did anything cool happen? Did you know I don't have school tomorrow? Mrs. Gratty got the stomach bug *in the middle of class*! It was so gross. Like *both ends* gross."

"Ray," I warned, lifting a brow. "Please. Spare us the details."

John huffed a laugh, already slipping back into his role as the steady center of the storm. "Tell you what," he said, crouching just enough to meet Ray's eye. "Why don't we both get cleaned up, and then you can sit with me while I eat supper? You can tell me everything, minus the graphic reenactments."

Ray nodded so hard I worried his head might pop off, then took off upstairs like a shot, the sound of his footsteps carrying down the hallway.

John and I wandered into the living room, our steps slow, unhurried, like we were both resisting the inevitability of the evening winding down. He ran his hands down the front of his jeans, leaving faint streaks of dust in their wake.

"Looks like I brought home a bit of the mine with me," he noted, grinning as he glanced at the smudges.

"You always do," I replied, my smile softening. "Wouldn't have you any other way."

He bent down and kissed my forehead, a familiar gesture that still managed to make something settle in my chest. "Thanks for holding down the fort," he sighed. "You make it look easy."

"It's a team effort," I affirmed, letting my gaze drift toward the stairs, where the aftertones of Ray's laughter still lingered.

In the kitchen, I returned to the stove and carefully ladled steaming soup into the ceramic bowls. It was my grandfather's recipe passed down over the years and a household favorite. Macaroni, hamburger, onions, tomato sauce, and just enough seasoning to taste like a fond memory. Simple, yes, but solid. It was comfort in a pot.

I placed the last bowl on the table, and as I did, the clean scent of pine soap wafted into the room, a subtle signal that John had washed up. A moment later, I felt his arms wrap around my waist from behind, warm and strong and still slightly damp. I leaned back into him without thinking, letting myself rest there just long enough before gently tapping his hand.

"Dinner smells amazing," he said, his voice low, planting a kiss on my neck.

"Well thank ya, darlin'," I drawled.

Heavy footfalls thundered down the stairs, and Ray reappeared in a blur of motion, sliding into his seat with an enthusiasm that always made me smile. His eyes were bright, cheeks still pink from scrubbing, and though he said nothing at first, his whole body practically buzzed with energy.

John settled into the chair beside him, their connection palpable and unspoken. Once upon a time, I had been Ray's whole universe. But lately, I'd noticed the shift, subtle at first, then clearer by the day. He was watching John now, learning from him. Looking to him for answers to questions he didn't even know how to ask yet.

"So," John began, lifting his spoon and blowing gently on the steam, "what'd I miss while I was working away underground?"

"Just some serious slingshot action!" Ray declared, already halfway through his first bite. "I hit *all* the cans. You should've seen it!"

John raised an eyebrow, feigning surprise. "Well damn, guess I've got some competition." A heartbeat passed as he considered his words. "Since you don't have school tomorrow . . . what do you think? Want to come help out at the mine?"

Ray's jaw dropped, eyes wide in disbelief, but before he could say a word, John turned to me, the unspoken question hanging in the air between us.

"If that's alright with your mother?" He asked, his tone gentle, but with that sly twinkle in his eye that always managed to charm us both.

Ray was frozen in place, not even breathing, hope practically vibrating under his skin. His whole body leaned into the silence, waiting.

I gave a small shrug, my voice casual, but my chest warm with affection. "Sure," I said, looking between them, "I'm fine with that."

In an instant, Ray launched himself out of his chair and flew across the room, arms flung wide, crashing into me with the kind of reckless, unfiltered love only a child can give. His arms wrapped around my neck so tightly it bordered on strangulation, but I laughed anyway, holding on as tightly as he did.

"Thank you, thank you, thank you," he chanted, breathless, the words tumbling out in a blur.

Then, as if suddenly remembering that he was almost a man, or at least believed himself to be, he pulled back, cleared his throat, and offered a more composed "Thanks" in a voice an octave lower than usual.

John and I caught each other's eyes across the table, and in that shared glance, something passed between us—recognition, pride, amusement, and a tenderness that needed no words. We both smiled, and seeing John reflecting my smile filled me from the inside, and everything else vanished.

That moment right there . . . that was the kind of thing I'd carry with me always. The magic of a Tuesday night. A bowl of soup passed hand to hand. A well-aimed shot. A boy so full of gratitude it nearly burst out of him, and a house alive with laughter and love.

6

TEN LITTLE PIGGIES, CATNIP, AND THE SKID MARKS THAT RUINED IT ALL

The short walk to Maeve's house was a welcome one. With each step, I felt the heaviness in my chest loosen just a little, and I focused on the present instead: the people who loved me, the warmth waiting inside Maeve's home, and the meal that would fill more than just my stomach.

Maeve came from money, *serious* money. Her family's ties to the Irish monarchy gave her more than wealth; they gave her access to a world most people only read about in books, and her home reflected that. A neoclassical mansion built just four years ago in 1906, its red bricks gleaming beneath the glow of the streetlamps and bright white pillars framing the entrance.

I didn't bother with the iron wolf door knocker, its gleaming eyes always watching. Instead, I turned the brass handle and stepped inside. The entry hall was still, except for the faint voices drifting from above. Candles danced in the sconces, casting soft shadows across the polished marble, and the scent of sandalwood layered with vetiver lingered in the air.

My heels touched the floor without a sound, each step steady and unhurried as I moved through the archway, the hem of my dress grazing the edge of the rug as I approached the staircase. Upstairs, the ballroom overlooked the front patio. Warm light spilled through the tall windows, skimming the polished floors like liquid gold. Violet spotted me first.

"Birdie!" She called out, beaming. Her hair was pulled into a long French braid, giving her an almost girlish glow.

All eyes turned toward me. A flutter of nerves sparked in my chest, but their warmth anchored me. Maeve, Elona, Violet, Emil, and Nell: My chosen family. The ones who pulled me back from the brink.

I moved to the grand oval table, hugging each of them in turn with a smile, a glance, and a silent thank you at every stop. I slid into the green velvet chair at the head of the table. Maeve had placed sunflowers in the center, my favorite flower.

Maeve broke the silence, eyes sparkling with amusement. "Well, Mass was a joyfully devious experience. I quite enjoyed the attention. Loads of familiar faces, male *and* female." She wiggled her brows and winked.

Violet laughed. "I bet our presence will cause a busy week at The Oily Cat. Can't say I'm complaining."

"Oh, there'll be a rush for sure," Elona added. "I'm *certain* I saw some stiff pants on the way out."

Everyone laughed, myself included, and the tightness in my chest from the day softened. This kind of easy teasing, this *camaraderie*, was balm for a soul too often left raw.

But then Emil's voice broke through the chatter. "May I say grace?"

Normally, I would have given the blessing, but not tonight. Tonight, I needed to let someone else carry it. I nodded.

Silence fell and we joined hands, Violet to my right, Elona to my left. Their touch was grounding, a wordless assurance saying, *We've got you.*

Emil began. "Bless us, O Lord, and these, Thy gifts, which we are about to receive from Thy bounty. Bless The Oily Cat in the upcoming week so that we may prosper. Watch over Maeve, Elona, and Violet while they're behind closed doors with the men and women of Your making. Watch over my wife, Nell, who so dutifully follows in Your word."

I could tell my name was next—the slight pause in his prayer, the crack in his voice, the way both girls on either side of me were rubbing my hand with their thumbs like they already knew.

"And Lord, please hold Bernadette close to Your heart tonight. For as You know, she will need to feel Your love and comfort more now than ever."

His words stung and I blinked hard. I couldn't fall apart, not yet, and certainly not here. "Amen." Emil whispered, barely louder than a breath.

"Amen." we repeated in unison, the word rippling softly through the room like the closing of a prayer and the opening of a wound.

I drew in a breath, letting the stew's aroma fill the space around us, rich and earthy, the unmistakable scent of Guinness beer and slow-roasted meat. My stomach gave a low growl in protest, but it was difficult not to focus on the deep emotion within my being that the day represented.

We ate in silence, the soft clink of silverware the only sound in the room. I reached for my napkin, soft linen edged with delicate Celtic knots, Maeve's embroidery. Each thread precise and thoughtful. Eventually, I found my voice. "Today . . . today marks two years since the worst day of my life," I began, swallowing hard. My throat closed up on the words, but I pushed through, one syllable at a time. "And I just wanted to say thank you. If not for you, Emil, Nell . . ." I looked between them, searching for their eyes. "I wouldn't be here."

The room stilled in the wake of my words. "There was a time," I recalled, my voice barely rising above the gentle scrape of cutlery, "when I welcomed death. When I wanted it. Truly wanted it. And some days . . ." I paused, glancing down at my hands, clenched so tightly in my lap that my knuckles had gone pale. "Some days, I still think about it."

The admission sat there, raw and unguarded. "But you saved me," I continued, forcing the words past the ache in my throat. "All of you. You helped me stand again. You reminded me there was something worth staying for, and I love you for that. I hope you know that. I hope you *feel* it."

My voice cracked on the last word. No one spoke right away. They didn't need to. Their eyes, full of knowing, said enough.

Nell's smile came first, carrying a warmth that spoke volumes. Emil gave me a slow nod, his gaze warm, the gesture simple but grounding.

Eventually, the conversation shifted, and by the grace of God or sheer stubbornness, it found its way to safer ground. Talk turned to the week ahead, to work at The Oily Cat. Clients we loved, clients we merely tolerated, and the usual gossip threaded with stories so wild they bordered on folklore.

"Literal shit," Elona blurted, finger pointed dramatically to the ceiling. "I pulled my finger out of his ass, and there was actual *shit* on it!"

"For fuck's sake," Emil muttered, the edge of his voice cutting as his expression curdled from stoic to disgusted.

We howled. Chairs creaked as bodies doubled over and glasses rattled on the table. I could barely breathe. "What did you expect?" I managed between gasps, my ribs aching. "The man had skid marks in his tighty-whities!"

"Honestly," Violet added, swiping at her eyes with the corner of her sleeve, "that guy should come with a damn warning label. I knew something was off the second he asked for a wet towel and whiskey in the same breath."

Maeve snorted into her wineglass, nearly spilling it. "Ah, sure, he's a lad of refined taste," she said, voice thick with sarcasm. "Clearly."

Elona leaned back in her chair, swirling her wine with one hand, the other draped dramatically across her chest. "You think *that's* bad?" She asked, eyes twinkling. "I had the Meow Man again last week."

Violet gasped so loudly you'd think someone had slapped her. "He's *still* around? I thought he moved to Billings!"

"Nope," Elona said, dragging the word out with all the disdain it deserved. She rolled her eyes so hard I thought they might detach. "Apparently he's back, and he's upgraded his act. This time, he wore a tail. A *tail*. And insisted I call him Sir Whiskerbottom."

Nell stared at me from across the table, eyes wide with horror, and I bit back a laugh. She looked genuinely appalled.

"Ah now, you poor thing," Maeve said between giggles, the corners of her mouth twitching. "Did he at least tip you proper?"

Elona held up a finger, regal as ever. "Generously," she said. "In cat treats."

I choked. Wine nearly sprayed across the table. "You're *lying.*"

"I wish I were. Left an entire bag on the nightstand like it was goddamn currency. Even wrote me a little note: *For the best feline trainer in the Rocky Mountains.*"

Violet was wheezing now, doubled over. "That man's kink is a whole veterinary emergency."

Elona raised her glass. "To fur, fantasy, and fucking delusion."

"Speakin' of emergencies," Maeve chimed in, gazing dramatically at the deep red wine in her crystal glass, "I had Mrs. Thompson again last night."

Violet straightened, blinking. "Wait, *the* Mrs. Thompson?"

"The very one," Maeve confirmed, her voice dripping with amused contempt. Her lips curled into a sly, satisfied smile. "Old money. Smells like rosewater and powdered shame. You know the sort."

"Oh, she's a *riot,*" Elona said, raising an eyebrow. "Didn't she once try to tip you with heirloom earrings?"

"Emeralds, love," Maeve corrected with a wink. "But that's not the point." She dipped her head, voice dropping to a deliciously conspiratorial tone. "The woman enjoys . . . a bit of attention to her toes."

"Elaborate." I demanded.

"I wish you wouldn't," Emil said quickly, his voice tight. Nell scooted a little closer and gave his arm a playful rub, as if to say, *Oh, come on. It's all in good fun.*

Maeve didn't miss a beat. "She has me ride her face. And while I'm bent forward, folded like a paper crane, suck on her toes. Slowly and with intention." She held our gazes, letting the silence build around the image. "After that, I rub a very particular lavender balm into them. Imported from France, mind you. Then, here's the crucial part, she asks me to kiss 'em. One by one. Softly. As though I'm sending each toe off to war."

Violet choked on her wine her face twisting. "I—why?!"

Maeve's shrug was elegant, almost bored. "She says it helps her relax. Helps her open her spirit, whatever that means." She took another sip of her wine, unbothered. "I say . . . it helps me afford cashmere. And I get my clit sucked in the process, so honestly, it's a win-win, aye?"

Elona was practically sobbing with laughter, wiping under her eyes with both hands. "So let me get this straight," she wheezed. "Mrs. Thompson gets her spiritual enlightenment from a face ride and a toe smooch?"

"Oh, aye, she claims it's deeply therapeutic," Maeve said, chin high. "And who am I to be questionin' the self-care rituals of an aristocrat?"

"Self-care?" I cackled.

"You laugh, but she swears it cured her migraines. Every time she moans, '*Maeve, you've got such gifted hands.*' "I'm thinkin', this is exactly how I die rich and slightly disgusted."

Violet leaned back in her chair, the stem of her wineglass dangling between two fingers, her head shaking in disbelief. "I swear to God, Maeve. You've got the strangest regulars."

"They're not strange," Maeve said with mock offense. "They're just . . . uniquely liberated."

"To uniquely liberated!" Elona toasted, holding her glass high.

"To toe-sucking therapy!" I added, laughing so hard I could feel the ache blooming in my sides.

"To emeralds, lotion, and spiritual enlightenment!" Maeve sang like a hymn, clinking her glass against mine with theatrical flourish.

The mood around the table was electric. Safe. Full of joy and memory and the strange intimacy that only shared absurdity can bring. In a place like The Oily Cat, laughter wasn't just levity, it was a survival mechanism, as essential as breath.

I leaned back, the edges of my mouth still curved from laughter, and let the glow of the room sink into me. The stew, the wine, the voices of the people who knew me better than I sometimes knew myself, it all stayed with me, clinging to my skin like warmth from a long bath. The ache in my chest hadn't left, but tonight, here, it didn't define me.

Emil stood with a stretch, his joints cracking in protest. "Always a pleasure, ladies."

"Oh, come on," I teased, smirking. "It's just a bit of shop talk!"

Nell rose with him, slipping her arm through his. "I love these dinners," she said, her voice soft, as if speaking any louder might shatter the moment.

Maeve waved her hand. "Leave the dishes. I'll handle everything."

I stood slowly, hugging each of them one by one. Giving long, tight embraces, like I could absorb a bit of their love into my bones if I just held on long enough.

"Well, my sweets," I said at the door, reluctant to leave the light, "I better be off. I'll see you tomorrow."

"You sure you don't want us to walk you?" Emil asked. His voice carried more than concern—It held the silent fear of someone who *knew* what I carried and how heavy it could get when the night got too still.

I touched his shoulder, grateful. "I'm okay tonight. But thank you."

He hesitated, then nodded.

Outside, the night was calm and crisp. The stars were scattered like broken glass across the sky. The moon, thin and pale, hung low, a waning crescent with just enough light to softly kiss the night.

I filled my lungs with the cool night air, savored the stillness for a moment, and then slowly let it fade. The silence wasn't what scared me, it was my thoughts. And by the time I reached my front door, they were screaming.

I wrenched the door open and rushed inside. The old wood groaned beneath my strain, protesting the intrusion. I slammed the door shut behind me, as if noise could seal the thoughts out of my mind. And then I dropped.

The floor beneath me was cold and unforgiving as I curled into myself, arms tight around my frame, rocking gently. The tears didn't fall all at once. They started slow, hesitant, and then, as though something deep inside me had cracked wide-open, they poured out fast and wild and hot and unstoppable.

My cries echoed in the emptiness, stretching out into the hollow corners of the house.

No one answered.

7

BOOM GOES THE DYNAMITE

THEN

The explosion tore through the entire town of Butte with the fury of God's fist. A thunderous sound that seemed to ripple through every corner of the earth, shaking it to its very core. I felt it first in the soles of my feet, a deep, reverberating hum that rattled through the wooden floorboards beneath me. The picture frame hanging on the wall above the chest in the living room trembled, its thin edges quivering. I watched the glass shudder, my eyes fixated on the family portrait inside, the one showing us on a summer trip to the lake, our smiles captured forever in that moment of innocence, before the world turned cruel.

Then the house shook violently as the walls groaned. Plates burst from the cabinets, smashing against each other in a cascade of shattered porcelain, and a scream caught in my throat. I dropped to the floor instinctively, my body going low as I dove under the coffee table, arms wrapping around my head in a futile attempt to protect myself from the chaos.

Dust rained from the ceiling, the air thickening around me in a murky haze. Everything was sound and no sound—furniture crashing, glass exploding, the low roar of fire, the high shriek of metal splitting. My heartbeat drowned out everything else. My breath was ragged, my heart pounded, and my hands trembled uncontrollably.

And then, silence.

It pressed down harder than the blast did. The absence of noise was suffocating, like the world had gone still just to listen to what had been lost. Smoke curled through the room. The smell of sulfur stung my throat, a sharp, acrid, scent that made my stomach churn. The dust had settled in the wake of the blast, and it now clung to the furniture, to the floors, to my skin. I couldn't focus on anything but the feeling of terror seeping into my chest.

It took a few moments before I could gather the courage to move, to peek out from under the coffee table where I had taken cover. My hands were shaking violently as I pressed against the floor, the wood beneath my palms slick with dust. Slowly, I crawled out from my makeshift shelter, my breath still shallow, my body tense, unwilling to let my guard down.

I continued toward the front door, my feet scraping against the floor as I moved. I didn't dare to stand yet, something in my gut told me to stay low, but the scream that rang out from the street sent a jolt of fear through me. It was high-pitched and full of raw terror. A sound so full of horror it could have stripped the marrow from my bones. I couldn't ignore it.

My pulse quickened and I sprang to my feet in one fluid motion, my breath coming in short, frantic gasps as I shoved open the door. The town was filled with smoke, turning the morning into a gray hell. Fires crackled in the distance and I could hear shouting somewhere beyond the mine. It all felt like a nightmare, but one I couldn't wake up from.

I didn't think, I just ran.

My feet pounded the dirt road with urgency, each step harder than the last, pushing me closer to the mountain. The panic was rising in me, tightening around my ribs. *John, Ray*. Their names rang through my skull, thrumming in my chest. I said them with every breath, every step—as if by calling them could somehow summon them back to me.

The ground tore at my feet, sharp rocks digging in with every step, but I didn't slow down. I didn't care about the pain in my lungs or the burning in my legs. Nothing mattered except getting to them.

I stumbled once, tripping over a large stone in the road, but my momentum carried me forward, and I found my balance again, pushing myself harder. My dress fluttered around my legs, and I barely noticed the dirt smeared across my skin or the way my breath hitched in my chest. All that mattered was for me to get to them.

I reached the mine. Smoke rolled from its mouth like breath from a dying beast. Men stood in front of it, their faces were pale and their expressions grim as they banded together. They formed a wall across the entrance, a wall of grief, and when they saw me coming, they moved to block my way. Their eyes were wide with panic, their hands trembling, and for a moment, I saw the fear in their faces, the same fear that gripped my heart.

I wasn't stopping, though. I couldn't.

I tried to shove past the first group of men, my body crashing into theirs with all the force I could muster. They stumbled back, but they didn't give way. I pushed harder, my hands outstretched as I fought my way toward the second group. "John! Ray!" I screamed, my voice hoarse and raw, but it wasn't enough. The men were all around me now, their hands gripping my arms, holding me back, their voices muffled by the pounding of blood in my ears. "Please!" I begged, but they didn't let me go.

I kicked and clawed, my feet finding purchase on the dirt road as I tried to break free. I felt the heat of tears behind my eyes, the sting of salt as they slid down my cheeks. "Please! I have to get to them! Let me through!" My voice was breaking now, cracking under the grip of terror that was choking me.

The men held me tight, their grasp unyielding.

"John! Ray!" My screams fractured the air as my body shook and my legs gave out beneath me before I collapsed to the ground.

The earth rose up to meet me, hard and unfeeling, as I choked on dust. On despair. My fingers dug into the dirt, but there was nothing to hold onto. Nothing to bring them back. The world around me fell into a muted, distant blur, and I was left with only the crushing weight of my loss. I was a mother trying to outrun her fate. I had lost everything.

Ray's tiny hands would never wrap around mine again. I would never get to hear him say "Love you most," with all the confidence like he was daring the universe to argue after I told him that I loved him more. I'd never get to see who he might have become or if he would have looked just like his father when he got to be his age. And John . . . I would never again find shelter in his arms, never again feel the hush of the world when he looked at me like I was the only light left in it. There would be no growing old together, no silver-haired mornings or tender, wrinkled hands brushing mine. The man I ached for with every breath, the father of my child, the fire in my blood, was now gone.

The sting of the truth slammed into me all at once, engulfing, unrelenting. The mountain had taken them both. The earth had swallowed them whole. And there was nothing I could do. The men around me had fallen silent now. Some bowed their heads, others turned away, unable to bear witness to the unraveling of a mother's heart. A gentle hand touched my shoulder, but I didn't look to see who it belonged to, it didn't matter. No human hand could reach me now, not where I'd gone. I was underwater. Drowning in grief. Suspended in this new reality where nothing would ever be the same again.

I stared at the entrance to the mine, at the black hole that had swallowed everyone I loved. A gaping mouth in the earth, as if hell itself had opened wide and taken them. I used to believe the mountain was alive—majestic, eternal, almost holy. Now, it was a grave. And I hated it for that. My fists clenched against the dirt, and I let my head drop until my forehead touched the ground. A silent offering to whatever gods were listening, or maybe just surrender. I whispered their names again, this time in reverence. Like a prayer. A lullaby I hoped might carry through the rubble and reach them somehow. A final goodbye.

Ray.

John.

I don't know how long I stayed there. Minutes? Hours? The world had lost all sense of time. The sky was darkening, and somewhere in the distance, the church bell began to ring. One for each soul they knew was lost.

One toll. Two. Three.

And then more.

And more.

Until the sound of the bell cracked something inside me I didn't know could still break.

And even though I thought the universe could take no more from me, she would rear her ugly head and prove just how wrong I was.

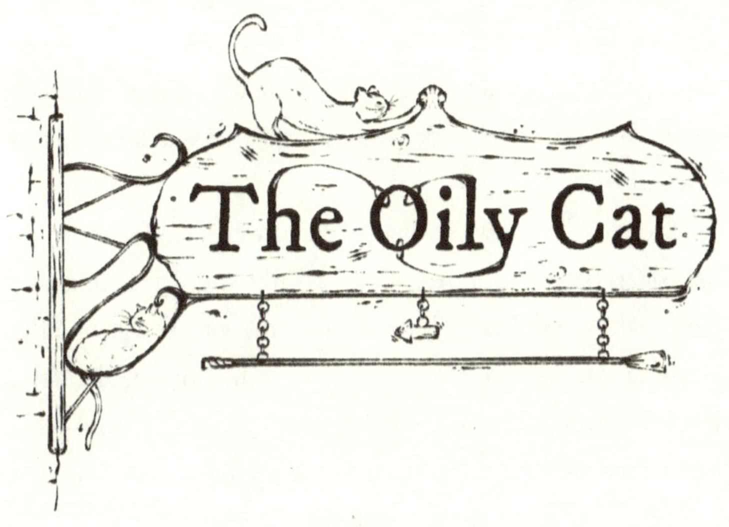

8

SOME MEN PAY IN COIN, THE FOOLISH ONES PAY IN BREATH

One of the many joys of owning my own business is choosing the hours. We don't open our doors to customers until late afternoon, giving Nell and I time to clean and stock the place. It's one of the few times of the day when I feel like the world slows down just enough for me to breathe. The rest of the time, it's a blur of bodies, money, and pleasure; an endless parade of raw, needy energy.

"Good morning, sweets," I call out to Nell as she walks through the front door. The rhythmic clicking of her heels across the floor is oddly comforting, a signal that another day is about to begin.

"Mornin'," she says with a tired but warm smile. She looks like sleep barely touched her—just like me. I glance at her from behind the bar, still focused on the whiskey glasses I'm washing, the scent of soap mixing with the burn of alcohol. I meet her eyes for a moment and know she feels it too—that bone-deep weariness, the kind that clings to you when you live a life that's always one breath ahead of empty.

"Did you get much sleep last night?" She asks while moving through the brothel, already knowing what my response will be.

"Not much, no," I reply, keeping it light. No use trading tired stories. If I were to ask her that question, I know the answer would be the same as mine. "The sheets are hanging in the back," I say, nudging the conversation forward. "They should be dry by now. Could you do a quick run-through of the rooms upstairs for the girls and make sure they're fully stocked on supplies?"

As she nods and moves toward the stairs, I spot the bundle of newspapers she's brought in and left on the counter—editions from New York, Chicago, San Francisco. They're always a few days behind, sometimes weeks, but they're a little indulgence I allow myself: headlines from far-off places, stories of lives I'll never live.

Most mornings I read through them before I touch a bottle or mop, grounding myself in someone else's chaos before diving into my own. But today, I'd come in later than usual, worn thin and slow-moving, so I hadn't had the chance.

"Mind putting those in my office drawer, Nell?" I ask, nodding toward the stack.

She reaches for them, and as she folds the top one in half, I catch a flash of bold type—**SHOCKING SCANDAL**—hovering above a blurred photograph of a gentleman in what looks like evening wear, mid-stride or mid-shame, it's hard to tell.

My eyebrows lift, and I smile to myself. "I do love a good scandal," I utter under my breath, more to the room than to her. "Remind me to read that later."

She doesn't look back, just chuckles softly and disappears upstairs.

By four o' clock, our tasks are done, and the girls start trickling in for what we half-jokingly call our pre-fuck ritual. This sacred rhythm we've carved into the bones of The Oily Cat feels like something holy. A final exhale. Our last little moment of sisterhood before the lights dim and the real performance begins.

Violet is the first to arrive, her lace dress floating around her as if it were a second skin, leaving little to the imagination. It's less a dress and more a statement, and Violet never misses the chance to make one.

I have a soft spot for her. She's wild in all the right ways, a creature of instinct and impulse, the kind of girl who doesn't bend for anyone. And in this line of work, that kind of defiance is more than charm—its armor.

Maeve follows soon after, her lips pressed into a thin line of determination as she slides onto one of the barstools. Elona is last to join, tossing her coat behind the bar as she hurries over to meet the others, her eager energy contagious. I pour five shots of whiskey, sliding them down the bar with practiced ease, making sure not a drop is wasted.

With the shot glasses set before us, I raise my own, my chest swelling with pride. I can't help but drink in each of my girls, taking in their beauty, their grit, their fierce resilience. I've watched them all rise from the streets, each one claiming her throne, queens of their own wild, unyielding domains. And every time I take a moment like this to stop and look at them, I'm left breathless and in awe of the strength they carry.

"Here's to the dicks, tits, and lips that you'll ride tonight. May they know just how lucky they are to get a taste of this." I say, with a playful wink.

"Whoo!" the girls yell in unison, their laughter filling the room like music. We slam our drinks back, the whiskey scorching our throats, lighting a fierce fire beneath our skin.

Maeve slams her palm down on the bar, steadying herself, her face snapping back to that cool, composed steel she wears so well. Next to her, Violet throws an arm in the air like she's swinging an invisible lasso, a wild grin on her lips.

"Let's stir up some trouble, girls—like a goddamn cattle stampede!" She hollers, earning an impressively theatrical eye roll from Nell, who mutters something under her breath about how it's going to be a "long night," though the corners of her mouth betray a smile.

At that moment the front door creaks open and Emil steps inside, boots heavy on the floorboards, his silhouette framed in sunlight.

"Emil!" Elona greets him, her voice sweet as honey, hands immediately on his shoulders for a quick kiss on the cheek. Violet, Maeve, and I follow suit, each of us sharing the same affectionate greeting. Nell's the last to share a kiss, but it's not on his cheek. She presses her lips to his in a kiss that's familiar and tender, full of the kind of love that blooms between soulmates.

"Evenin', ladies," Emil says, tipping his hat and depositing his coat behind the bar. "A man could get used to this treatment. Don't go spoilin' me now."

Nell laughs, smacking him playfully on the shoulder. "You'll be begging for more soon enough."

We spend the last hour running through our plan for the evening. In the corner, the grandfather clock chimes, the melody resonating through the room, a gentle reminder that it's time. Emil makes his way toward the door, boots echoing softly on the worn floorboards. He pauses, hand on the handle, before turning back at us. "You ladies ready?" He asks.

The answer is a resounding "Yes!"

Each of the girls has taken their position by now: Violet perches on the windowsill with her leg dangling off the edge, her lace dress rising to reveal the soft curve of her thigh.

Maeve lounges in her favorite chair, legs spread wide enough to send a clear message to any man brave enough to approach.

Elona stands, one strap of her dress teasingly hanging off her shoulder, ready to pounce on the first man who walks through the door, while I'm leaning against the banister, silently observing the strategy of it all, watching my girls prepare to do what they do best.

The first wave of men floods in, the ones who work down in the mines: regulars with familiar faces. We greet them all by name, our voices sweet and inviting, guiding them to the bar, where Nell waits with a smile and a stiff drink.

The music begins next. In the corner, a man settles at the piano and coaxes out a soft, soothing melody. The sound fills the air, and Violet glides across the room, a drink already in hand. She offers it to the man at the piano before easing down beside him on the cushioned bench. Her fingers dance over the keys, each stroke seductively slow, a show of pure temptation. She arches her back just enough so that the strap of her dress falls a little too far, her breasts pushing up and straining against the lace. The man almost chokes on his beer, and I catch the look in his eyes, the same one I see in the eyes of so many men who walk through these doors. It's a hunger, an overwhelming desire to claim something that's just out of reach.

Meanwhile, Elona is locked on to her target, a tall, broad-shouldered man whose abs, though sadly hidden beneath his shirt, are legendary enough to earn a reputation of their own. Abs that look like they were carved from stone. But it's not his abs that we all talk about. No, it's the way his cock can go for hours, never tiring, never failing. Why any woman would want that kind of endurance, I'll never know. But indeed, he's a rare breed. A man who takes as much delight in giving as he does in taking.

Elona's eyes glint with a knowing desire. She's been circling him like a cat for weeks, and today she'll have her turn to claim him . . . and she'll most likely be walking gingerly for days after. I take care of the business between them, making sure the price is agreed upon before Elona leads him up the stairs, a small, satisfied grin on her face as she takes him by the hand.

I'm about to return to my post when I feel a hand on my ass, followed by a pinch, and I sigh, already knowing what's coming. Turning slowly, I face the man with the lusty eyes and the stupid confidence of someone who thought the rules didn't apply to them.

"Are you up for grabs?" He asks, voice dripping with arrogance.

I point to the wooden sign by the staircase. "Sir, can you go on ahead and tell me what rule number four says?"

He squints, brow furrowed, like reading was suddenly a monumental task. "A-and . . . n-no touching whiii—without pe-permission."

"Good," I say, my voice still sugary sweet. "Say it again, like you actually mean it."

"And no touching without permission," he repeats, a bit edgier this time, his voice losing that lazy slur.

"And below that, we have our consequences, Mr. . . . ?"

"Mr. Tiddly," he says, puffing out his chest like the name means something.

"Mr. Tiddly," I repeat with a razor-thin smile. "It's clear that you've broken one of our rules. And we take rules very seriously at The Oily Cat."

His eyes narrow. "C'mon now, it was just a little pinch. You're really gonna get your knickers in a twist over that?" He huffs, rolling his eyes like a brat denied dessert. "You work in a whorehouse. Thought you girls liked a bit of rough."

That earns a few sidelong glances from the other patrons.

I lean in slightly, dropping my voice to a low simmer. "Isn't it a bit extreme to touch a woman without her permission, Mr. Tiddly?"

"What's extreme is you acting like some kind of queen," he mutters, loud enough for the room to hear. "You think because you've got rules on a wall and a fancy bar, you're better than the rest of us?"

I squared up to him. "No. But I know I'm better than *you*."

His cheeks flush red, but he keeps going, digging in deeper. "What, you get one little business and now you think you're some untouchable bitch?" He sputters. "News flash, sweetheart, underneath all this, you're just another hole."

Then he spits in my face and the room stills.

I don't flinch. Instead, I wipe the saliva off with the back of my hand, then drag it across the hem of my skirt like it was nothing more than dust, never breaking eye contact.

His smirk is gone and that's when I know, I've already won something he doesn't even realize he's lost. "Tsk-tsk, Mr. Tiddly," I whisper, voice low and lethal, every syllable sharp enough to draw blood. "You've just broken rule number three."

I lean in, close enough for him to smell the metallic edge of my perfume. I say it slowly, savoring the moment like the first bite of something forbidden. "No. Back. Talk."

His eyes dart, panic blooming on his face as he starts shaking his head, lips fumbling. "I didn't mean, look, I didn't know . . ."

"Oh, hush now," I coo, my voice syrupy sweet. "It'll be over before you know it."

Behind him, Emil appears, as if summoned by the scent of fear.

Mr. Tiddly's breath hitches, his fight folding in on itself like paper in fire, and I step back just slightly, giving them space. Leaving him to face his consequences.

Because that's the thing about rules. They don't mean much until someone pays the price for breaking them.

Emil's hand wraps around Mr. Tiddly's neck, his grip tightening until the man wheezes, eyes bulging. "Second offense," I say with cruel calm, "you'll be left broken and bleeding in an alleyway." Emil nods once and drags Mr. Tiddly through the back door like he weighs nothing at all. The door slams behind Emil and Mr. Tiddly, the final punctuation to a lesson well learned.

For a moment, the room is still, suspended in silence. Glasses pause in midair, jokes are left half finished, and even the music halts, the pianist's hands frozen above the keys.

But then, like a wick catching flame, life returns.

The piano picks up again, soft at first, then swelling into a sultry, bluesy rhythm that breathes warmth back into the walls. Violet gives a little shimmy where she stands, her smile curling like smoke. "Well, *that* was exciting," she purrs, swaying back toward her piano man, who looks appropriately terrified and aroused.

Elona cackles as she reappears at the top of the stairs, adjusting the strap of her dress with a satisfied glow. "Did I miss the fun, or was that just foreplay for the rest of the evening?"

Maeve lifts her whiskey glass, half full, untouched through the whole ordeal, and tosses it back in one smooth motion. "I give the whole show a solid eight outta ten. Points lost for spitting . . . too predictable."

Nell leans over the bar, casually wiping down the wood like nothing happened. "Don't worry, ladies, he won't be returning. Emil doesn't take out the trash unless he means to leave it somewhere *far* from our doorstep."

I give a small smile then: my girls didn't miss a beat. Storm or no storm, this house belongs to them. To us.

I pull a fresh bottle of whiskey from beneath the counter and refill everyone's glass with a generous pour. The liquid splashes gold under the low lights, catching the glint of sequins, skin, and power.

"Alright, ladies," I shout, raising my glass once more. "To soft beds, hard bodies, and a night that pays more than it takes."

"Cheers!" They chorus, the room once again crackling with warmth and wickedness.

The Oily Cat slips right back into its rhythm, hips swaying, laughter reverberating, drinks flowing like sin in a bottle. More men pour in, all smiles and desperation, none the wiser that the fire they feel between their legs is matched only by the fury and grace of the women who run this place.

Outside, the world might be hard and cruel. But in here? We make our own rules.

And God help the man who dares forget them.

9

IF HEAVEN WON'T HAVE ME, I'LL TAKE A ROOM IN HELL

THEN

I'll be honest, I don't remember much of the funeral. The only thing I can recall is wishing I could be with them, my husband and son. Even surrounded by the mourners, their voices a blur of sympathy and sadness, I felt utterly alone. It was as if I were watching my own life from the outside, trapped in this numb shell that couldn't grieve because it didn't know how. They spoke, and I'm sure their words were kind, but they didn't reach me. I could barely hear them over the thunderous silence inside my own head.

Thinking about it now, I wish I had paid more attention, not just to be present for the sake of my loved ones, but because maybe, just maybe, I would have seen the shadows of what was coming, what they were going to do to me.

The days that followed the funeral blurred together like the tears that stained my pillowcase, each day more unbearable than the last as, neighbors and fellow church members of St. Ann's dropped by with their condolences and casseroles.

I didn't bother with the mundane things that used to be part of my routine—getting dressed, combing my hair, pretending that everything would somehow be okay. I didn't want to live in the world anymore. I was too raw, too exposed, my soul shredded into too many fragments by grief and self-loathing. I had no idea how to move on, and I certainly didn't care to. My only desire was to lose myself in the darkness, to be swallowed whole by it.

So when the knock came, I didn't flinch. I wasn't startled. By then, I'd sunk too far, my mind heavy and sluggish in that thick tar-black fog where nothing mattered, where even the sound of someone at the door was just another ripple in the static. I didn't realize I was moving toward the door until I was already there, hand on the knob, eyes staring at the chipped wood like it might open all on its own.

I heard voices, low and rough, and for a moment, I thought they were imagined. Echoes born from the fractured corners of my mind. But no, there were men out there and they were real. My stomach twisted with something unfamiliar . . . fear, maybe? Or was it dread? It was hard to tell; everything inside me felt like it belonged to someone else.

I held the door handle, my finger numb and unresponsive. Maybe I just wanted to get it over with. Maybe I thought, in my desolation, that nothing could make the world worse than it already was. I didn't expect the door to be shoved open with such force, the copper lock hitting my face with a sickening crack that sent a shock wave of pain through me. I barely had time to register the assault before I was on the floor, my head spinning, a warm trickle of blood running down my cheek.

"Close the door!" One man barked, his voice harsh and distant. A second figure loomed over me, pinning my arms above my head, his knees grinding into my palms as pain shot through me.

"Bernadette . . ." The voice of the third man was like thorns scraping across my skin. "I've had my eye on you for a long time."

The words didn't make sense at first, they were muffled by my own shock, but then . . . my body reacted, because my mind could not. His hand was creeping up under my skirt, and everything inside me screamed.

I fought back. I thrashed and kicked, panic flooding through my veins as I screamed into his grasp. But the man's weight was too much. I was trapped, held down by a force that felt like it was slowly crushing me, making me disappear into nothing. His other hand clamped over my jaw, forcing me to silence myself. All I could do was whimper now, helpless, a prisoner inside my own body.

"You're a beautiful woman, Bernadette, so beautiful," he growled, his breath hot and foul against my ear. "I've always wondered what it would be like to be John . . . to bed you every night. That man didn't know what he had."

I tried to scream, forcing every ragged breath from my lungs, willing sound to rise, to break free and reach someone, anyone who might hear me, who might come. And then I felt him against my hips, his hands, rough and shaking, fumbling at his belt with a clumsy desperation that sent a cold bloom of horror spiraling through me.

My body locked, every nerve frayed and useless, as the instinct to fight drained out of me. The edges of my vision dimmed, curling inward with a grim finality before I closed my eyes, and in that narrowing dark, a single thought clung to me: I didn't know if I could survive what was coming, and I didn't know if I wanted to.

But while he touched me, while he destroyed me in a way I didn't think I'd outlive, a violent sound split the air—a thud, a crack—and my eyes flew open. The man above me froze, confusion flashing across his face, but he didn't have time to make sense of it before a familiar voice filled the room. Emil's voice rang with rage. "Not today!" He growled.

Then he dropped. The man who had been violating me crumpled forward, his body jerking in a grotesque spasm as Emil's hands closed around his throat, tight, and full of fury. The merciless pressure of justice meted out by flesh and bone. And then came the sound. A snap, so jarring and final, that it shattered the silence of the room like a trap springing shut. Swift, brutal, and irrevocable.

For a moment, I lay there, frozen, my mind struggling to catch up with what my eyes had witnessed. The room felt impossibly still, my chest tight, heart hammering in disbelief. The man who had pinned my hands above my head shuffled back, fear making him stumble, before I realized Emil was at my side, his hands steadying me, as he helped me to my feet.

I didn't know if I felt relief or more fear, but as my mind began to clear, I sensed another presence entering the room. Nell, Emil's wife, the woman who worked the bakery stand at our local farmer's market. Her eyes were a mix of burning fury and icy calm as she swung the casserole pan across the face of the second man. The sound of impact was harsh, but the follow-up was worse.

The man stumbled back, stunned, but as he lunged to retaliate, Nell grabbed the oil lantern from the mantle, swinging it through the air with an almost graceful violence. The fire caught him instantly, and in seconds he was covered in flames.

I couldn't tear my eyes away, couldn't stop watching as his screams mixed with the sickening scent of burning flesh. Nell didn't flinch, not once, not even as the fire began to burn her hand, her own pain barely registering on her face as she continued her assault, sending the man sprawling across the kitchen floor.

I didn't know how to process the chaos, how to make sense of the brutality that had erupted within the walls of my own home. My skin ached with the leftover surge of adrenaline, every nerve stretched thin, yet even that physical tremor was nothing compared to the weight of the trauma I'd been carrying for far too many weeks. Everything blurred together—shouts, movement, the smell of blood and fear—too fast for my mind to separate one moment from the next. But when I turned, I saw him, the last man. The one who had helped hold me down. And Emil had him on his knees. His body twisted, broken, positioned like some grotesque offering laid out before me, like a gift. The man's eyes, lit with the first real trace of fear, met mine. But there was no mercy left in me.

I didn't need words. A single motion toward the stairs and a subtle flick of my hand was all it took. Emil understood immediately, as if he'd been waiting for the command all along.

The man jerked back on instinct, panic flashing across his face as his shoulders tightened, his body coiling like he might try to run. But Emil was faster. He moved without hesitation, slipping behind him in one smooth, practiced motion, his arms snapping forward to wrench the man's wrists behind his back before a scream could form. The struggle turned wild and desperate, all flailing limbs and useless resistance, yet Emil handled him with chilling ease. And then the man's head struck the step with a sickening thud that echoed up the staircase.

I drew in a long, steady breath, forcing air into my lungs as I tried to ground myself for what waited ahead. Fury, hate, and desperation churned beneath my skin—a volatile storm with no clear beginning and no end in sight. The emotions surged upward, too powerful to contain, rising until there was nowhere left for them to go but forward.

This was the moment it had all led to, the breaking point, the reckoning. Everything I'd buried, everything I'd endured, converged now with perfect, terrifying clarity, and it had found its target.

With all the rage I could muster, I brought my heel down on his head, once, twice, and lost count after the twelfth stomp. Using my cries of anger and pain be the engine that drove my knee back and forth until there was nothing but splattered brains and shards of skull decorating my floors.

My breath came in short, uneven bursts, my chest rising and falling as the last traces of fury slowly drained from me, leaving behind hollowness and shaking. Emil and Nell didn't speak, didn't move, but their presence held me steady when I might have otherwise unraveled. They understood, without judgment, what had just happened, and somehow, that unspoken understanding was enough to keep me grounded.

For a single biting second, the reality of what I'd done hit me, but I didn't let it take hold. Instead, I turned my focus to Nell. To her injury. To something tangible, something that could still be saved. I swallowed, my throat dry and tight, and when I finally spoke, my voice came out more clipped than I intended "Nell," I said, a sense of urgency in my words, "we need to get that hand tended to."

As I spoke, Emil's attention shifted instantly to his wife, and I watched as his expression changed immediately to concern, softening the hard lines of his face. He stepped toward Nell with urgency, placing a reassuring hand on her shoulder. The gesture was so simple, yet it struck me hard, a stark contrast to the rough, brutal hands I'd just escaped, the ones that had tried to tear me apart. His touch wasn't just gentle, it was loving. Intentional. A tender act of care in the middle of all this wreckage. It reminded me that compassion still existed in the world, even when horror tried its best to drown it out.

I rushed to gather what I needed, moving through the house like a ghost, my mind disjointed. My steps were automatic, driven by necessity rather than thought, as I staggered past the lifeless forms of the men who had taken part in my violation. I collected what I could—carbolated Vaseline, bandages, a bottle of laudanum—the bare essential for tending a wound. My hands trembled as I set them on the kitchen table, glass and tin clinking against the wood.

I turned to her and nodded toward the table, a silent cue that Emil instantly picked up on. He guided her into the chair, his hands firm but careful on her shoulders. I pulled out the chair beside her and sank into it, my movements slow, steadying myself as I prepared to begin.

I worked carefully, peeling away the charred remnants of Nell's shirt where it clung to her raw, blistered skin, my hands trembling even as I forced them to be steady, to be gentle. Out of the corner of my eye, I caught Emil flinch. It was small, barely more than a wince, but it cracked straight through the mask he'd been holding onto. He looked away, jaw tightening, his throat bobbing around words he didn't speak. I sensed it wasn't the injury itself that broke him but the sight of her like this—vulnerable, hurt. And in his eyes, I saw it all: the sorrow, the helplessness, the guilt. He hated that he hadn't been able to stop it.

I kept my focus on the task, knowing that what I was about to see would not be pretty. Nell was trying to hide the pain, but I could see it in the set of her jaw, the way she refused to make a sound, but her eyes gave her away. Without a word, I slid the bottle of laudanum across the table toward her, pushing it within reach. It wasn't a suggestion. She needed it.

When I finished, I leaned back, my eyes trailing over the shape of her hand, now wrapped in clean, white bandages. The sight of it felt like a minor victory in the wake of everything else. My fingers lingered just a moment longer, brushing the edge of her skin, desperate to grasp onto something that could feel like home, before I finally let go.

She sat still, her face carved in stoic control, not a sliver of pain betraying her before her voice broke the silence. "And what about you?" She asked.

I dropped my gaze, letting it settle on the bloodied cloth and scattered remnants of our efforts—anything but her. "What about me?" I echoed, the words softer than I intended. It wasn't an answer, it was a deflection, and we both knew it.

Nell shifted in her seat slightly, bandaged hand resting on the table between us, palm up like an open invitation. "You think you tending my burns is going to stop me from seeing what they did to you?"

My hands stilled, and my jaw tightened as the words rose. "I'm fine," I lied.

Nell leaned forward, her voice low with empathy. "You're not. And it's okay that you're not. But don't go burying it. That kind of pain? It doesn't stay buried, it rots, it eats through the good parts."

I pressed my lips together, to keep everything inside. I didn't have words for it, the *right* words for it. Only fragments, only heat behind my ribs that wouldn't cool. "I feel like I'm . . . leaking," I whispered, surprising myself, "like if I stop moving, it's all gonna pour out of me. Every scream I swallowed, every second I couldn't fight back."

Nell didn't speak right away. Instead, she reached out with her good hand, her fingers brushing mine. "Then don't stop moving," she said gently. "But don't pretend you're not bleeding. We see you, Bernadette. Emil and me, we're not going anywhere."

My throat tightened, and my eyes burned, but I refused to cry. "Thank you," I managed, the words thick on my tongue tasting foreign and heavier than they should have.

Nell gave me a small, tired smile. "You don't have to thank me. You just have to keep going."

I swallowed, taking a shaky breath while the room seemed to grow heavy, steeped in the residue of violence and pain. But Emil's voice yanked me back from the edge of my thoughts.

"Well, what shall we do with these sorry sacks of shit?"

I looked over at Emil, his gaze already fixed on the bodies. There was no space for hesitation or second guessing now. What's done was done.

"I save almost all of my old newspapers and paper bags," I said, the words tumbling out in a single, urgent breath. "We take them out back, cut them into manageable pieces, wrap them into paper bags, and haul them into the mountains. We scatter the remains for the wildlife to feast on. After that, we burn the bags, make sure there's nothing left.

Emil thought on that for a moment and then gave me a nod.

We helped Emil drag the bodies to the backyard, where he hung them upside down beneath the pine tree before slicing their throats. Their blood ran steadily into the tin buckets that had once held soil and fertilizer for my garden. Nell and I stayed behind to clean the house while Emil handled the rest—the cutting, the packaging, the hauling into the mountains under cover of night, and burning the evidence. It was well into the early hours by the time he was finished, and all we could do was sit in the aftermath.

"I have never been more thankful for a casserole in my life," I said, my voice dry, attempting to break the awkward silence with a hint of humor as we sank onto the couch. "It's a shame I never had the chance to taste it, though hearing it collide with his skull was almost satisfying enough."

Emil didn't react. He sat silently beside Nell, his eyes fixed on her bandaged hand, looking utterly spent and drained to the last reserve. Nell offered a faint, barely there, smile.

"We'll be staying here for the night," her voice was firm but kind, and I didn't argue. "And you wouldn't have liked that piece-of-shit casserole anyway." She added with a wink. "But I'll fix you up something real nice tomorrow."

I leaned over and kissed Nell's forehead gently before standing and making my way toward the stairs. As I passed, I gave Emil a look, one filled with unspoken gratitude. "Good night," I said, my voice barely audible as my hand touched the banister.

"Good night," they both replied, their voices merging in soft harmony, as if we had somehow found a fragile moment of peace in the middle of everything.

I scrubbed my skin until it burned. Letting the water run scalding over me, turning my shoulders first pink, then an angry red, but still I didn't stop; I couldn't. I needed to strip their touch off me like it was a film of rot. It felt as though if I just kept going, if I pressed hard enough, stayed under the heat long enough, I might somehow cleanse myself of it entirely.

I wanted to erase them: their breath against my neck, the weight that pinned me, the cruelty that lingered long after they were gone. Yet no matter how fiercely I tried, the water carried nothing away.

The bruises stayed, blooming on the surface of my skin, and when I finally collapsed into bed—skin damp, hair knotted, heart plummeting—the silence wasn't a comfort, it was a cage. My ceiling stared down at me while my mind spun in slow, punishing circles, pulling me deeper into the reality I was too exhausted to escape. I just lay there, haunted, like something freshly buried. And then, when all the numbness had settled, the rage came. It simmered low in my gut, a murderous heat, that only seemed to grow.

"Damn you, John," I whispered into the dark, my voice splintering around his name. "You get heaven. You get Ray. And I'm the one left here with the ache, with the emptiness you left behind, trying to pretend it doesn't tear through me every time I breathe."

And then I cried myself to sleep.

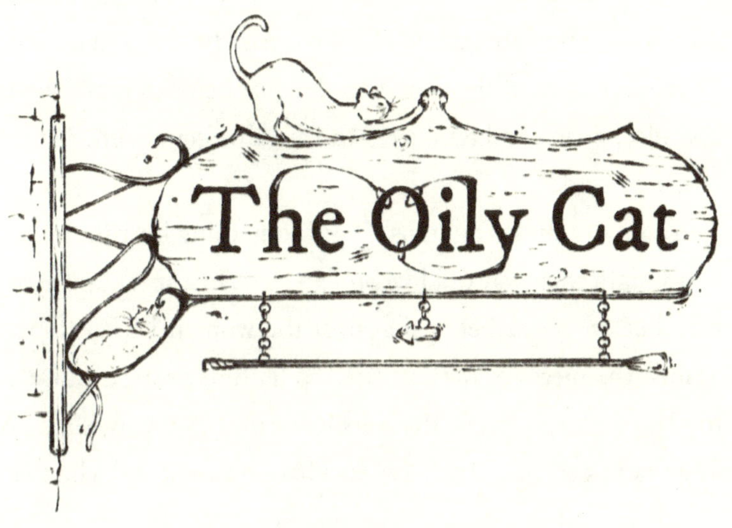

10

FORGIVENESS IS OPTIONAL, BUT BLOOD IS MANDATORY

THEN

"Forgive me, Father, for I have sinned. It's been . . . a long time since my last confession."

My voice barely rises above a whisper in the quiet of the church. I don't know how long it's been—months? Years? Confession was never a door I thought I'd need to open: I'd build my life on careful steps and clean hands, a mosaic of silence with no cracks to spill secrets through.

Father Cyrus doesn't answer right away. For a moment, there's only the faint rustle of his robes as he shifts, followed by the soft creak of the worn wooden seat beneath him. Then his voice, steady and familiar, "You are always welcome in the house of God."

"I . . ." My throat tightens. "I did something horrific." The words fight their way out like broken glass. Just speaking them feels like an act of betrayal against the woman I used to be, against the pieces of her I've tried so hard to protect. But it's too late for loyalty now; that version of me has already slipped away, fading somewhere between what I endured and who I've now become.

The confessional is silent, yet the air feels altered, as if my demons have drawn closer, summoned by the sound of my voice, waiting for the moment it falters so they can take hold and lay claim to what's left of me.

I push the words out. "The worst part is, Father . . . I don't feel guilty." I admit. "I wish I did. God, I wish I did. But I don't." I draw in a slow breath. "And if I'm being honest," I say finally, voice barely above a whisper, "I would do it again."

There's a pause, and when he finally speaks, his voice is edged with caution: "What is it that you did, my child?"

"I murdered three men." I say, and the words feel wrong here, as if the sacred walls shouldn't hold such confessions. And yet, they belong to me now.

Silence seems to fill every corner before he whispers, "Why would you do that?" And something unsteady slips into his voice.

"They hurt me." Just three words. Those were my justifications and I felt them to be enough.

I wait and give him time to say something, anything, but only silence answers. Though I can't see him, I feel the weight of all that he's choosing not to say, pressing heavy through the thin screen that separates us. I don't blame him. Honestly, I'm not sure I could find the words either.

"They broke me," I go on, the words gathering strength now. "They didn't just touch me, they dismantled me. Piece by piece. They took my body, my spirit, and stripped it all away until there was nothing left. I fought them. God, I fought. Every second of it."

And then I tell him everything.

I don't dress it up. I don't offer comfort or euphemisms. I give him the truth, unfiltered, as jagged and ugly as it really was. I tell him how their bodies crashed down on mine, how their hands locked around me, how their laughter, stinging and cruel, sliced deeper than any knife could. I describe the way it felt, being devoured from the inside out. How I wanted to vanish, to die just to stop feeling it. And while I didn't die, something else did. Something deep inside me, something old and primal ripped loose, clawing its way to the surface. It had no humanity, it wasn't kind, but it knew how to survive and that's what saved me.

"Then Emil and Nell found me," I say, my voice dropping to almost nothing.

"My god," Father Cyrus whispers almost like he's bracing for what comes next.

"I couldn't stop what happened after that," I continue. "Truth is, I didn't even want to. Justice found them. And when it did, when I saw what became of them . . . I felt alive again. Like taking the first deep breath after drowning."

I don't tell him about the blood, how warm it was, how it seeped into the whorls of my fingerprints. I don't confess the details no one should have to bear: how we tended to the bodies afterward, how we wrapped them carefully before leaving them to the wild animals. I don't admit how I watched the light drain from their eyes . . . and never once looked away. I don't say how good it felt. How *right* it felt.

Finally, after what feels like an eternity, Father Cyrus speaks, his voice hesitant, almost distant, as if he were unsure of his own words. "Very good, my child."

I freeze. "Very good?"

The words strike me like a slap across the face. It doesn't make sense. My confession, this confession of horror and violence, is *very good?* My insides twist into a knot, and I feel a strange, chilling emptiness wash over me. I had expected rebuke, condemnation, anything but approval. My mind scrambles for answers, for any kind of explanation. But there is none. His words don't offer clarity or redemption, they only leave me more confused, more lost.

"You think . . ." My voice is unsteady now. "*This* was good?"

His voice shifts, lower now and textured with sorrow. "I think," he says, slowly, like the words might splinter in his mouth, "that you've carried a burden no soul should be asked to bear. I think you survived something unimaginable, and in surviving, you lost something vital. But not everything." There's a quiver in his voice now. A crack in the calm that tells me he's not unmoved. He's shaken and he's *trying* to hold his shape, but the edges of him are fraying.

"I've heard many confessions," he says. "But never one like this. Never one that felt like . . . prophecy."

What the fuck? *Prophecy*. As if this was divine. Holy. I didn't come here to be sanctified . . .I came here to bleed.

"I didn't come for absolution!" I snap, the words lashing out before I can soften them. "I came because I needed to *say it*. Out loud. I needed to hear it echo back. That I did it and that I'm *not sorry*."

"You want the truth?" He says, voice suddenly hard-edged. "The men who did this, if they stood before me now, breathing and whole, I would not weep for them. Not a tear. But that does not mean what you've done has no cost. And it will cost you, Bernadette."

He knew the sound of my voice. He knew it was me all along.

"But you are not beyond saving," he goes on, the steel in his tone softening into tenderness. "Not in the eyes of God. Not in mine."

I close my eyes. I don't believe in salvation anymore, not the kind he's offering, wrapped in scripture and stained glass. But I listen anyway.

"Let us say a prayer," he says, and there's no room for refusal in his voice. It's gentle, yes, but firm and immovable. I take the rosary in my hands, cold at first but now warming under my touch.

Father Cyrus begins his prayer, but the words that leave his mouth are not what I expect. They are not filled with the softness of mercy or the righteousness of judgment. They are filled with fire, with a fury that matches the rage I feel inside.

"God, the Father of mercies," he begins, "through the death and resurrection of His Son, He has reconciled the world to Himself and sent the Holy Spirit among us for the forgiveness of sins. But even so, evil continues to break free. It continues to tear at the souls of Your children, defiling and destroying them in ways that should never be possible. Father, it is evil that has touched this devoted child of Yours. But fear not, for she has been given Your angels. She has fought back, and through Your strength, she has banished the darkness."

His words are raw and powerful. They feel almost like a sermon of revenge, as though he too is ready to stand against the forces that hurt me. There is an intensity in his voice, a sense of righteousness that I had never heard before.

As his prayer continues, I feel the tears slip down my face, one after the other. The beads of my rosary grow warm beneath my fingers as they absorb every drop of pain, every ounce of anger. The prayer no longer feels like a request for mercy, it is a cry for justice. A cry that has been buried deep within me since that night.

Father Cyrus's voice wavers, as though the truth strains against his throat. "Through the ministry of the Church, may God give you pardon and peace. And I absolve you from your sins in the name of the Father, and of the Son, and of the Holy Spirit."

As he finishes, I don't rush to respond. My hand, trembling slightly, moves to my forehead, down to my chest, then to my left and right shoulder. I trace the shape of the cross slowly, feeling every movement, as the final words slip from my lips in a whisper: "In the name of the Father, and of the Son, and of the Holy Spirit."

For a long moment, I don't open my eyes. I don't want to leave this space. This is the last sanctuary I will ever know, and I will never again be the same woman as the one who entered this confessional.

"Bernadette?" Father Cyrus's voice breaks through my thoughts. "I am so sorry," he whispers, his voice cracking like the moment has broken something in him too. I can hear the muffled sound of him choking back tears, and my heart aches. Is he sorry for me, for the things that happened to me? Or is he apologizing for the fact that, in some way, he too had witnessed the loss of innocence that couldn't be regained?

"Me too," I say, voice tinged with acceptance.

11

POLITE IN PUBLIC, FILTHY IN THE PLAYROOM

The Oily Cat didn't judge. It *absorbed*. It inhaled shame, lust, grief, and longing in equal measure and exhaled something that almost tasted like redemption. Tonight, the air pressed in with a strange density, and something electric crawled beneath my skin. The oil lamps along the hallway burned low, casting elongated shadows on the floor. Light flickered against dark-paneled wood, and for a moment, everything existed in slow motion.

The sounds from downstairs were muffled, but I could still make them out—the low roll of conversation, the distant clink of glass, and the occasional burst of laughter that rang hollow.

The scent in the air was as familiar as my own perfume. Tobacco, cheap cologne, and the unmistakable musk of arousal—of expectations soon to be bartered and bought. It clung to the curtains, to the velvet chairs, to skin, and no one left the Cat without carrying some of it with them, whether they realized it or not.

I stood in front of the mirror, adjusting the lace of my corset. The fabric was tight, cinched in just enough to make my breath shallow, but I preferred it that way. The corset, the heels, the bloodred lipstick, they weren't just for show, they were part of the performance. They were my armor. I ran my fingers along the hem of the corset, checking for fraying, even though I knew it was perfect. I had a ritual before every night began, and I didn't deviate. Rituals made chaos feel manageable, and here, chaos wasn't just expected, it was currency.

A soft creak came from the hallway beyond my door, boots on wood, a signal that the night was beginning. I made my way downstairs, the old banister cool beneath my fingers, as the murmur of voices swelled with each step.

Violet was holding court, perched like usual on the armrest of the worn velvet sofa near the entrance, spinning one of her well-polished lies. Tonight's tale? A brief stint in the circus. Contortionist. Acrobatic marvel. The kind of fantasy that made rugged men like the miner beside her imagine her folding in ways that had nothing to do with the rings or trapeze, and she knew exactly what she was doing. Violet didn't tell stories for amusement, she told them to disarm, to draw men in like a slow pour of honey over a knife's edge. Her laugh cut through the fog of tobacco and whiskey and the poor bastard beside her didn't stand a chance. He was already leaning in too close, already halfway gone.

Further into the parlor, Maeve played her own little game. She was draped over the back of a loveseat, her hair a red veil that shimmered with candlelight. The man in front of her, older and desperate, was whispering like he thought secrets might unlock something in her. But Maeve wasn't listening, not really.

Her eyes were scanning the room, catching every movement, every drink poured, and every whisper shared. She looked disinterested, almost bored, but I knew better. She didn't waste her energy on pretending to care. Maeve dealt in scarcity; her attention, her smile, her touch, nothing was given freely. And that's what made men want her more. She had the air of someone who'd once had everything ripped away and now kept every piece of herself behind lock and key.

At the bar, Elona and Nell were locked in another one of their heated debates. I didn't need to hear the words to know it was about something pointless, but passionately defended.

Politics, probably. Morals, maybe. Or simply the illusion of choice. Elona gestured wildly, one long-fingered hand slicing the air while the other clutched a glass of dark liquid, and her cheekbones caught the light like daggers.

She had that same feral glint in her eyes that made men mistake her for a challenge, not a threat. Until they tried something, then they learned that Elona wasn't built for softness, she burned too hot. Too bright. The kind of woman who made you think about your own mortality with a devious smile. And the fools kept coming anyway, drawn like insects to the inevitable fire.

Emil stood by the door, arms crossed, unmoved by the heat and noise of the room in front him. His attention moved constantly, tracking everything without ever looking impressed by it, his expression unreadable.

I stepped into the parlor, the piano put out a slow and aching tune in the corner that was just melancholy enough to make everything feel more romantic than it deserved. A couple of miners sat hunched at a table near the back, slurring through a game of cards, their laughter clumsy and rough-edged. At the bar, a lone man nursed his drink, eyes fixed on Maeve like she was a puzzle he was desperate to solve.

I felt their stares before I ever saw them. That familiar, unwelcome heat, crawling up the back of my neck. And when I finally looked, nothing had changed. That same unmistakable blend of hunger and conquest burned in their eyes, as if wanting me was enough to claim me. As if I were something to take, not something that could bite back. Maybe tonight, I'd let them believe they were the ones in control.

And maybe tonight, I'd remind them how wrong they were.

I crossed the room, letting my hips sway with lazy confidence, until I reached Violet, still perched on the couch armrest. Her attention was half on the miner beside her and half on me, eyes lighting up as I approached.

"Birdie, darling, you look delicious tonight," she purred, lips curling into a smirk.

I winked. "Hopefully I taste just as good as I look."

The miner swallowed hard. Violet caught the shift in his expression and chortled. "Well, we do aim to please, don't we?"

"Only when they earn it." I teased, my eyes scanning the room.

Then I saw him. The one who'd been watching me from the corner booth since I walked in. He was trying to look casual, leaning against the table as if he hadn't been burning holes through me since the moment I stepped downstairs.

Sweet thing. He probably thought he was being subtle.

I took my time crossing the room, my heels clipping against the floor with just enough bite to slice through the noise, and with each inch I closed, I could sense the tension in him coiling tighter.

I stood before him, an inch too close, close enough to make him nervous, and could feel the heat roll off him. Could see the way his breath hitched, how his hands twitched at his side like they were fighting the urge to move.

"Do you want me?" I asked, daring him to pretend that he didn't. If he was going to eye-fuck me all night, why not let him experience it properly?

I watched his throat work as he swallowed, his Adam's apple shifting up and down.

"Yes," he whispered, the word breaking on it's way out.

I let my fingers trail along his collar, my nails dragging lightly over the fabric, and I felt the stutter of his heartbeat through the thin cotton. He was unraveling already, bit by bit, one teasing touch at a time, and the power of it surged through me. This raw desire twisted into something I could mold, control, or even break if I wanted. I hadn't let this side of me out in weeks, and now, it was hungry.

I leaned closer, brushing my lips against the warm pulse at his neck, tasting the salt of his skin, my teeth grazed him lightly. "Then you'll have to pay for it first," I murmured, my breath hot against his ear as my hand slid lower. "That's how you'll earn every inch of me." His body trembled under my touch, cock already straining against his pants, begging for attention he hadn't earned yet as he fumbled for his wallet.

With the cash in my hand, I caught his wrist and pulled him through the crowd, guiding him upstairs to one of my favorite playrooms. At the center, a large circular bed dominated the space, draped in black silk sheets. In the corner stood an ornate padded chair, its leather arm and leg straps gleaming, ready to bind and expose. Nearby, a wooden chest table held feathers, oils, and a coiled whip waiting for its turn. But the real star was the tall, multi-paneled mirror spanning one wall, reflecting every angle of surrender.

"Strip," I commanded, my voice impatient. "Turn around and face the mirror. I want you to watch yourself."

He hesitated, looking at me like he wasn't entirely sure he had heard me correctly. Then he reached for his buttons, fumbling slightly, his shirt falling open to reveal a chest dusted with dark hair, his muscles tightening with nerves. His pants dropped next, cock springing free—thick and veined, already leaking pre-cum from the tip. He stood there, naked and vulnerable, eyes locked on his reflection as I circled him like a shark.

I stepped behind him, my hands sliding over his shoulders, down his arms, feeling him shiver. "Don't speak unless I tell you to," I ordered, my fingers wrapping around his cock, stroking slowly from base to tip. He gasped, hips bucking involuntarily, but he kept his eyes on the mirror, watching my hand work him—squeezing the shaft, thumb circling the slick head, milking out more of that clear fluid. His balls tightened under my palm as I cupped them, rolling them gently, then tugging just hard enough to make him groan. "You're already shaking."

"I—"

"Don't. . .speak. . .unless I ask you to." I repeated, releasing him abruptly.

His jaw flexed, but he nodded in agreement.

"You're pretty when you're obedient," I whispered, my lips brushing the shell of his ear, "but you'll be beautiful when you beg."

He let out a sharp breath as I met his eyes in the mirror, his reflection unsure and needy. I stepped back to untie the delicate satin ribbon at the top of my bodice, allowing the fabric to fall away, and my breasts to be fully exposed. My nipples were hard and aching in the cool air, while his gaze devoured them in the mirror.

"You want these?" I asked, my tone mockingly sweet as I trailed one finger down my breast, then lower, slow enough to torture. Knowing that anticipation ripens best when it is forced to wait.

"Yes," he rasped, breathless.

I stepped beside him, so we were both in full view. His restraint, my dominance, reflected back in perfect symmetry. "Then earn it." I challenged, as I crossed to the vanity, the drawer sliding open with a soft creak.

Inside lay the flogger, its dark leather strands coiled and when I lifted it, the tails spilled over my palm in a slow cascade. I trailed the tails along his back first, watching goosebumps erupt across his skin. "Feel that?" I asked, not giving him enough time to answer before I pulled back and snapped it forward, the strands whistling through the air before cracking against his ass. He jerked, a sharp hiss escaping his lips, red welts blooming instantly where the leather kissed his flesh.

"Count them," I demanded, striking again, harder this time, the tails wrapping around his hip, stinging his thigh.

"One," he rasped, voice breaking.

I built the rhythm, each lash deliberate: a light flick across his shoulders, making him arch; a heavier thud against his lower back, forcing his cock to twitch. The flogger's tails bit into his ass cheeks, spreading heat that radiated down his legs, his skin flushing from pale to angry pink. "That's it baby, you take the pain so well." I praised with the next snap, the leather thudding against his chest.

"Five," he gasped after a particularly vicious one that left parallel lines across his pecs, the pain twisting his face in the mirror, but his cock throbbed harder, betraying his hunger.

"You love this, don't you? Getting your skin striped while your cock begs for more."

By the tenth strike, his body was a canvas of welts and bruises, trembling under the assault, but he held position, eyes never leaving the reflection. I paused, breathing heavy, my own pussy aching with wetness, clit pulsing from the power rush.

Dropping to my knees before him, I met his gaze in the mirror. "Watch me fuck myself," I moaned, as my hand slid up my thigh, pushing aside my skirt to expose my pussy, lips swollen and slick. Fingers parted my folds, dipping into the heat, coating themselves in my arousal before circling my clit. "See how wet you make me? How badly I need you inside me?"

He whimpered, and the sound vibrated straight to my core, making me throb. I pinched my nipple with my free hand, rolling it roughly, tugging until it burned, all while my other fingers plunged deeper, fucking myself, the wet squelch echoing in the room. His hands clenched at his sides, desperate, struggling to hold back. I wanted the collapse, the surrender, I wanted *everything* from him . . . and he was going to give it to me.

"Beg," I commanded, my voice husky as I edged closer. "Beg for it, and then maybe I'll let you come."

"Please," he groaned, voice raw. "I need it—fuck, please."

I let my lips curl into a smile while looking up at him. It was a small victory, a deliciously sweet one. He was beautiful like this—flushed, restrained, caught between pleasure and uncertainty, and I savored the way his pulse fluttered beneath the surface, as though seeking permission to race.

"Good boy," I purred, standing slowly. With a firm hand on his chest, I pushed him back onto the chaise until I towered above him, taking his wrists in my hands and lifting them above his head. His arms stretched, obedient, offering themselves up without hesitation. I reached behind; fingers finding the loop in the binding and pulled the strap tight around his wrists. The leather kissed his skin as it cinched closed, just tight enough to anchor him in place, to make every twitch a reminder of his choice, while leaving his nerves alive and humming with anticipation.

"Too tight?" I asked

He shook his head.

"Good."

The candle waited beside the chaise; its thick beeswax body bowed from prior use. I lifted it carefully, the flame trembling in the draft of my movement, casting dancing shadows that licked across his exposed skin. Tilting the candle just so, I watched the first molten drop gather at the edge, swelling until it broke free and plummeted. It landed on his chest in a golden bead, sizzling as the heat seared his flesh, a blooming sting that drew a ragged gasp from his lips. His body jerked against the leather straps, muscles tensing in the bonds, but he held still, eyes locked on mine with a mix of shock and hunger.

The wax cooled almost instantly, hardening into a fragile seal over his skin. I pressed my thumb into the softening edge, feeling the warmth under my touch, and smeared it slowly across his chest, marking him. "Pain clarifies devotion," I whispered, watching the way his breath fractured in response.

His nipples tightened under the lingering heat, chest rising and falling in quick rhythm, and I traced the wax's path with my gaze, noting how it accentuated the rapid thrum of his pulse. Another drop followed, this one trailing lower, toward the taut line of his abdomen, promising more exquisite torments to come.

"Still with me?" I asked.

"Yes."

My smile sharpened. "Good boy. Now fuck me."

Straddling his lap, I positioned myself over his cock, the head nudging my entrance, slick with my arousal. "Suck," I ordered, shoving one breast into his mouth. His lips latched on eagerly, tongue lashing my nipple, teeth grazing just enough to send sparks down my spine. "Yes!" I moaned, sinking down slowly, inch by torturous inch, his thick cock stretching my pussy, filling me completely. The burn was exquisite—his girth splitting me open, veins dragging against my inner ridges as I bottomed out, my ass slapping against his thighs.

My eyes moved to the mirror. "Look at yourself," I ordered, ensuring his gaze returned to the mirror where candlelight flickered across his skin, across leather, across the thin ribbons of hardened wax tracing his chest. "Look at what obedience does for you." He was the perfect picture of surrender.

"Beautiful," I whispered as the mirror caught every motion: the brush of my fingers, the arch in my back, the flash of control that turned me into something holy and dangerous. It was power made flesh.

I rode him hard, my fingers tangled deep in his hair, grinding my clit against his pubic bone with every upward pull, then slamming down to take him deep. His eyes started to roll back and I had to remind him that his only job was to watch. "Don't take your eyes off us," I growled, grabbing his chin to force his eyes to the mirror. We watched—me impaled on him, breasts bouncing, pussy lips gripping his shaft as it moved in and out, coated in me. His bound hands flexed uselessly above him, hips thrusting up to meet me.

“Watch me devour your dick." I gasped, planting my feet flat on the cushion for solid leverage. My hands gripped my knees, fingers digging deep into skin as I bounced faster, thighs burning with the strain.

I leaned in and bit his lower lip, teeth sinking in until he bucked wildly inside me, the pain fueling his desperation. My pace quickened, inner muscles clenching around his cock, milking him as tension coiled in my belly.

"Oh my fucking god!" He panted around my nipple, voice muffled and frantic as he sucked harder, tongue swirling wildly while I shattered. An orgasm ripped through me, my body convulsing as I gushed around his thick length in hot spurts.

“Fuck, yes—cum for me!” I cried, nails raking his wax-marked chest, drawing thin lines of blood that mingled with sweat.

He followed a heartbeat later, his entire body arching beneath me, our cries rising together. I stayed on top of him, panting, still pulsing around him as the last tremors of our release faded into the heavy silence. The room buzzed with heat, with sex, with a well-earned heady satisfaction. My thighs ached; my lips were swollen from too much kissing. And I was still starving.

I slowly got up, turned toward the mirror across from the chaise lounge, and met my own reflection. Hair wild, lipstick smeared, skin flushed and glistening, I looked feral, dangerous, divine even. *Holy hell,* I thought, watching the slow rise and fall of my chest. *No wonder they keep coming back.*

Behind me, he groaned softly, a sound that was half pleasure, half surrender. He was completely wrecked, and I loved it. Leaning down, I traced a slow kiss along his jaw, savoring the way he flinched beneath the gentleness. "You were fun," I whispered.

I stood, adjusting my corset, running my fingers through my hair like nothing about me had just been laid bare. I faced forward, refusing to look back until I reached the door.

"Thanks for the release, darlin'," I said with a satisfied grin.

He nodded, panting, his hands still strapped above his head. I watched his chest rise and fall, the red marks blooming on his wrists around the restraints. Beautiful, fragile, and temporary. Then I turned, letting the heavy door swing shut behind me, knowing that I'd be back for round two shortly.

12

IN THE NAME OF THE DADDY, THE BASTARD, AND THE HOLY WHORE

This town had always been unforgiving to those who dared to step outside its rigid expectations. The streets of Butte, lined with worn-down houses and gossipy neighbors, didn't leave much room for 'difference', and I had become the embodiment of that difference.

"She lost them both, and now look at her," one woman would mutter as she passed by in the market. "A widow can't be left alone for long. She'll find another way to fill the hole in her heart."

"Did you hear? That brothel of hers, The Oily Cat, they're committing all sorts of devious acts. I heard she's got men holed up in there like rats in a trap," another voice would hiss, harsher than the first. "She might've been a decent woman before, but now . . . now she's making deals with the devil himself."

If they thought shame would stop me, they didn't understand the type of woman I'd become.

I found myself lingering outside the brothel, watching the empty street stretch into the dark while the lights inside The Oily Cat spilled onto the pavement. The wind cut through my coat, but I barely noticed. I remembered a time when John and I had walked these very streets, side by side, our arms brushing together as we shared laughter and dreams. Back then, we had been accepted; now I was nothing more than a figure of scorn.

As I stood lost in thought, a voice pulled me from my daydream. It was the familiar biting tone of a local resident, an older woman whose face seemed to have been etched by bitterness.

"Funny, isn't it?" The woman sneered, crossing her arms with all the authority of a schoolmarm. "You're still here, running this place. I heard you were a good woman once. But now? I can hardly look at you without thinking of all the men you've led astray. How low you've sunk, Bernadette. Not that you care what anyone thinks, I suppose."

I gave her a cool smile, before I took a step forward, meeting the woman's eyes directly, refusing to back down. "Low, am I?" I asked, my voice measured. "Funny, I don't feel particularly low. In fact, I feel more *alive* than I ever have."

The woman scoffed, "You're nothing but a sinner, running this house of—"

"House of what?" I interrupted, arching an eyebrow, my lips curling into a small but wicked smile. "A house where women can take control of their own lives? Where we aren't forced to bend to society's expectations? A place where we can make our own choices?"

The woman flinched, but I wasn't done. "You see, it's easy to throw stones when you're hiding behind a veil of respectability. But I'm not the one whose husband needs to *pay* to sleep around, am I?" I let the words settle for a moment before I moved closer, my voice just a shade sweeter. "Funny, isn't it, how judgmental people get when their own lives aren't as perfect as they pretend?"

I held my words back, letting the moment press against us, before I broke it. "It must be exhausting to carry so much judgment around," I said, my tone composed enough it almost felt like a compliment, "but I don't have the energy for it. Life's too short." I gave a slight shrug and walked away, leaving the woman behind with her own tangled thoughts.

I stepped into the warmth of the brothel, my heart racing with triumph, my eyes scanning the room before I caught the familiar sight of Violet lounging with her long legs draped over the arm of the couch, as though the world had been designed for her comfort alone. She held a glass of brandy in one hand, swirling it with idle elegance "You look pleased with yourself," she chimed, eyes glinting.

I smiled, my earlier conversation fading into the background. "Just a little chat with the town's moral compass," I replied dryly, taking a seat at the bar.

Maeve glanced over from the far corner, where a pair of men were trying too hard to impress her. She barely gave them a nod.

"She'll run home and pray for your soul," Violet drawled.

I smirked. "She can pray all she wants. God stopped listening to prayers about me a long time ago."

Elona let out a huff of laughter from her seat on the barstool. "If God ever did listen, I'd have been struck dead at least six times by now."

"Seven," Maeve corrected from across the room.

"I was being modest." Elona tossed a peanut at Maeve, missing by a mile.

Maeve didn't look up. "You were being delusional."

Violet raised her glass. "To delusion. May it keep us charming and employed."

I allowed myself a small smile as I slid behind the bar, offering Nell a quick five, which she graciously accepted. The wood was warm from the gas lamps and the touch of too many desperate hands. I wiped down a glass out of habit more than need, while over in the corner, someone played a lazy piano tune that didn't match the mood, but didn't ruin it either.

Then the front door creaked open on its stubborn hinges, letting in a gust of cool night air, and with it stepped a man in a fitted vest. He was tall and broad-shoulders, and his cheeks were tinged with a flush that might have come from whiskey, nerves, or maybe both. He paused just inside the threshold and scanned the room like he wasn't sure if he was brave or stupid for walking through our doors tonight.

Elona's smile sharpened into something dangerous. "Oh, look," she said, sliding off her stool with a feline grace, "tonight's donation to the church of sin has arrived."

He held his hat in one hand, the brim damp and misshapen, clutched tight as if it might shield him from whatever he'd just walked into. I watched the subtle twitch of his fingers, the way his shoulders hovered somewhere between tension and defeat, and I could almost hear the thoughts rattling around in his head: *Turn around. Leave. You don't belong here.* But his feet told a different story. Planted firm on the warped floorboards, they'd already made the choice his mind was too scared to voice. Poor bastard didn't even realize the hardest part wasn't walking in, it was surviving what came next and Elona was already halfway to him.

"Evenin', sugar," she purred. "You look like you wandered in by mistake. Lost your way to confession, maybe?"

The man blinked, and his jaw shifted like he was about to speak, then thought better of it. Elona reached out and touched his chest, barely a graze, like she was testing the fabric of his vest for quality or searching for a heartbeat.

"Name's Elona," she said, though it hardly mattered. He wouldn't remember it tomorrow, and if he did, he'd never say it aloud. Not to anyone that mattered.

After the money was exchanged, she took his hand and turned, leading him toward the stairs, the same way she might lead a dance partner to the floor. They disappeared up the staircase, her laugh trailing behind them, while I returned to the bar, flipping over a chipped shot glass and filling it with my favorite whiskey.

Violet sipped on her brandy. "Think he'll cry?"

Maeve, still in the corner, glanced up. "I'd bet my left tit on it."

The piano faltered for a brief moment, its notes slipping uncertainly before pushing forward with a jagged, off-key tune that rang unevenly through the room. Slowly, people began to trickle in—first just two at a time, then more and more, until the space was steadily filling with the sound of voices and movement. Chairs scraped against the floor, voices overlapped in rising chatter, and the space came alive. The piano shifted gears, breaking into a quicker, livelier melody that instantly put me in a good mood. Finally, the night had found its rhythm.

That is until an unexpected sound cut through the music. At first, it was soft, barely audible over the clink of glasses and the hollow piano. But then became clearer—a sharp gasp trapped in his throat, followed by another, deeper sound that was impossible to ignore, and the bar fell into a particular hush only the guilty and the curious know well.

The sound filtered down from the ceiling, through the thin plaster, as a slow, dragging moan filled the silence. Then a cry, high and bright, that shattered the silence completely. Somewhere in the corner, someone let out a chuckle, breaking the tension, while nearby, another person shifted uneasily on a barstool, the scrape of wood against the floor.

"Well," Violet said, swirling her brandy again, "either she's killing him, or saving him.

Maeve shrugged. "What's the difference?" She asked casually, and that earned some nervous, wayward glances from the men sitting at the nearby tables, eyes glinting with a mix of amusement and caution.

13

THE PEARLY GATES CAN KISS MY ASS

THEN

The weather was pure shit. It was only drizzling when I first stepped outside, just enough to be irritating, but not enough to justify turning back. Then, like some kind of sadistic mist trap from the heavens themselves, it began to pour the moment I reached the part of town with no awnings, no trees, and no hope of cover. Naturally, I'd left my umbrella at home, a decision I began to regret with increasing intensity around the second block. I paused on the church steps, letting the rain soak into my hair, trail down the line of my neck, and cling to my dress until the fabric grew heavy against my skin. The wind picked up, and I let my eyes fall closed, bracing against a rush of cold air. And there, in the roar of the rain, I let my thoughts drift to John.

I used to meet him on evenings like this, when the world had folded in on itself, soft and gray and utterly private. He would bring me wildflowers he'd found out in the fields, wrapped in crumpled old newspaper, because he knew I hated anything that felt too perfect or polished. He used to tell me I looked beautiful when I was soaked to the bone, as though the rain couldn't put out the fire burning inside me. I'd laugh, saying he needed his eyes checked. He'd laugh too, but he never stopped looking at me like I was something worth surviving for. And now he was gone.

Now they were both gone. Ray's smile, gap-toothed and full of innocence, haunted me more than the loneliness. When I buried him, I buried pieces of myself too, pieces I never got back. The storm pressed down on me, mirroring the weight of my grief. It was both cleansing and cruel, relentless in its truth.

I made my way through the entrance of the church, my hands gripping the rosary that dangled from my wrist. The beads felt cold against my skin, and the familiar scent of incense clung to the air like it always did, wrapping around me like a shroud. Inside, the quiet of the church felt unusually oppressive. It had always been a place of solace, but today it felt like the very walls were holding their breath, waiting for me to speak the words that were going to change everything.

Father Cyrus had been my confessor for years, not just a priest offering absolution, but a man who had witnessed every shade of me: the good, the bad, and the messy, unguarded parts I rarely showed the world. The lines etched into my face were familiar to him, as were the subtle sparks in my eyes, whether I was about to crack a sarcastic joke or silently carry a secret too heavy to speak aloud.

He wasn't the kind of priest who delivered lectures or fired off brimstone-laden sermons. Instead, he carried a warmth that gave a feeling of safety, as if you could lay bare every truth and every lie without fear of judgment. I could hear his voice in my head, as if he had already expected something like this from me: *I know you, Birdie, you're not someone who hides her truth.*

I took a deep breath, silently willing my heart to stop racing, and made my way to the confessional booth at the back of the church. The sound of the rain tapping against the windows followed me, a steady percussion to match my nervous steps. I pushed open the small wooden door and settled into the narrow seat, the wood creaking softly underneath me. While the confessional was by its nature a confining little box, it offered a strange kind of refuge.

Father Cyrus was already there, waiting in the other side of the booth, his presence unmistakable in the gentle rhythm of his breath and the soft rustle of fabric as he folded his hands. I couldn't see him, but I could picture him clearly—silver hair neatly combed to the side, glasses perched low on his nose in that familiar, grandfatherly way.

"Ah, Birdie," he greeted me, his voice a rich rumble. He didn't use my full name anymore; to him, I was always Birdie, a nickname that had, at some point, overtaken Bernadette.

I leaned back slightly. "Not sure if it's a compliment that you recognize me before I even speak, Father," I said, dryly. "Could mean I've spent far too much time in this booth."

He snorted, the sound soft. "Or that you've always had a distinct way of entering a room, even one you're not seen in. So, what brings you here today, my dear?"

I raised an eyebrow at him, a smirk tugging at my lips. "Father, I'm surprised you haven't moved to a warmer place by now. You know, somewhere where people aren't so prone to confessing sins about, oh, I don't know . . . running brothels?"

The screen between us was a mercy and a torment all at once. I couldn't see his face, only imagine it, but I heard the smile in his voice, heard the slight huff of laughter he tried, and failed, to suppress. "Running a brothel, you say? Well, I suppose I'll have to hear this confession before I pass judgment."

I folded my arms over my chest and let out a short bitter laugh. "Good thing you're sitting down, Father. I've got a lot to say, and I'm not interested in keeping it short and sweet today."

He shifted slightly on the other side of the screen. "I'm listening, Birdie," he said, the warmth never leaving his tone. "Go ahead."

I stared down at the rosary in my hands, fingers running over the cold, smooth beads. I'd held them so many times, clutching them during every confession, every moment of doubt or regret. They were my security, the last thread that had kept me tethered to something resembling normalcy. But today they felt different. Today they were just . . . beads. Taking a deep breath, I turned my eyes back towards Father Cyrus, trying to steady my shaking hands before the words came tumbling out. "I opened a brothel," I said flatly. My voice didn't waver, but it was quieter than I'd intended.

When Father Cyrus spoke, his voice carried no judgment, only that same calm patience I had come to count on. "And how did that come to be?" He asked gently.

I let out a short laugh, but it had no humor to it. "Well, it wasn't exactly part of my life plan, Father. But you know what they say: When life hands you a pile of wreckage, you might as well build something out of it."

"Is that what you did, Birdie?" He asked. "Built something from wreckage?"

"Hell, yes. And let me tell you, it's a damn fine wreckage I've got to work with." I shot him a sly grin, though he couldn't see it. "You wouldn't believe how many men there are in this town who think they deserve a bit of company. A drink, a little something extra . . . and a place to forget their miserable lives. It's like they just can't help themselves, Father."

Father Cyrus chuckled. "I'm beginning to think you've got a flair for sarcasm, my dear."

I stared at the ceiling, searching for the words. "What can I say? It's a gift." My eyes narrowed, a spark of heat burning behind them. "I named it The Oily Cat."

"The Oily Cat?" Father Cyrus repeated, his voice full of surprise. "Well . . . that's unique."

"Yeah, I know. A classy name, huh?" I couldn't suppress the grin that tugged at my lips, but there was an edge to it now, the kind of edge that comes from being both defiant and unapologetic. "But it works. They come in, they get what they need, and they leave. No strings attached. No judgment. Just money for me and a bit of peace for them."

"You know I'm not blind, Birdie," he said, his voice still gentle but edged with concern. "I know this town has its share of places like that. But *you*—you've never struck me as the kind of woman who would choose that path. So tell me . . . why a brothel?"

"I had nothing left. *Nothing*. After John, after Ray, it felt like the world had swallowed me whole. And when those men attacked me, when they took what little I had left, I had a choice. I could crawl into a hole and die, or I could do what I needed to survive. And I chose survival."

"And you've found peace in this . . . work?" He asked.

I snorted. "Peace? Father, if you think I'm walking around holding hands with angels, singing hymns all day, you've got another thing coming. But I've found control. I've found a way to make sure I don't let the world push me around anymore. If I'm gonna play in the muck, I might as well own the damn swamp."

There was a long pause and I know he was studying my words, searching for the layers beneath them. He'd seen the wife, the mother, the widow, the woman driven to the edge. But now he was seeing someone different, a woman who had taken her pain and turned it into power. "You know, Birdie," he spoke finally, "the world will try to break you down, again and again, it doesn't care about your pain or your choices. But it's clear to me that you've done what you had to do to rebuild yourself. You've found strength in a place where many would have crumbled."

I sighed, rubbing my fingers over the smooth beads of the rosary, feeling their familiar comfort seep into my bones. "I don't know about strength, Father, I just know I needed to survive. And if that means doing something I never thought I'd do, then so be it."

Father Cyrus's voice softened, almost a whisper now. "I think you've always had strength, Birdie, you just didn't know where to look for it. And maybe, just maybe, this is where it's led you."

"You don't think less of me?" I asked, the vulnerability in my voice a stark contrast to the bravado I'd been carrying thus far.

Father Cyrus huffed. "Not in the slightest. But I do worry, my child, this path . . . it will be hard. It will demand things from you that you may not have anticipated. But remember, you are never alone, not truly, not with the faith you carry."

I gave a wry smile, letting his words sink in. "You're a good man, Father, but don't go getting soft on me now. I still need you to keep me in check, keep me from crossing the line."

"I'll do what I can, Birdie," he said with a chuckle, "but I think it's clear you're not someone who needs a lot of saving."

I stood up, smoothing the folds of my dress. "No, I suppose I'm not. But a little guidance never hurt."

"You'll have it, always." Father Cyrus said warmly. "And if you ever need someone to talk to, know that I'm here."

I nodded, turning to leave. The door of the confessional creaked again as I pushed it open and walked back through the church ready to step back out into the night. The rain was still falling in steady sheets, but for the first time in a long while, I felt like I had made peace with myself—not with my sins, but with the woman I had become. I wasn't the woman I thought I'd be, but I was the woman I needed to be.

"Take care of yourself, Birdie," Father Cyrus called after me.

"You too, Father," I replied, offering a small, genuine smile before stepping out into the storm.

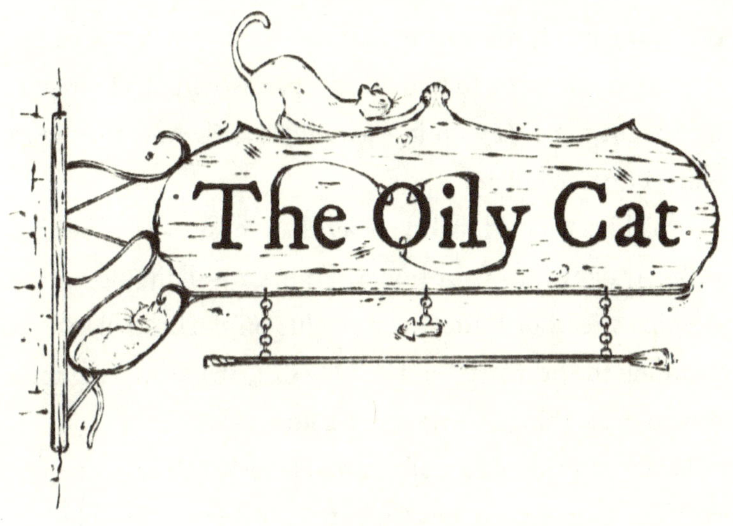

14

WHEN GOD TURNS HIS BACK, I OPEN MY ARMS

I couldn't sleep. I'd been lying there for what felt like hours, the sheets tangled around my legs, staring into the dark, my thoughts refusing to settle. Every time I closed my eyes, something surfaced, voices, faces, unfinished conversations.

My body was still, but my mind was moving too fast, cycling through memories I hadn't asked to revisit.

I shifted under the sheets, hoping for stillness that didn't come, and finally rolled onto my back, staring up at the ceiling. If sleep wasn't going to find me, the past would. And tonight, it brought the girls with it, each one, exactly how they were when I first met them.

It had been a cold night, colder than most, where the chill sinks straight into your bones. I'd been walking down the sleeping streets of Butte, my thoughts on the brothel, always planning the next step for The Oily Cat, always looking for a way to make things a little easier, a little safer.

I had nearly passed the alley when I saw her: Maeve. She was standing by the curb, her back straight despite the chill, the light of a nearby lantern catching the fire in her red hair. It was her hair that first drew my attention, fiery and wild. But what caught my eye most was the look on her face when she approached me, one of determination, of someone who had no intention of being controlled.

"Are you Bernadette?" She asked, her voice rich, with a lilt from a faraway place.

I stopped immediately, my heart skipping. There was something about her that felt so familiar, as if I'd known her in another life. "I am," I replied, caution in my voice.

Something changed in her then. I saw it. The shift was palpable, as if she was letting go of a pain she had been carrying for far too long. It was in the way she exhaled, the way her shoulders dropped just slightly. Like maybe she'd found what she was looking for. She paused, and the corner of her mouth lifted into a slight smile.

Hours later, she sat across from me in my office, still in that funeral dress, looking like she hadn't eaten a proper meal in days. "I ran," she explained. "From Ireland, from my family. From a life I never wanted . . . I read about you in the papers. You and this brothel of yours. They called you trouble, but to me, it sounded like freedom."

There was a look in Maeve's eyes I recognized straight away, not just the desperation of someone running, but the restless hunger of a woman trying to find herself before the world decided who she was. She didn't tell me much, at least not right away, but she didn't have to. I'd seen that kind of fire before. It wasn't weakness that brought her to my door, it was defiance, and I respected that more than most things.

I watched her as she told her story, listened, and said nothing. But I could feel the story weaving between us. Different ghosts, same shadows. Maeve entered my life, unapologetic, strong, and full of life and energy. She became the spark of The Oily Cat. Its heartbeat. And in turn, I was inspired, proud of the place I had built, proud of the women I had brought together.

Then, there was Elona.

I'd met Elona late on a sunny afternoon, not far from The Oily Cat. The sun was beginning to set, and as I passed the edge of town, I noticed her. She sat alone beneath a tree, sketching in a notebook, her long braids falling over her shoulders as she worked. I'd seen her around before but had never paid her much attention. She was from a far-off tribe and had become a solitary presence in town, always keeping to herself.

Over the next several days, I found myself passing that stretch of ground again and again, and she was always there—sketching the landscape or the people who wandered past. She was alone each time, settled beneath the same tree, day after day, her gaze distant but intent on her work.

One afternoon, I decided to approach her. "You have a talent," I said fondly, watching her eyes lift to meet mine. "Your art is beautiful."

She nodded, almost as if the compliment was nothing new, but she didn't offer much else. Her gaze lingered on me for a moment, weighing whether to say something, but then she went back to her sketching. I stood there for a while, watching her draw, the silence between us comfortable. But the more I watched her, the more I realized: Elona was truly alone, and she had no place to go. The few times I had seen her walking through town, she never seemed to interact with anyone.

"You know," I began gently, "I think you'd find a good home at The Oily Cat. It's not just a brothel, it's a place where women come to find themselves, to heal, to create. You don't have to be alone."

She stopped drawing and looked up at me. There was a flash of something in her eyes, something almost hesitant, but there was also curiosity and maybe even a spark of hope.

"I could offer you a place there, if you want," I continued, my voice steady. "I think you'd be a good fit."

Elona remained silent, but I could tell the offer had planted a seed. She didn't give me an immediate answer, but she didn't turn me away either.

Days passed, and I continued to see her sitting in her usual spot. I wondered if Elona was considering my offer, or if she had simply gotten used to the steady rhythm of her life there. Then, one evening, I was walking home from the market when I noticed her again, this time standing near the entrance of The Oily Cat. She hesitated for a moment as if gathering the courage she needed, then she stepped forward, her eyes lifting to meet mine.

"I think I'll take you up on your offer," she said. "I could use a place to stay. My name's Elona, by the way."

Relief washed over me, and I smiled warmly at her. "You're always welcome here, Elona. I'm glad you've decided to come."

She became a part of The Oily Cat as a woman with a story that was still unfolding. I watched her grow within these walls, her art becoming more confident, her presence more vibrant. I knew she had the potential to make a name for herself beyond this town, and I hoped, one day, she would.

And finally, there was Violet.

Violet's story didn't begin like the others'. She came to us on the coldest of nights, nearly swallowed by the dark, nothing but bone wrapped in torn cloth. I found her crumpled in the alley behind The Oily Cat, barely breathing. When I knelt beside her, something in me cracked, though I'd long thought my heart too calloused for that kind of breaking.

She was starving, yes, and half frozen, but there was a spark in her eyes, dim but defiant. The kind of fire that clings to life even when the world's done everything to put it out. "Help me," she whispered, barely audibly, her voice ragged.

I didn't ask her who she was or where she'd come from. That could wait. I just took off my coat and wrapped it around her shoulders. "You're safe now," I said. "We'll get you warm, and then we'll figure the rest out."

Violet had been cast aside long before she ended up at my door. Raised in an orphanage, tossed out the day she turned eighteen like yesterday's news. No family, no home, just the cold truth that no one was coming for her. She tried selling her poetry at the market, little scraps of her soul written in ink, but the world doesn't stop for beauty when it's hungry. No one listened, no one cared. The world had discarded her just like it had so many others.

And yet . . . there was something about her. Even in her desperation, she carried herself like a girl who saw the world in verses. Her words had a raw, aching beauty to them, a poet's soul, bruised but still burning. She wasn't just meant to survive, she was meant to matter. Her poetry, raw, aching, and full of strength, reached deep into the hearts of those who heard it. Her words carried sorrow and hope in equal measure, becoming a balm for us all.

Now, in the silence of my room, I lay still and let my eyes fall closed, a soft smile curving at my lips. The women they had become stirred a fierce and unshakable pride within me that I carried like a second heartbeat. The restlessness in my mind faded, and I drifted into sleep, knowing that no matter what comes, The Oily Cat, and the women I'd come to love, would always be my greatest triumph.

15

HAPPY BIRTHDAY, DARLING...HOW LUCKY ARE YOU TO BE SURROUNDED BY PSYCHO KILLER WHORES?

The comforting scent of roasted pork and freshly baked bread filled the air with a mouth-watering aroma. It was Emil's birthday, and the women had claimed the brothel's kitchen with a focused energy that turned chaos into celebration. Pots clattered, steam curled toward the ceiling, and the soft sound of our voices wove through the space. At the center of all the work, though not yet present, was Emil, no doubt going about his day with his usual, unassuming steadiness. He wouldn't be expecting this, and that was part of the plan. Tonight wasn't about flashy gifts or grand speeches, it was about giving something back to the man who had given so much to us.

Maeve, with her wild, untamable hair and restless energy, was the first to voice what everyone else had been dodging. She moved like barely managed chaos, arranging the silverware with the kind of care usually reserved for rituals or farewells.

"Do you think he'll be surprised?" She asked, her eyes darting toward the door, her fingers tracing the delicate pattern of ivy leaves etched in faded gold.

I stood by the stove, stirring the final dish with absolute focus. It had to be perfect. My gaze lingered on the doorway, nerves and excitement curling in my stomach. I hope so," I replied, adding more seasoning to the pot. "He's not one for fuss, but he deserves this."

Elona, one hand placing candles on the cake, the other cradling a glass of whiskey, grinned over her shoulder. "Oh, he's gonna love it," she said, voice bubbling with excitement. "Just make sure he's had a drink or two before he realizes we've gone full sentimental."

I smiled, almost in spite of myself. "He doesn't need whiskey to know we care, Elona."

"Maybe not," she said with a shrug, "but it doesn't hurt."

Violet set the glasses in place one by one, aligning them with care. Nearby, Nell lingered in the doorway, a bundle of Emil's favorite wildflowers cradled loosely in her hands. Color warmed her cheeks as an unfamiliar, almost luminous anticipation softened the edges of her usually unreadable expression. She was his wife, his anchor, the only person who could soften him with a look and undo him with a touch.

"I can't wait to celebrate him," she said, placing the bouquet in a vase at the center of the table.

"I know," I acknowledged, moving beside her to help adjust the stems together.

"He's never liked attention," Nell added.

The words had barely left her mouth when the door creaked open, and Emil stepped inside, shadow stretching ahead of him. He stopped short at the sight of us gathered there, excitement radiating from our faces. His brow tightened in confusion as he looked from Nell then to me, searching for clues. His gaze drifted to the gentle sway of candlelight, over the table and across the careful love folded into every detail.

"I—" he began, then stopped. Words seemingly got stuck somewhere behind his ribs. For all his strength, this kind of vulnerability was unfamiliar terrain.

Maeve beat the silence. "Happy birthday, Emil!" She chirped, unapologetically earnest, launching herself toward him, arms wide and catching him off guard. A funny sight, watching him try to brace for impact.

Nell reached him next, placing her hands on his shoulders like she'd been doing it forever. "Happy birthday, my love," she said, softly. "I love you so much."

Everything else seemed to fade away as they kissed, a kiss built over years of choosing each other, again and again. Nell pulled away first, slowly, as if reluctant to break the spell. Emil stood frozen for a heartbeat too long. Then his jaw slackened, and he rubbed the back of his neck, his tell that he was overwhelmed but trying not to show it.

"You didn't have to do all this," He said in a low voice.

Elona handed him the whiskey, brow arched, dared him to resist. "Oh, but we did. Now sit, before I start singing."

Violet, from behind the candles, added softly, "It's for everything you do. For all the ways you keep us safe."

Emil looked at her then, something unspoken passing between them. He didn't respond, not verbally. He didn't need to. His gratitude was in the way his posture eased, in the way his fingers curled gently around the glass. We had closed the brothel for the night, no clients, no noise, just this. A cherished pause in our otherwise chaotic lives. As Emil took his place at the head of the table, the women gathered around him, serving him first from each dish.

Elona raised her glass, voice rich adoration. "To Emil," she declared, "the man who gets it done. The man who makes sure we're all still standing, even when we don't know how. The man who never asks for thanks, but damn well deserves it."

"To Emil!" Our shouts rang out, and the clinking of glasses sounded like armor falling to the floor.

His lips twitched into a shy, almost uncomfortable, smile. "I don't deserve all this," he mumbled.

"You do," Nell replied with a sparkle in her eyes, "but don't get used to it. We're not *that* soft."

A few muffled laughs stirred around the room. Even Emil let a smile slip, and for once, he didn't fight the love being offered. Then Maeve, still glowing from the wine and warmth of the moment, clapped her hands once to get everyone's attention. "Okay," she said, her grin a little softer now, less teasing and more meaningful, "time for the tradition."

Emil blinked. "What tradition?"

"The birthday circle," Nell said, sliding her chair a little closer to his. "Everyone at the table shares one thing they love about the birthday person."

Emil opened his mouth to protest, but Violet gave him a look that made it clear he didn't get a vote.

"And . . ." Maeve added, raising a finger like she was delivering the twist in a thrilling novel, "at the end, *you* have to share one thing you love about yourself."

Elona let out a low whistle. "That's the hard part, darling."

Emil gave a half smile, still skeptical. "Sounds like a trap."

"It's a tradition," Nell corrected, "and it's happening."

There was a pause while everyone took a minute to think. Then Violet began. "I love how you listen," she said, her gaze steady on the birthday boy, "even when you say nothing, you hear everything. You remember the things the rest of the world forgets."

Next came Elona, who swirled her whiskey like it might help her find the words. "You never let us drown," she said simply. "Even when you can't change the ending, you're still there. You show up."

Maeve leaned across the table toward Emil, her elbows knocking silverware aside. "You make me feel safe," she said softly. "Sometimes I think my fairy guardian angel must've sent you, because he knew I needed someone like you, someone kind. Someone who'd love me. Who'd remind me of my worth, *really* remind me, like a father should've. Like mine never did." She gave a small shrug. "You make me feel loved." Emil met her gaze across the table, a vulnerability passing between them before he broke eye contact, looking down at the worn wood beneath his hands.

I hesitated, then looked him in the eyes. "You see the best in broken things," I said, "in broken people. In all of us. Even when we forget the good is there."

Nell was last, her voice tender. "You love without asking for anything back. And somehow, you still think that's not enough."

The silence that followed was different now, heavier, but not uncomfortable. The kind of silence that stays with you, that invites reflection instead of retreat, and no one rushed to respond. Her words had found their mark, not just in Emil, but in each of us. You could feel it in the way no one looked away, the way breath was held just a moment longer than usual.

Then all eyes turned to Emil expectantly.

He cleared his throat, rubbed the back of his neck again. "This is . . . weird," he said, earning a few soft laughs. He stared at the table for a long moment. Then, finally, he said, "I think . . . I like that I don't give up. Even when I want to."

His words were fragile and real. And somehow, that small confession cracked open an understanding in each of us, a recognition that he finally let us see what it cost him to carry everyone else.

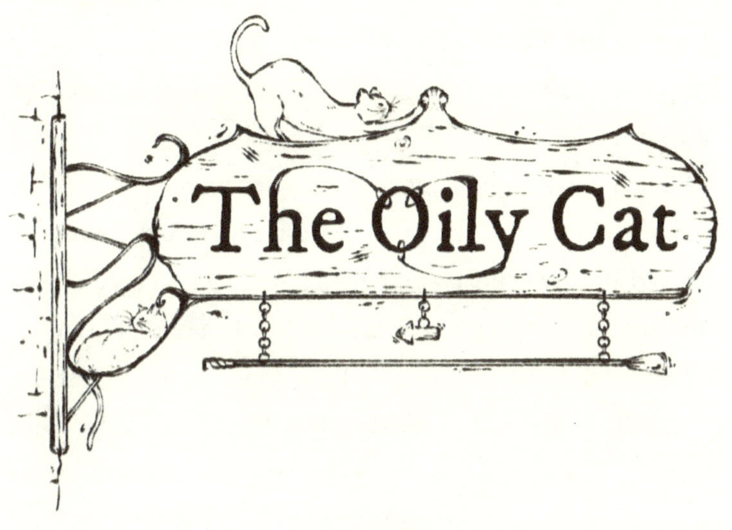

16

HELP ME, I'M A WHORE

THEN

The past few months had stripped everything down to nerve and instinct. I felt like I was on a knife's edge, with every step needing to be exact. As the wind began to pick up, I pulled my coat tighter, the rough wool scratching my neck, and pressed forward. My boots clacked against frozen cobblestones, the rhythm steady, betraying none of the storm brewing inside me. The town was stirring around me, the creaking wheels, traces of far-off laughter, and the low hum of early risers. And then there were the eyes, seen and unseen, watching and judging. Pretending not to see me while seeing everything. But today, I didn't have time to shrink under the whispers.

Emil and Nell's place sat at the edge of town, smoke rising from the chimney as the smell of fresh bread carried through the cold air. My stomach tightened at it; I couldn't remember the last time I'd had a decent meal. I knocked once, the sound almost harsh in the stillness, and the door opened almost immediately. Nell stood in the doorway, her apron dusted with flour, dark eyes taking me in. There was no judgment in her expression, only a calm patience that made it harder to pretend I was fine.

"Bernadette," she said gently, "you're freezing. Get in here before you catch your death."

I stepped inside, letting the warmth wrap around me. It smelled like cinnamon and home, and for a moment, it was Sunday morning all over again. Ray humming off-key, John's laughter spilling from the kitchen, and the ache of their absence folded itself seeping into the comfort.

"I'm not staying long," I said. "I need to talk to you. Both of you."

Nell closed the door behind me and placed a hand lightly on my arm. "We've always got time for you, sweetheart." Her touch was brief, but it steadied me more than I wanted to admit. She gestured to the kitchen. “Emil’s just finishing breakfast. Come, sit. You look like you haven’t slept in a week.”

“I haven’t,” I admitted as I followed her into the cozy living room.

Emil entered a moment later, wiping his hands on a towel, his boots thudding against the wooden floor. His face was its usual unreadable canvas, but his eyes softened when they found me. He crossed the room without a word, the towel still in his hands, and came to stand beside Nell, the two of them a matched set, weathered but unyielding. “What’s going on?” He asked with no preamble.

I didn’t waste time. “It’s The Oily Cat.”

Emil exchanged a glance with Nell, something unspoken passing between them.

“I need help,” I admitted. “Emil, I want you at the door. I need someone who can hold the line when things go bad. And they will, you know they will.” Emil didn’t respond immediately. He studied me, arms crossed, weighing things the way he always did, carefully and thoroughly.

Nell looked at me with a tenderness she didn’t try to hide. “They’ve been pushing you harder lately, haven’t they?”

I nodded. “They want the place gone. They want *me* gone. But it’s more than that, they don’t like that I gave the girls somewhere to go, somewhere safe.”

Nell pressed her lips into a hard line, holding back the words she wanted to say. She stepped closer, tenderly brushing a stray curl from my forehead, looking at me with a protective sadness. "I figured you were building something bigger than they understood," she said, "and you don't strike me as the kind of person that backs down."

My throat tightened, but I didn't look away. "I'm not backing down, I'm asking for backup."

Emil finally spoke. "You sure this is the best way to fight them? It's not just bar fights you're dealing with, it's politics. It's names with money behind them."

I met his gaze evenly. "I'm not asking you to fix it, I'm asking you to keep the walls standing while I do." His face softened. Then I added, quieter, "You saved my life, Emil. That night . . . you didn't hesitate. You didn't ask what it would cost, and I haven't forgotten that."

"I remember," he said, and I saw it, the brief flash of pain he usually kept buried. The consequences of the choices they'd both made, and how this town had repaid them for it. I looked at Nell. "You both know what it's like to be pushed out, to be told you're not worth the trouble."

She shook her head slowly. "You're worth all the trouble, Bernadette, always have been."

Emil finally nodded. "Alright, I'll do it. But not just for you, for what that place means, what it *could* mean."

Tension slipped from my shoulders, a sigh escaping my lips, but I didn't let myself settle. Not yet. There was still more to ask. "I want the women to be safe, that's number one, and I know you can keep the peace. But Nell," I said, turning to her,

"I could use your help too. The books, the schedules, tending the bar, and making sure no one takes more than they give."

She paused, taking in my words, her gaze locked on mine, measuring the stakes. Then came that look: calm, resolute, ironclad in its certainty. There was no need for reassurances because it wasn't trust offered, it was commitment declared. "If Emil's in," she ventured, "I'm already there."

"Thank you," I said, beaming, smiling bigger than I had in months. I stood up tall from the chair, my head held high. The road ahead was fraught with danger, but now, for the first time in a long while, I felt the glimmer of hope. The Oily Cat would stand, I would stand, and together, we would protect each other.

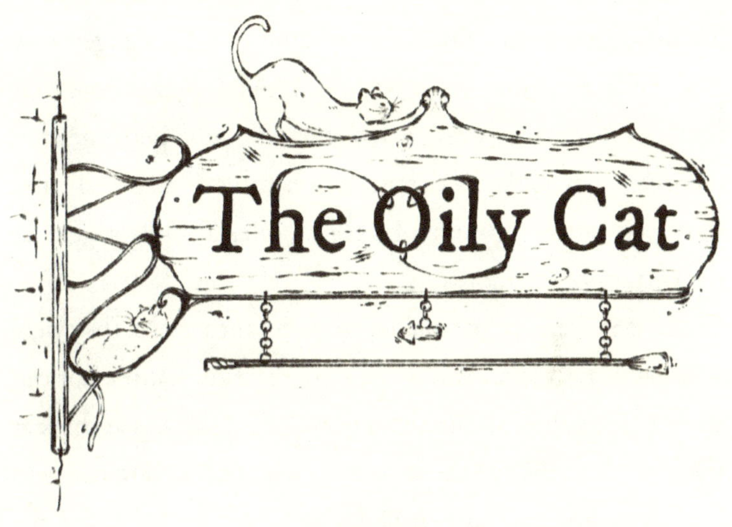

17

ALLOW ME TO INTRODUCE MYSELF

The girls hadn't lied when they said they wanted to start attending Sunday Mass more regularly. I'd had no reason to doubt them, not when their conviction made me feel like I was the one hesitating without cause. Still, they hadn't set foot inside St. Ann's until a few weeks ago, and I wasn't sure if the promise was meant to last or just said in passing. And yet, there I was, making my way up the cathedral steps with a strange, unfamiliar eagerness. Either way, I walked toward my usual pew with a flutter in my chest that felt dangerously close to hope. Only . . . it was occupied. Three women sat there, immaculately dressed and draped in silk, perfume, and menace. They looked like temptation stitched into flesh, and they were sitting in *my* spot. A slow, wicked smile tugged at the corners of my mouth.

Oh, they weren't just making good on their word, they were making a spectacle. And if the congregation hadn't noticed them before, they certainly did now. The irony was as thick as the incense in the air: the same men who dropped folded bills into the collection tray every Sunday, now kneeling beside the very women they'd paid to sin with the night before. I nearly laughed aloud. *Three whores walk into a church, a redhead, a blonde, and a brunette.*

I sauntered toward them, a sugary smile in place. "My darlings," I sang, arms wide like I'd stumbled upon old friends in a foreign land. They rose to greet me with matching grins.

"Told you we'd keep our word," Elona reminded me, her voice all confidence. "Regular Mass attendance. Starting today."

Maeve flicked her fan in a way that could rival any duchess in Versailles and added, "Last time was such a treat, I do hope this morning offers similar delights." She waved her fan toward me in a lazy, yet deliberate motion, sending a soft breeze past my cheek.

I settled beside Violet, her lace-trimmed gloves pristine and perfectly fitted. She shifted gracefully, giving me room without needing to be asked. I patted her hand, and she smiled; behind that composed expression, I caught the familiar glint, the spark of devilry that always lingered just beneath the surface.

The opening chords of the piano swept through the cathedral, silencing idle chatter and curious whispers. I welcomed the ritual of it, but the comfort was short-lived. Because it wasn't Father Cyrus at the altar . . . it was a stranger. He was young, collar crisp, standing at the podium with a confidence that belonged more in a courtroom than a cathedral. But beads of sweat dotted his brow, betraying the nerves he tried to hide.

"Brothers and sisters," he boomed, far too loud for a room built on solemnity, "I am Father Frederick, and it is my great pleasure to lead you in Mass this fine Sunday."

The shift in the room was immediate; a ripple of unease rolled through the pews. This congregation ran on tradition, and change, even in cassock form, did not go unnoticed.

Maeve leaned toward Violet, voice low and lethal. "Ah, the dramatics of men who think they're the main act."

Violet clapped a hand over her mouth, her shoulders trembling as she fought, and failed, to smother a laugh. I bit the inside of my cheek, keeping my gaze fixed on the stranger as he recited his prayers in a practiced cadence, like a man who'd memorized them in a mirror and paused between verses just long enough to admire himself.

"I praise You for fresh starts and new beginnings," he intoned. "Your mercies are new every day . . ."

Maeve rolled her eyes, her voice dropping just enough to slide beneath the noise of the room. "Save us from the theatrics," she murmured, barely louder than a breath. "Fierce talk for a man who'd come undone at the first real touch, I'd wager."

Another muffled laugh slipped from Violet, Elona quickly following suit, and my ribs ached with the strain of holding mine in. *Where the hell was Father Cyrus?*

The man continued, sounding heavy-handed and over-enunciated. A sermon dressed in costume. He spoke of redemption, hammering the word into every sentence like it might summon salvation through sheer repetition. *Redemption through repentance. Redemption through discipline. Redemption through denial.*

It was all very performative, every phrase neatly polished, delivered like a script he didn't quite believe but desperately wanted us to. I could feel Maeve practically vibrating beside me, her patience fraying with every pious proclamation. Violet's shoulders trembled again, this time not from laughter but from holding it all in. Finally, as the congregation echoed a polite, restrained "amen", the church doors creaked open, and there he was: Father Cyrus.

He entered with the unbothered grace of a man who'd walked into hundreds of rooms filled with chaos and claimed them as his own. The tension melted at the edges of the congregation. His presence didn't demand calm, it *invited* it. He made his way to the front, nodding to Father Frederick with a warmth that felt like a curtain being drawn open. "My dear brothers and sisters," he said, his tone rich, "forgive my absence. I thought it fitting to let Father Frederick introduce himself and lead this morning."

A nervous chuckle slipped from somewhere in the back—whether at the performance, or the silent relief of Father Cyrus's presence, I couldn't tell.

Father Cyrus raised his hand gently, and the murmurs fell away. "Change, even when well-meaning, often arrives before we're ready to receive it," he said, his voice even but unmistakably resonant. "And yet, what is faith, if not a daily practice of welcoming the unknown with grace?"

His gaze swept over the congregation. "We gather here each week, not because we are already whole, but because we are trying to be. Trying to do better, to be better, for ourselves, for our neighbors, and for the God who sees us as we are, not as we pretend to be. We are not perfect, but we are present."

A pause, a breath, not one soul shifted in their seat. "Let us be patient with newcomers, let us be kind with change, and let us never forget that even those who wander the farthest are not beyond the reach of mercy." He offered a final nod. "Peace be with you all." And then he stepped back, letting the silence reclaim the space with no fanfare or flourish. Just truth, spoken plainly. As the congregation began to disperse, the girls and I lingered.

"Bernadette." I heard my name, spoken by a familiar voice.

I turned, my smile starting to form before fully facing him. "Father Cyrus," I replied, his name a joy on my tongue.

He gestured toward the younger man beside him. "I'd like you to meet Father Frederick."

I extended my hand. "Lovely to meet you, Father."

He took it, firm and practiced. "The pleasure is mine . . . Bernadette, was it?" His gaze swept to the others, lingering an extra beat on Violet. I saw it, the admiration, that spark of curiosity men get when they see something they want but know they shouldn't. Typical. Still, he masked it well, and when Father Cyrus asked if we'd enjoyed the sermon, I smiled sweetly. "Oh, it was quite . . . memorable."

Maeve made a noise in her throat. "Bit much, if you ask me."

I gave her a look, somewhere between warning and affection, and held it a moment longer, as if to remind her just how serious I was. She met it without flinching, unbothered, maybe even a little amused. Father Cyrus laughed, clearly entertained, but poor Father Frederick looked like a boy who'd wandered into the wrong saloon. Elona, bless her, chose that moment to drop the match into the tinder. "Well, at least the good Father gave the town something new to whisper about besides the whores in the back pew."

Violet added, her smile sugar and sin, "Who'd have thought we'd ever get this far?"

I turned back to Father Frederick and decided to twist the knife, just a little. "You'll have to forgive us, Father. We joke about being whores because, well . . . we *are*. I own a brothel."

His eyes widened, disbelief momentarily breaking through. His jaw didn't quite drop, but it twitched, a subtle betrayal of the shock he tried hard to mask. Father Cyrus stepped in, gentle as ever, and explained my history and my so-called "community contributions." I gave him a silent 'thank-you'. No need to push the poor new priest off the edge. Still, I wasn't done with him. "So," I asked, changing gears, "what brings you to Butte, Father Frederick? I assume it's more than just shadowing our dear Father Cyrus."

He glanced away, brushing over it quickly. "Think of it like an internship," he voiced. "Father Cyrus is letting me learn from him before I move on to St. Patrick's in Arizona."

"You're not staying, then?" I asked, a note of sincerity slipping in beneath the curiosity.

"No, ma'am. But I'm grateful for the time here."

I gave a small nod. That was enough for now. "Well," I chimed, turning to the girls with a subtle flick of my wrist, "it was lovely to meet you, Father Frederick. Father Cyrus, I look forward to your next sermon." We swept past them, the soft rustle of skirts and quickened steps echoing off the polished floorboards as we made our way down the aisle. The voices of the few remaining parishioners faded behind us, swallowed by the heavy wooden doors just ahead.

"Until next time, Birdie," Father Cyrus called out.

"Try not to miss me too much, old man," I called back over my shoulder, just loud enough for him to hear. He chuckled, low and genuine, the sound following me as the doors closed.

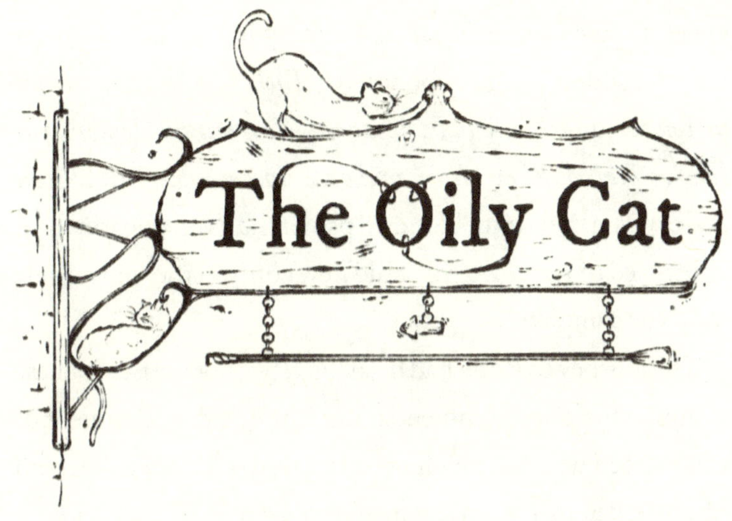

18

...I WOULD MUCH RATHER BE THE PREDATOR

HIM

From the moment I saw her, I knew I wanted her. She looked untouched by the rot of this world, like something God had crafted in a moment of indulgence.

And I knew I had to be the one to have her.

Despite the sanctity of the moment, my body betrayed me. Beneath the vestments, beneath the collar, the beast stirred. I had spent hours, *hours*, last night and this morning on my knees, begging for deliverance. Pleading for the Lord to burn the wickedness from my bones. *My Father in Heaven, thanks to You for this chance to begin again. Cast out the demon that lives in me. Make me clean, make me untouchable.* But I knew better. Even then, with bloodied palms and a voice hoarse from whispered prayer, I knew I could never outrun the thing inside me. Not completely.

The journey to Butte had been long, but not unusual. These things, transfers, recommendations, the quiet reassignment of sin, happen without much noise in our world. There is a kind of unspoken mercy among men of the cloth. We protect each other and we absolve one another long before confession is required. No priest is ever cast out, not truly. Not when we carry His name. When Father Cyrus extended his invitation for me to lead Mass this morning, I accepted with the same gracious humility I'd practiced for years, voice soft, eyes shimmering with gratitude. But beneath that calm, I was overflowing. This was my redemption. My resurrection.

The sacred ritual of dressing, the tactile comfort of it, never failed to soothe me. "Give virtue to my hands, O Lord," I recited, scrubbing them raw under the cold tap, "that being cleansed from all stains I might serve You with purity of mind and body."

The amice, the alb, the cincture, the stole, each layer slipped on like armor, each prayer a ward against the darkness that still lingered within me.

"O Lord, who hast said, My yoke is easy and My burden light . . ."

Amen.

St. Ann's was modest, worn but proud. The stained glass shone color across the pews like spilled wine while the air carried the scents of incense and age. The church was quiet when I arrived, almost reverent in its stillness.

Until she walked in.

At first, I thought she might be a trick of the light. The kind of distraction the devil sends just before Mass to test a man's resolve. But no, she was real. More than real. That updo, carelessly perfect. The strands that defied gravity and fell like whispers over her shoulders. The curve of her neck, the arrogance in her posture. She didn't fidget, she didn't smile, she didn't *ask* to be seen. And so, of course, I couldn't look away. I tore my eyes from her long enough to reach the pulpit, but every word I had written now felt stale and lifeless in my throat. I forced my voice to steady.

"Good morning," I began. "Today, we gather to reflect on the theme of redemption."

Redemption. The irony tasted bitter.

I delivered the sermon like I always did, confidently, articulately, and steadily. I quoted the Psalms, I spoke of the mercy of Christ, I gave them what they came for. But under it all, my mind spun with impure thoughts, with devious thoughts.

Thoughts of her.

I imagined the silk of her dress between my fingers, the small gasp she might give if I whispered scripture against her neck. I imagined her eyes, those piercing, devastating eyes, darkening just for me.

The things I could do to her.

I felt the heat rise beneath my garments, the cruel trick of the body at odds with the spirit. I pressed my thighs together and shifted behind the pulpit. The robes, bless them, concealed my shame. I clenched the sides of the podium and pushed the fantasy down.

"Forgiveness is not earned, it is given. And we must learn to give it to ourselves, as He gives it to us." The words came easy, the lie came easier. When Father Cyrus appeared at the end of the service, his presence grounded the room in a way mine could not. He smiled that unassuming smile of his, offered a warm explanation for his brief absence, and welcomed me with a grace I neither deserved nor returned. We descended the pulpit together to greet the congregation. I said all the right things and smiled at all the right times, but my eyes kept slipping toward the back, toward *her*.

I couldn't stop watching her.

She lingered with the other girls, laughing and speaking in hushed tones. But there was something . . . *commanding* in her silence, something that made her more dangerous than any woman I'd ever met. "Father," a voice interrupted my thoughts.

Mrs. Henderson. Sweet, wrinkled, and ever faithful. "That was a lovely sermon," she beamed, "You have a way with words."

I smiled. "Thank you, Mrs. Henderson. You're very kind." But I'd barely heard her. My mind was across the room, locked on the woman who had *ruined* me with a single look. The church emptied slowly, and the air grew lighter. I held my breath as I closed the distance with my new obsession, finally allowing myself to take a deep inhale as our bodies were only inches apart. As if I could simply breathe her in.

And then, finally, she stood.

Closer now, close enough to smell her. Sandalwood and lavender, clean but sinful in the way purity sometimes is. I tried to not let the images that danced in my mind show on my face, but the woman before me, the one who I now knew as Bernadette, seemed to sniff out my sinister craving for one of her own rather quickly. Her gaze met mine and didn't flinch, and there was something edged behind her eyes, something that told me, clear as day, that she saw through me. *She knows*, I thought. *She knows what I want.* She turned slightly, gesturing behind her. "And this," she said, "is Violet."

Violet.

My fixation, my punishment. And, if I could have my way, my salvation.

19

SHARING IS CARING

"Maeve, darling, you really must stop consuming all the charm in this room. The rest of us are suffocating on what you leave behind," I drawled, fanning myself with a playing card as I lounged deeper into the velvet armchair, ankles crossed.

Maeve didn't so much as blink. She sat perched atop the parlor's mantel like a bored gargoyle with immaculate features, one leg swinging idly and a cigarette balanced between her fingers. “If I’m hoarding charm,” she said, exhaling a thin stream of smoke in my direction, "it’s only because you keep stockpiling all the bad decisions.”

“Touché,” I grinned. “But admit it: My bad decisions make for excellent stories.”

Maeve arched a brow, lips curling. “Your bad decisions *are* the stories. You’re basically the Greek chorus and the tragedy, rolled into one irresistible corset.”

Before I could fire back, the front door creaked, and Violet swept into the room. Rain clung to the hem of her skirt, molded to her thighs, damp and translucent in places. “If only we could escape,” she sighed, her gaze already lost to the window and whatever faraway world lived beyond it. “To the lands of Byron and Keats . . .”

“Byron would’ve adored you,” Maeve said lightly. “You’ve got the sorrow of a widow and the face of a woman who poisons men for sport.”

Violet’s lips curved into a smile.

I folded my arms, watching her with open amusement. “You’d miss us if you escaped. Who else would heckle you at your poetry readings and bring gin to your emotional spirals?”

Violet gave me a sidelong glance. “I don’t spiral. I unravel gracefully.”

Maeve flicked ash into the fireplace. “You unravel like a damn silk stocking caught on a man’s belt buckle.”

Violet turned, her expression hovering between fondness and exasperation. “At least I’m not stuck in a loop like you, Maeve. Same night, different cock. Hoping one of them tells you you're clever.”

“Please,” Maeve scoffed, sliding off the mantel. “I already *know* I’m clever. I just want someone rich to say it with diamonds.”

Before I could sharpen that into something more dangerous, Elona arrived, her laughter announcing her long before she crossed the threshold. She wore her red dress, the one that made her look like Satan’s mistress, her heels clicking across the floor.

“I’m with Maeve,” she declared, already halfway through a glass of something amber. “Let’s skip the tragedy and write a farce. Something with mistaken identities and erections in the wrong rooms.”

“Sounds like last Tuesday,” I muttered.

Elona winked. “Exactly. Life imitates farce, darling.”

The room swelled with laughter again. That was our magic. It wasn’t just the perfume, the silk, or the practiced touch, it was this: the sisterhood of women who had nothing, and still gave each other everything.

As the night wore on, the customers started arriving, their presence always bringing a palpable shift to the energy of the brothel. Then the door creaked open again and a man stepped through, tall and rough cut. His coat hung heavy with rain, his boots were muddy, and his jawline was sharp enough to make a nun reconsider her vows. He looked like he'd been in far too many fights but won just enough of them to walk into a brothel like ours and think he could afford not to kneel.

Elona and I noticed him at the same time.

"Trouble," she whispered under her breath.

"Delicious trouble," I corrected, already straightening, my attention fixed on him as I crossed the room.

He looked me over as I introduced myself, his intense eyes locking on to mine, as if assessing me, sizing me up and cataloging every inch of me.

"Looking for something?" I asked.

The sound of his voice sent a ripple through me, "I believe I've found it."

My thoughts ran wild, racing ahead into dangerous territory. *Me too.* The things I would let him do, the ways I could unravel for him—it all flashed through my mind, vivid and tempting. A faint smile curved my lips, the thought lingering just long enough to betray itself in my expression. I didn't need to speak; he saw it. I knew he did.

I glanced toward Elona, giving her the signal.

She caught it instantly, stepping in with effortless confidence. Her hand slid across his chest, fingers tracing the fabric. The touch was casual, claiming, but her laughter, her flirtation, it was all part of the dance we'd perfected.

And I was more than willing to watch the show.

"Fifty for the night," I said, as Elona played with his collar, her fingers trailing over his chest with predatory grace.

He gave a single nod. "That works. I just need a place to disappear for a while."

"Then welcome to paradise, sweetheart." Elona teased, already guiding him to the stairs.

I gave Emil a subtle nod, signaling for him to take charge while I stepped back to observe, lingering just behind them, content to watch from the shadows and witness what was about to unfold.

Elona turned to face him, the low light settling over her, catching the red silk as it followed the lines of her body. She paused just inside the room, letting him take her in, holding there as if the moment belonged to her. As the door closed behind us with a soft click, I slipped into the corner, hidden from view, an audience to their performance and eager to witness every moment.

"Come here," she said softly. He crossed the room, his gaze fixed on her with the desperate hunger of a man who hasn't eaten in days, and sat at the edge of the bed.

Elona moved to him, her fingers finding the buttons of his shirt. She worked them free one by one, exposing his chest slowly. Leaning in, she brushed her breath against his skin and kissed him gently.

"Tell me what you want," she whispered, her lips brushing his neck.

His eyes darkened. "I just want to forget."

Her smile was softened as she looked at him. "Then let's make you forget everything."

Her hands traced over him, following the shape of his body as his chest rose and fell. His breath hitched when her mouth found the hollow beneath his collarbone. She lingered there, pressing a kiss, tasting him, claiming him between heartbeats.

"I want you to touch me," she breathed against him. "Every inch of me." She slid the straps of her dress from her shoulders, the fabric surrendering, falling slowly to her waist.

Elona pressed her body against his, and their lips met again in a soft, tentative kiss. It was electric, igniting a fire within the room. She guided his hands to her waist, encouraging him to explore. "Touch me," she begged.

He stood in one swift motion, unfastened his belt, and stepped out of his trousers before sitting back down on the bed. His hands roamed across her back, pulling her close to him until her nipples brushed his lips, his hot breath playfully teasing them to life. He gave a firm flick of his tongue, sending a shock of arousal throughout her body, her eager moans drawing my hands down between my thighs as I leaned my body firmly against the wall.

The kiss deepened, and I lost myself in the moment, surrendering to the passion that engulfed them. I could feel the world outside fading away, leaving only the three of us in our own cocoon of intimacy.

He reached for her hips, lifting her as her legs wrapped around him. His hands were large, hesitant at first, until she pressed closer. Then the hesitation was gone and the kiss deepened with a fierce hunger, as though they were trying to taste each other's soul.

His hands roamed down her back, gripping her curves. Their bodies moving in a rising rhythm, hips finding hips, friction sparking with every grind, every breathless gasp.

I bit my lip and slipped one hand down between my thighs, sliding beneath the edge of my garter belt, where my fingers found heat and slickness instantly. The pleasure was immediate as I circled my clit, slowly, watching Elona straddle him.

She reached between them, her fingers wrapping around his length, guiding him to her. Hovering there, she teased him with the heat of her body, her breath coming in shaky gasps before she sank down onto him, taking every aching inch.

His head fell back with a ragged groan. "Fuck," he hissed.

Elona moaned low in her throat, riding the delicious stretch. She moved in fluid, rolling waves, like she knew exactly what he wanted and how he wanted it. Her hands on his shoulders, her breasts bouncing with each thrust.

My breath quickened as my fingers moved faster, circling my clit with tight, practiced pressure. I was soaking. Drenched. My other hand traveled up to my heaving chest, fingers finding my hardened nipples, rolling and pinching them between my thumb and forefinger. The wet sound of Elona's body taking him was enough to push me closer to the edge, and I shoved my hand into my mouth to stifle the building moan.

His hands gripped her hips hard, guiding her, thrusting up into her with a rhythm that made the headboard tap the wall. They were lost in each other—sweat-slicked, breathless, wild.

Then he flipped her.

Elona gasped as he bent her over the edge of the bed, her red dress pushed up around her waist, her ass high and waiting. He grabbed her hips and drove into her with a groan that felt like it had been building for years.

"God, you're beautiful," he choked, breath ragged. The sound was raw, a mixture of relief and need, that stirred something dangerous in me.

I nearly came right then while Elona cried out with every thrust.

He growled something low and filthy into her ear, one hand on her hip, the other snaking between her thighs to rub her clit.

"God, yes," she gasped. "Don't stop—don't fucking stop."

I was already on my knees, my dress hiked up and legs spread, as I fucked myself. Fingers thrusting in time with their rhythm, biting my lip to stifle my whimpers.

His hands found her chest, gripping her breasts with possessive strength, his thumb brushing over her hardened nipple. The sensation made her gasp, and she arched her back, pushing against him, desperate for more.

"You feel so fucking good," he growled, as Elona's body shuddered beneath him.

"Yes . . ." she gasped, her words a broken plea. "Don't stop."

Elona's hands grasped the edge of the bed as he pounded into her, the rhythm growing faster and more intense, while she met him with equal force, her body rocking to meet each thrust. Her breath came in sharp, quick bursts.

His pace grew wild, harder, as Elona's moans turned into cries of pure pleasure. Her whole body shook, and he wasn't far behind. His muscles tightened, jaw clenched, a broken growl ripping from his throat as he came hard inside her, hips jerking in sharp bursts.

They collapsed into a tangle of limbs, Elona laying boneless beneath him, and a slow, satisfied smile curved her lips as he kissed the back of her neck, still buried deep inside her. She let out a breathy laugh, more exhale than sound, then shifted to the side, curling lazily into the cushions.

He straightened, chest still rising and falling. His skin was damp with sweat, lips parted as he caught his breath. Then his eyes found mine.

I was still on my knees. My body trembling, slick and flushed, every breath a ragged aftershock of my climax. My dress had ridden up my thighs, and my fingers, wet and glistening, rested between my legs.

He saw all of it. All of me. And a slow smile spread across his face.

Elona collapsed into the pillows, still panting, watching us now with that slow, knowing smile—the kind that said, *your turn now.*

He dropped to his knees in front of me, eyes locking on to mine before they slid down to the mess between my thighs. A low, appreciative sound rumbled in his chest as he caught my wrist in his hand and brought my glistening fingers to his mouth. His tongue swirled around them, tasting me, sucking every drop as if it were nectar.

My whole body tensed.

He moaned low in his throat, like I was the richest thing he'd ever known. "You taste like a fucking dream," he said, voice rough and ruined.

I parted my lips, breathless. But before I could speak, he took my wrist and guided my hand back between my thighs.

"Show me again," he whispered, mouth grazing my ear. "I want to watch you."

Spreading my legs wider, my fingers slid over my clit, before plunging back into my wetness. He watched intently—his eyes fixed on the way I moved, the way my hips started rocking, chasing the high all over again.

He kissed down my jaw, my throat, my shoulder. Hot, open-mouthed kisses that burned into my skin.

And then he pulled me down flat, laying me gently onto my back, my legs falling open for him, as he stared at me, spread wide, like I was art.

He dropped between my thighs, breath ghosting over my wet, aching pussy. And then—*God*—his tongue. The first stroke of it made me gasp, my back arching off the floor. He licked me like he'd been starving for it. Like he needed to memorize the taste of me.

His mouth sealed over my clit, tongue flicking and circling, the pressure just right. My thighs clamped around his head, but he didn't stop. He growled into me, hands gripping my hips, holding me in place like a man determined to drag pleasure out of me by force if he had to.

I came hard, again, with a cry that could have cracked the ceiling. My hips jerked, my hands flew to his hair and my world shattered.

But he didn't stop. He kept going—driving me higher. A second orgasm barreled through me, then a third. I was shaking, sobbing, coming undone under his tongue.

"Please," I begged. "I don't think I can take any more".

He looked up at me with amusement, "Yes, you can."

He pulled me up, crushing his mouth to mine in a deep, devouring kiss that let me taste myself on his lips. He positioned me on all fours, my ass presented like an offering while Elona watched from the bed, her fingers trailing lazily over her own body.

He thrust into my pussy first, each slam of his cock stretching me, filling me. One hand on my hip, the other sliding into my hair, gripping tight as he pulled my head back. Elona's gaze fueled the heat, her hand dipping between her legs to touch herself in sync with his movements, lips parted as she moaned with us.

"Not yet," he teased, pulling out to circle my clit with his thumb, making me whine in frustration. Then, slowly, he pressed the head of his cock against my ass, inching in with deliberate care. The stretch burned, then bloomed into ecstasy as he filled me completely. My orgasm hit like lightning, body convulsing around him, milking every drop, and tearing a scream from my lungs as my vision went white.

He came seconds later, roaring my name into the crook of my neck, collapsing over me, both of us gasping for air. Elona crawled over to us and we stayed like that—sweaty, tangled, and absolutely spent.

20

THE KIND OF GIRL THEY DON'T PAINT

ELONA

I stood before the grand double doors of the gallery, my heartbeat steady, though I felt a nervous flutter deep inside my chest. I smoothed the worn fabric of my coat, once a rich burgundy that had deepened to a muted wine with the passing years, and adjusted the strap of my leather portfolio before lowering it to my side. Each step toward this place, this moment, was an act of courage which I had rehearsed in my mind countless times.

The district that the gallery was in was a place of wealth; of polished marble and gilded frames. Elegant buildings with tall windows loomed over me, sunlight flashing off the glass and casting colorful reflections. It was something that had always seemed to be just beyond my reach. But it wasn't just the art I craved; it was the validation. It was the recognition, something that had always been unavailable to me, especially in a world that still saw me as "other."

Through the gallery's window, I could hear the muted sound of voices as their hands swept and circled before each painting, the faint clink of glasses, and catch the subtle click of polished shoes against cool, gleaming marble floors. Art lovers, critics, and collectors mingled in the light, their eyes roaming from one expensive painting to the next. But for me, it wasn't the abstract pieces or the clean lines of modern art that called out to me; it was the charcoal drawings that I carried, my own small rebellion against the sterile perfection that filled these walls.

The women in my drawings, strong, raw, and defiant, embodied everything I had fought to hold on to in my life. They were more than just images; they were stories, my stories. The untold histories of women like me, women who had been erased, neglected, or forgotten by the world. In each stroke of my charcoal, I had found a voice, a way to communicate the power and beauty of those who had survived against all odds.

Taking a deep breath, I pushed the doors open. The warm air from the gallery kissed my skin as I stepped inside, and for a moment, I felt like a stranger, an intruder in a world that did not welcome me. I scanned the space with careful eyes, noting the silent, lifeless art adorning the walls that pretended to offer something more than just an aesthetic.

My gaze swept through the crowd until it landed on the man I was looking for, Mr. Bennett, the gallery owner. He stood near the center of the room, solidly built, his frame carrying an easy weight that made him feel rooted in place rather than simply occupying it. His hair was perfectly arranged, every strand disciplined into submission, and his glasses sat low on his nose, while his eyes did most of the talking—cool and assessing. They moved over the room until they found me, and something shifted. The calculation softened just enough to pass for warmth, replaced by the polished courtesy of a man long accustomed to artists who never quite belonged in his world, yet kept trying to earn their place in it.

"Miss Elona," he said, stepping forward. "Good to see you, come right in."

I offered a tight-lipped smile. I could already feel the tension in my body; the small pulse of anxiety that had started the moment I stepped into this space. Every inch of this gallery reeked of privilege, of rarity, and of the silent judgments that waited to pounce.

"I've brought my work, Mr. Bennett," I said, my voice steady despite the nerves that prickled my skin. "I'd like to show you some of my drawings that I think would be a good fit for your gallery."

Mr. Bennett's gaze dropped to the portfolio in my hands, but there was hesitation in his eyes and a slight shift in his posture, almost imperceptible, but enough for me to notice it. He glanced over his shoulder at one of the attendants, a tall, thin woman in a sleek black dress, and then nodded toward an empty corner.

"Of course. Let's have a look at them in private, shall we?" His voice remained smooth, yet there was an undercurrent to his words that made my stomach tighten. I nodded, following him through the crowd while every glance from the art lovers felt like a challenge, a reminder that I was not meant to be here, not meant to be seen.

We arrived at a small, secluded corner of the gallery, where Mr. Bennett gestured toward a low table. "Please, have a seat," he offered, his tone almost condescending. "Let's take a look at your work."

I carefully placed my portfolio on the table, my fingers trembling slightly as I began to unlatch it. I had rehearsed this part, the introduction, the explanation of what each drawing meant to me, the personal stories behind each line, but now, as he loomed across from me, the words seemed to vanish.

Before I could open the portfolio, Mr. Bennett cleared his throat and adjusted his glasses, his posture defensive. His fingers folded together in a steeple and then he spoke in that soft, too-measured voice that always made my skin crawl.

"You know, Miss Elona," he began, "we appreciate your interest in having your work featured in our gallery. However. . ." He let the word hang, the finality in it suffocating. His gaze drifted toward the crowd, ensuring no one was listening. "Your work is, I'm sure . . . very well done, of course," he continued, "but—"

My fingers tightened around the edge of the portfolio, my pulse quickening. "But?" I prompted, my voice cool, though I could feel the rage beginning to bubble up in my chest. This was familiar. I knew exactly where this was going, the same words, the same thinly veiled dismissal.

He leaned back, shifting his gaze to my hands as if inspecting them for signs of weakness. "Your style of work is . . . unique, certainly. But, Miss Elona, as we discussed before—" his eyes lowered once more, settling on my hands in a way that made me feel small "this is an exclusive space. A space for the finer artists, for those whose work appeals to a very specific clientele. Your. . . style of work is striking, but perhaps. . . it doesn't quite fit the image we're looking for."

I could feel it now, the familiar sting of rejection. It was all too clear: My art, my voice, my identity didn't fit into the carefully curated world of refined taste he championed. He wasn't looking at my work, at the raw, unapologetic power of the women I drew. He was looking at me, at who I was and what I represented. And I was, in his eyes, an outsider. My voice remained calm, though my chest tightened with frustration. "What exactly do you mean by 'doesn't fit the image'? I thought you wanted authentic, powerful art that challenges the viewer. That's what I've brought for you."

This time Mr. Bennett's lips curved into a sly smile. "It's not about authenticity, Miss Elona, it's about refinement. The people who visit this gallery. . ." He paused, his voice dripping with condescension. "They expect something different. They expect something. . . more palatable."

I could feel my jaw tightening, the words already forming on my tongue. "You don't want to display my work because I'm Indian." I said firmly, my voice cutting through the pretense.

Mr. Bennett faltered for a moment but quickly regained his composure. "I wouldn't say that, Miss Elona. It's just a matter of what fits with our gallery's. . . vision—"

"Stop." I stood up, unable to stay seated any longer. My portfolio felt like stone in my hands, his rejection settling deep, but I kept my expression steady. "I'm not here for your polite lies. I've seen your 'refined' art before. It's all the same: a white canvas, a clean line, something easy to digest. My women are not easy to digest, but they're real, and you're afraid of that." The room shrunk down to an airless box but I fought the suffocating feeling.

Mr. Bennett made a nervous, uncertain noise. "It's not personal, Miss Elona. I'm merely trying to help you understand—"

"I understand perfectly." My voice came out steady, even if everything inside me wasn't. "I never needed your help." I straightened my back, lifted my chin, and turned toward the door before he could say anything else. By the time I crossed the gallery, I was fighting back tears.

Outside, the cold hit hard, wind slicing across my face and sucking the air from my lungs. I huddled deeper into my coat, dragged in a breath and trying to steady myself, but it only made the burn behind my eyes worse. Mr. Bennett's belittling words whispered of an age-old truth: In a world built on polished privilege, my people, the bright threads of my heritage, would always be deemed unworthy by men like him.

21

WORTH THE TOUCH, NOT THE NAME

ELONA

I slipped inside The Oily Cat with my shoulders already tight, my boots hesitant on the floor. I kept my head down, tracking the familiar lines in the wood, hoping muscle memory might kick in and save me the effort of pretending.

It didn't.

Golden light poured through the space, soft and honeyed, the kind that should have felt like home, but instead, it brushed over me too knowingly, too bare—like it could see every doubt I carried in with me and refused to let me hide. I kept walking anyway, the strap of my bag pulled tight across my shoulder, fingers locked around it hard enough to leave dents. My sketchbook pressed against my ribs, but it didn't steady me the way it should have. If anything, it made it worse. *What if I'm worth nothing at all? What if my art is trash?* The thought came uninvited, curling inward, and my chest tightened until breathing felt like an effort.

The day had dragged its claws across me. I'd walked into the gallery with my best dress and a head full of maybes. But that hope had been shattered with every passing moment. The soft, dismissive glances, the polite but hollow smiles, capped off by Mr. Bennett's cold words: *Your work doesn't fit our image.* It stayed with me, that moment, lodged somewhere inside my chest. I'd been turned away before, it wasn't new, but today it felt like a punch in the gut. I had known it was coming, of course. People like me, people from my world, never got the same chances, never were seen as worthy. The gallery had only confirmed what I'd always known: I wasn't their idea of art or beauty.

Upstairs, the girls were already slipping into their nighttime selves—heels clacking, corsets tightening, voices rising and falling. Violet's laugh curled down the staircase, followed by Maeve's edgier one, and I didn't need to see them to know the scene: perfume clouds, painted lips, someone fussing with a loose curl in the mirror as if it mattered more than air. Their noise made it easy to slip past the saloon unnoticed. I didn't look toward the mirrors; there was no point. Whatever version of me had once reflected there had already unraveled somewhere between Mr. Bennett's smile and that damn gallery floor. I just kept moving, head down and bag clutched. My heart was still trying to pretend it wasn't broken open and leaking all over the floor.

Behind the bar, I slipped out of my coat, revealing the black lace gown underneath, the one I saved for nights when I didn't want to be looked at like a meal. It draped over me loosely, brushing my skin without asking much of it. It wasn't the kind of dress that drew much attention, yet, I could still feel like something worth looking at, without giving myself away.

One by one, the patrons slipped through the door, coats damp from the fog, pockets heavy with expectations. I moved the way I was supposed to—sipped the drinks, offered the smiles, touched an arm here or there like it meant something. It was muscle memory more than anything. My grin held, but it pinched at the corners. My voice lifted when it needed to, light and warm, like sugar stirred into something bitter. They laughed and I laughed back. I even moaned when the moment called for it—soft, practiced, without a drop of pleasure behind it. Just another part of the performance. Something in my throat that sounded like me, but wasn't.

BERNADETTE

I noticed immediately, of course. Elona was distant and had seemingly detached herself from what was happening around her. Her eyes were glassy, her movements sluggish. I watched her from across the room, my eyes narrowing in concern. The brothel was winding down, the night bleeding out slowly, and the air had that stale, used-up feel. Most of the men had already slunk off into the dark, and the girls were slipping out the front door one by one, bound for their homes and whatever peace waited there for them. But Elona stayed behind in the lounge, alone, with a half-empty glass of whiskey perched before her. Her eyes looked through the room, distant and unfocused, while her fingers traced the rim of the glass.

Unable to stand the sight of her slipping further into that empty space, I eased across the room, my boots barely making a sound on the worn floorboards. Settling down beside her, I found the edge of the armchair, close enough to catch the faint heat she gave off, but careful not to cross the fragile line she'd drawn around herself. Leaning forward, elbows resting heavily on my knees, I kept my voice low. "Elona, what happened?" The words carrying urgency and concern.

She offered no reply, simply blinking slowly as if trying to muster the strength to speak. When her eyes finally met mine, there was a raw vulnerability there, a spark that hinted at both pain and hope. But almost as quickly as it came, that tenderness was replaced by a hard, guarded look. "Nothing," she whispered flatly, the word scarcely audible, "just a bad day."

I frowned, "Don't give me that. You've been moving around like someone just trampled your heart."

Elona's lips curled into a bitter smile. "I'm fine, Birdie, really. It's just the usual shit. People like me don't get to do things like that," she said, a dismissive flick of her hand toward the artwork that hung above the bar. She recounted her jeering dismissal from the gallery, a place where her work was never given a fair glance.

She continued, nearly inaudibly, "I shouldn't have tried. I knew exactly how it would end." Each word bore the ache of a lifetime measured in doors slammed shut and chances never given.

My own frustration flared as I leaned in closer. "I don't care who 'they' are, Elona. You deserve more than to be trampled on by folks who see you as less because of where you come from or the color of your skin." My tone was fierce, a protective blaze ignited by years of watching her fight. Her eyes widened briefly, and in that instant, I saw her vulnerability mixing with a deep, unspoken fury. She steadied her voice before uttering, "You don't understand."

Gently, I reached for her hand, offering something solid in the storm she was caught in. "Maybe I haven't walked your path," I said, "but I know what it is to be treated like you don't matter. I've seen you shine, Elona. And I'll be damned if I let anyone make you feel anything less than brilliant."

A tender, fragile smile began to glisten on her lips, a spark of relief and hope breaking through the gloom. "Thank you, Birdie," she whispered. "I really needed that."

I gave her hand a firm squeeze, "Anytime, darlin'."

Elona sat a little straighter now, her eyes clearer. But as I sat beside her, watching her fingers still nervously trace the glass rim, something cold settled in my gut. They thought they could dismiss her. Like she was nothing more than a girl with charcoal on her hands and too much ambition in her eyes. Like talent had to come wrapped in silk and pedigrees to be considered worthy. I wasn't going to let that stand.

So, while Elona sat there trying to swallow the bitterness of the world, I made a silent vow: They were going to see her. And they were going to remember her name.

22

THE ART OF REVENGE

No one ever says the rules out loud in a town like this, but break them, and you'll know them fast enough. Mr. Bennett never cared about the lines he crossed; he thought people like Elona were just background noise, forgettable. But today wasn't going to be a quiet day. Today was the reckoning, and I was done waiting for justice to show up on its own.

Mr. Bennett, the self-styled king of the art world in Butte, paraded around in his poorly tailored suits, his nose always tilted upward as if he was above everyone else. I had watched Elona walk out of the brothel after she told me about her experience at the gallery several nights ago, her eyes still red with disappointment and something shattered inside me. I couldn't let it go, not when I knew that there was still a fire burning inside her, that her work was demanding to be seen.

The gallery gleamed with its sterile, godly aura: a temple of exclusion. White walls, pristine floors, paintings hanging at regular intervals. The space was like an imitation of art, perfect in form, yet empty in substance. He had rejected Elona without even sparing her a second glance, blinded by his own warped views.

I walked in like I owned the place. The black portfolio under my arm held the essentials, but it was the power of my presence that would do the real work. Mr. Bennett stood next to one of his latest exhibits, incrementally adjusting the already perfectly straight painting. The moment I cleared my throat his eyes cut toward me with surprise.

"Miss Bernadette," he said, his voice dripping with forced politeness. "What a surprise. I wasn't expecting you today."

I let a smile curl at my lips. "Oh, I'm sure you weren't," I said, my voice honeyed with a hint of sting, "but I've come to show you something. Something . . . quite extraordinary."

Mr. Bennett's gaze moved to the portfolio under my arm, his eyes narrowing ever so slightly, and that gleam of curiosity was all I needed. He straightened, his posture shifting like a dog that decided the scent was worth the chase. "What's that?"

I shifted forward slightly, my tone purposefully tantalizing. "A collection of charcoal drawings, portraits of women. Stunning work, Mr. Bennett, I'm sure you'll appreciate them."

The skepticism still lingered on his face, but it was slipping. "Hmm, I see. Well, we're not exactly taking new submissions right now—"

I cut him off smoothly. "Oh, I'm not submitting, Mr. Bennett." I said the words slowly, savoring the power in them. "I've been told that my friend's work might be better suited to a . . . private collection." I placed just the right emphasis on "private collection," the words sliding from my tongue like an invitation to an exclusive, unspoken world. His eyes brightened. "Well," he said, his voice low, "I'm intrigued. Show me."

I pulled the portfolio out from under my arm, opening it slowly. His face, usually so smooth, betrayed the slightest hint of hesitation as he peered down at the first drawing. The charcoal portraits jumped to life with a depth that made even the sterile gallery feel too confined. The women in those portraits had power, grace, and vulnerability, the kind of presence that couldn't be ignored. His fingers hovered over the first page, skimming the surface as though unsure how to touch something so real.

"These are. . ." he faltered, voice filling with surprise, "remarkable. The depth, the shading, the realism. . . it's incredible."

I waited, my eyes fixed on him, knowing exactly what he was thinking. I could see the wheels turning in his mind, the internal struggle between his own rigid biases and the undeniable quality of the work in front of him. I let him stew for a moment, enjoying the silence. "I'm glad you see it." I said, my voice oozing with just enough sweetness to make the venom underneath that much more poisonous. "The artist who created these . . . she's truly extraordinary."

Mr. Bennett nodded, his posture tightening as his mind kicked into overdrive. "Yes, yes, these could be the next big thing. We should feature her in the upcoming exhibition; this could make a name for her."

My lips curved into a knowing smile. "I'm sure it would," I said, measuring each word. Then, casually, "But you see, I've already reached out to another gallery in Bozeman and they're *very* interested."

His eyes narrowed, just slightly.

I turned toward the door. "Still," I added, glancing over my shoulder, "if you'd like, I'll go ahead and get her." Before he could answer, I was already moving, pulse quickening with a simmering satisfaction. I didn't need to look back to know his gaze was still on me.

Stepping outside, I found Elona waiting, her shoulders slightly hunched, uncertainty clinging to her and the sight tugged at me. Beneath that hesitation, I saw what so few ever did: a brilliance, and a strength that didn't shout, but endured. She was so much more than anyone, least of all Mr. Bennett, could ever begin to understand. I placed my hand gently on her elbow, guiding her forward. "Come on," I said softly. "Let's show them what they've been blind to."

Her brows furrowed in confusion. "Birdie, I . . . I can't. I'm not—"

"You can," I said gently, but with absolute conviction. I smiled, pride unmistakable in my eyes. "You can do anything, Elona. Now go in there and make him regret ever treating you as anything less."

I opened the door wide, ushering her inside like a queen stepping rightfully into her palace. Mr. Bennett's eyes flicked up, meeting Elona's, and for a brief, taut second, his face twisted in disbelief. Apparently he couldn't quite reconcile the woman standing before him with the artist he had only just begun to appreciate.

"You mean . . ." His voice cracked. "She's the one who created these?"

I stood behind Elona, my gaze fixed on Mr. Bennett, watching the realization dawn on him. "Yes, Mr. Bennett," I said, relishing the moment, "she's the one. But I believe you've met before?" I took a step forward. "Now, perhaps you'd like to discuss that exhibition?"

There was no hesitation this time, no arrogance, just stunned silence. Then Mr. Bennett cleared his throat, struggling to recover from the full impact of his own ignorance. His voice trembled slightly as he spoke. "I . . . I had no idea. Please, Miss Elona, we would love to feature your work." He gestured to the portfolio. "I must have these."

"Well," I said coolly, "the Bozeman gallery didn't seem to have any issue with the color of Elona's skin. It made no difference to them, only the art mattered." I let that sink in, then added, "And really, that's what a true gallery is meant to be about, isn't it? The work, not the artist."

His mouth opened, then closed again.

"Of course," I continued, "we've already begun discussions with them. Pulling out now wouldn't be simple, and frankly, Mr. Bennett, if you want Elona's time, you'll have to make it worth it to her."

Mr. Bennett turned toward Elona, his expression pale.

"Miss Elona . . ." he said, voice softer now, almost pleading. "I was wrong, I see that now. Your work. . . it's extraordinary, and if you'll allow it, I'd be honored to feature it here. To feature *you.*" He hesitated, as if weighing the cost of humility. "I can't change what I didn't see before. But I'd like the chance to make it right."

Elona blinked, still catching up to the moment. She drew a steady breath and met Mr. Bennett's gaze, her voice clear. "I'd be honored to have my work featured. But I'll need to see if our values and ideas align well enough for a working partnership. Please feel free to write up a proposal with numbers, and I'll get back to you." Then her eyes found mine, a silent thank-you passing between us, her lips curling into the faintest, grateful smile.

I winked at her, pride in my chest nearly bursting. The tables had turned.

We walked together toward the door, Elona's fingers brushing the handle.

"You go on ahead," I said gently. "I just need a word with Mr. Bennett."

She stilled, her hand lingering on the copper. "Birdie—"

"It won't take long," I assured her, shaping my voice into something warm, something that would have passed for harmless, if she didn't know me as well as she did. "Go."

She searched my face, trying to find the truth hidden in the smallest corners of my expression, but exhaustion weighed heavier than suspicion. She was too worn down by the fight, by the emotions spent over these past few days, that whatever questions lingered, she let them go. And after a beat, she nodded, before slipping outside.

I waited.

One heartbeat. Two.

Until the echo of her footsteps thinned and vanished into silence.

Only then did I turn the lock.

Click.

When I turned back, Mr. Bennett was already watching me, his posture no longer the easy, curated poise he wore just seconds ago. His gaze flicked toward the door behind me before returning to my face.

"Miss Bernadette. . . ?" He asked, uncertainty in his voice.

I didn't say anything. Just watched him, studying every shift in his expression before I moved. Each step carried me farther into the center of the gallery, my heels soft against the pristine floors.

"Elona might forgive your poor manners," I said at last, my voice level, smooth enough to mimic kindness if one didn't listen too carefully. "But I don't operate on forgiveness."

His throat bobbed, the movement betraying his unease. "I think," he began, choosing each words carefully, "there may be a misunderstanding. I've already expressed—"

"No," I interrupted. "You've performed an apology." A faint smile touched my lips, though there was no warmth in it. "There's a difference."

He moved behind the wooden counter, his eyes narrowing as he recalibrated, searching for a way out of this. "What exactly is it that you want from me?"

I tilted my head, considering him the way he might consider one of his acquisitions—assessing composition, searching for flaws, wondering where the structure would fracture first if enough pressure were applied.

"Interesting question," I murmured.

Above us, the gallery lights hummed awake, spilling a harsh, headache-bright glow across the room. I drifted toward one of the white walls, stopping just close enough to catch the faint ghost of my reflection in the varnished surface of a framed piece.

"You didn't reject her because she lacked talent," I continued, my tone almost conversational now, as though we were discussing something as mundane as brushstrokes or framing. "You rejected her because you thought her value was determined by the color of her skin."

"That's not—"

"It is," I said softly, cutting him off. "And what you did—what you relied on—was the assumption that she wouldn't come back."

His expression tightened, the words catching somewhere between offense and exposure. "What are you implying?"

I turned then, meeting his gaze fully, and let him see, really see, that whatever pretense had existed before was gone now, stripped down to something far more honest and far more dangerous. Mr. Bennett shifted, the movement small but telling as I stepped toward him, my heels striking the floor.

Once.

Twice.

Each sound closing the distance until it was no longer polite, until the space between us felt charged in a way that had nothing to do with proximity and everything to do with control.

"I'm not implying anything," I said evenly. "I'm making sure you understand exactly what kind of mistake you've made."

For a fraction of a second, he held my gaze, clinging to whatever kindness he thought still lived there.

Then I reached into the pocket of my dress and by the time he realized what I was holding, it was already too late. The knife flashed once beneath the gallery lights before I drove it through the back of his hand, the blade sinking deeply enough that the tip lodged into the wood of the counter with a dull, splintering crack that vibrated up my arm.

His body jerked hard in response, a broken sound tearing free from his throat as he tried to pull back, causing the wound to open wider. He frantically screamed before my free hand came up, clamping firm over his mouth.

"Careful," I murmured, leaning in close. "You wouldn't want to make a scene in your beautiful gallery."

His breath came sharp against my palm, uneven and shallow, his eyes wide and full of fear. Up close, I could see it clearly now, the understanding, the dawning realization that I was in fact, as crazy as they said I was. And that brought me a sick kind of joy.

My gaze dropped to the wound, blood pooling, spilling over his skin, and dripping down onto the polished surface below.

"Let this be the part you remember," I said, my fingers tightening around the handle, anchoring him in place. "Not the apology you performed. Not the sale you nearly lost." I twisted the blade. "But this."

He let out a muffled cry, his breath stuttering against my palm as tears slipped down his face.

I eased my hand from his mouth, turning the blade once more before pulling it free, the wood and bone yielding with a reluctant scrape as he cried out in pain. I dragged the blade clean across the front of his shirt, the gesture almost absent-minded, before slipping it neatly back into my pocket.

I stepped away, smoothing my dress as though nothing at all had happened.

At the door, I paused, glancing back over my shoulder. His injured hand was clutched to his chest now, his body curled inward, but he hadn't moved from where I left him.

"Do be more careful next time," I said lightly. "Not everyone is as forgiving as Elona."

Then I unlocked the door, turned the handle, and stepped out into the sun as if I were leaving nothing more than an ordinary meeting behind me.

"Have a nice day, Mr. Bennett."

23

PRACTICE WHAT YOU PREACH

HIM

I had been in Butte for nearly a week and already a gnawing unease had begun to take root deep within me. The town, with its charming streets and humble homes, had welcomed me with open arms. The people were kind, perhaps naively so. The whole town seemed to hold great respect for Father Cyrus, as though he were a god amongst men, with his broad smile, gentle words, and calm demeanor. And truthfully, I could see why they admired him. His presence was steadying, his faith apparent in everything he did. But there was one thing that I could not understand: the brothel. It wasn't the existence of it that troubled me, per se, it was the way the townsfolk, and Father Cyrus himself, seemed to accept it with a level of tolerance that seemed to me both appalling and irredeemable.

My mind swirled with confusion as I paced the small rectory with my hands clasped tightly behind my back. How could they, these good, God-fearing people, simply overlook the sinful presence of that establishment in their midst? The brothel, with its open doors, its welcoming embrace of men and women who sullied their souls in acts of lust—how could Father Cyrus, a priest, allow such an abomination to exist under his watch? How could he stand idly by, offering grace to the women who worked there and the men who frequented it?

My thoughts spiraled. I had heard the whispers around town, the rumors about Bernadette, the owner, and her business. She had been to church, in fact she was a regular, and she was even respected by Father Cyrus. It was inconceivable to me.

I remembered the first time I met Bernadette and her girls. They had entered St. Ann's on a Sunday morning, wearing lavish silk dresses that looked far too expensive for women who supposedly lived a life of sin. They had seated themselves with such casualness, such ease, as though they were just like any other parishioners, and Father Cyrus had welcomed them with a smile, rather than rebuke. He had even joked with them, as if they were just old friends, not the harbingers of moral decay that I, and any other ordained man of God, understood them to be. I did, however, notice the way the other townsfolk had reacted. They had judgment in their eyes and a clear sense of disapproval. But still, it was almost as though the brothel were simply another business in town, no different than a bakery or a hardware store.

"Disgusting!" I blurted aloud.

My hand tightened into a fist as I paced the room, my footsteps echoing through the rectory. The walls, adorned with simple religious symbolism, seemed to close in on me, each crucifix staring down at me with a silent reprimand. I felt trapped in a sea of hypocrisy, but it wasn't just the brothel that plagued my thoughts, there was something else. Someone else.

Violet.

I had seen her at church, seated in the pews with Bernadette and the other girls, her long, angelic blond hair falling in gentle waves around her shoulders, her skin pale and flawless. She had a mysteriousness about her, something dark and dangerous but also irresistibly beautiful. Violet didn't laugh like the others, didn't smile like the others. She just watched, with those dark, brown eyes that seemed to strip me bare every time her gaze found mine. I caught myself watching her during the sermon, again and again, my mind a twisted pit of filthy thoughts that made me want to vomit. It was her fault: Violet's.

She haunted my every waking hour. She was the cause of every desperate, shameful night spent touching myself alone in the dark, begging for release from a craving I knew was sinful but couldn't stop.

Every time our eyes met, a sick knot twisted deep in my belly, half longing, half hatred, for her, for myself, for this unbearable desire that clawed beneath my skin. I tried to drown it out with prayers, with scripture, but when she was near, my body betrayed me. I was meant to be pure. A man of God. But instead, I was a slave to her shadow, trapped in a cage of lust I built myself.

I clenched my fists until my nails bit into my palms, but the images stayed, vivid, relentless, crawling beneath my skin like worms. My mind wandered to the brothel, that cursed place festering at the edge of town. A place that seemed to hold all the answers to my confusion, yet none of the salvation I craved. The rage boiled beneath my calm façade. How dare that place exist? How dare she? And why does Father Cyrus allow it?

A part of me wanted to believe that perhaps the old priest was doing the right thing. After all, the townsfolk loved him, respected him, and if they truly had been living in sin, would they not have turned on him long ago? But another part of me, the part that tugged at my very soul, rebelled against this idea. I had been taught that sin must be confronted, that those who stray from the path must be brought back to the light. Yet here in Butte, in Father Cyrus's church, there was no confrontation, no judgment, no salvation.

How can I accept this?

"Father Frederick," came the voice of Father Cyrus from the doorway, cutting through my spiraling thoughts.

I turned abruptly, my face a mask of frustration and confusion. My hands trembled slightly, a clear sign of the inner turmoil that had consumed me in recent days. "Yes, Father Cyrus?"

Father Cyrus smiled warmly, his presence so calm and steady that it only made my frustration grow. "You've been in here a while. I thought you might want to join me for a walk. The weather is beautiful today."

I clenched my jaw but nodded, following Father Cyrus out of the rectory and into the sunlight. We walked side by side, the comforting hum of the town surrounding us, the sound of children playing and merchants haggling in the distance. The day was bright, and the sky was a deep, cloudless blue that seemed to mock the darkness inside of me.

We walked in silence for a while, the soft crunch of gravel beneath our feet filling the space between us. Father Cyrus, as always, seemed at peace with the world, his slow, deliberate steps in perfect harmony with the rhythm of the town. But for me, each step was a heavy reminder of everything I couldn't shake. I was hyper-aware of everything, the warmth of the sun on my face, the cool breeze tugging at my cassock, the steady pulse of the town around me. It was all too normal, too perfect, and yet, I felt like an outsider, like a man standing on the edge of something I could not be a part of.

Father Cyrus led me down the familiar path, past the white picket fences and quaint houses, until we reached the town center. The brothel loomed in the distance, its faded sign swaying slightly in the breeze, its entrance marked only by a small, simple door. The building was modest, unremarkable in its outward appearance, but to me it represented everything that was wrong with Butte. Its very existence was a stain on the town's otherwise pristine image. My stomach churned as we drew closer, and I couldn't help but feel a deep sense of disgust. My chest tightened and a coldness settled over me as though something unseen was pressing down on my shoulders, urging me to turn away. But I couldn't.

Father Cyrus stopped at the entrance of the brothel and turned to face me. "I know it's hard for you to understand, Father Frederick," he said, his tone gentle. "But this town, these people, are good, despite their flaws. They live their lives, they struggle, they fight their demons, and I believe they deserve grace. All of them."

My eyes narrowed, a mix of disbelief and anger flashing across my face. "You're okay with the brothel? You condone it?"

Father Cyrus's eyes softened, but his voice remained firm. "I don't condone it, Father Frederick. But I understand it. People fall. They make mistakes, and sometimes, they need a place to go where they can find solace, even if it's in the arms of another."

"Solace?" My voice rose slightly, though I quickly tempered it. "Sin is sin, Father Cyrus. The women who work there—" I stopped myself, biting back my frustration. "They are prostitutes. It's not a mistake. It's not something they deserve forgiveness for. It's something that they choose every day. And you . . . you just let it go on. You let them sit in your pews, you let them take communion, and you do nothing to stop it."

Father Cyrus's gaze hardened for a moment, and I braced myself for a rebuke, but instead he simply smiled, though there was something sad in his eyes, something that made my chest tighten. "You've been taught well, Father Frederick," he said. "But you have a lot to learn. God's mercy isn't just for the saints, it's for the sinners too, all of them. Even the ones who sell their bodies, and even the ones who find solace in their weakness."

A cold knot twisted in my stomach, and my thoughts turned again to Violet, to her face with that distant, knowing look in her eyes. *How could she, how could anyone find solace in something so revolting?* The question hung in my mind, unanswered.

Father Cyrus patted me gently on the shoulder, guiding me away from the brothel. "Come now, Father Frederick," he said softly. "Let's continue our walk. There's more to see here than this place."

I didn't trust myself to speak. I nodded stiffly, following Father Cyrus as we walked away, our footsteps fading into the background of Butte. The brothel, still looming behind us, remained a silent witness to all that had been said, and all that had been left unsaid.

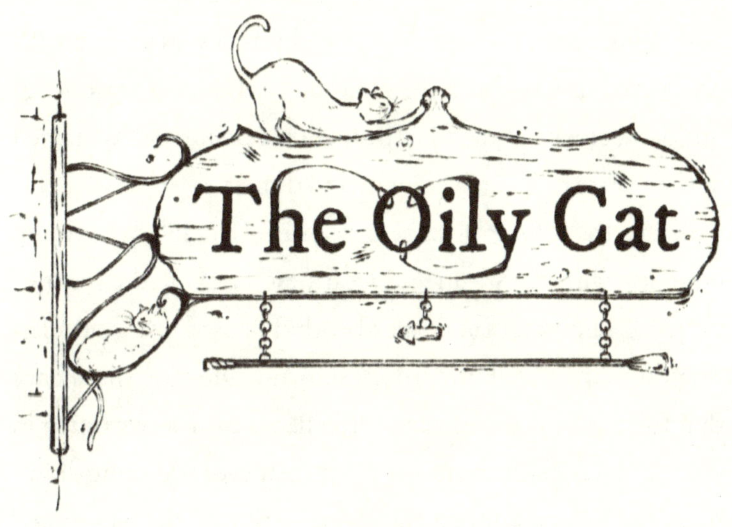

24

IF YOU DON'T HAVE ANYTHING NICE TO SAY...

As I made my way to St. Ann's, the wind clawed at my coat, dragging dust and sleet through the streets of Butte like it was trying to skim the town clean. Spring didn't come easy to this place; it scraped its way in, rough-edged and stubborn, just like the rest of us. The sharp tap of my heels on the cobblestones announced my arrival long before I reached the side door that doubled as the entrance to the shelter. The humble offering of St. Ann's to the unwanted misfits of the town only opened once a month and was always packed with unclaimed mothers and the children born out of season and out of wedlock. These were people that polite society named in their prayers, but never invited to dinner.

Inside, the sounds of sighs and shifting feet filled the room, mingling with the steam and weariness, carrying the scent of overcooked potatoes and weak broth. I paused just inside, letting the warmth lick my frozen skin and allowing the silence that followed my entrance to settle like dust. Every woman in the room went still. Some dropped their eyes and some didn't bother. I briefly scanned the room until my eyes fell on *her*, Mrs. Henderson, standing ramrod straight by the fire, gripping her ladle like a weapon, jaw set so tight I could practically hear her molars grind.

I offered her my slowest, most deliberate smile, making certain I showed my teeth. "Mrs. Henderson," I purred. "How's the soup today? Still taste like penance?"

Her eyes narrowed into slits, mouth curling like she was deciding whether to scold me or summon God Himself. "Bernadette." She spat my name like a curse. "You shouldn't be here."

I stepped further into the room, brushing snowflakes from my shoulders. "Well, that's funny, I thought this was a place for the forgotten, the fallen, and the barely hanging on. You sure I'm not exactly where I belong?"

A few of the women looked away, but I read it in their expressions. Some smirked, some winced, and some wanted to applaud. That was always the game in these places; some loved to hate me, some hated to love me, and most weren't brave enough to admit they'd ever darkened my doorway when the world got cold.

"You think feeding the poor absolves you?" Mrs. Henderson hissed.

I let my smile widen. "Oh honey, I don't need absolution. I'm not here to be saved, I'm here because I remember what it was like to be hungry and scared and invisible. You think I do this for atonement?" I edged nearer. "I do it because hardly anyone else does." That shut her up.

I turned away before she could sharpen her tongue again and spotted the reasons I kept coming back to this godforsaken place: the kids. They were huddled near the hearth, knees drawn to chests, hands wrapped around chipped mugs of broth. One little boy caught my eye, his big brown eyes too large for his pale, pinched face. I walked over and crouched beside him. "What's your name, sweetheart?"

He clutched the mug tighter, his small fingers white around the handle. He looked to his mother, the question already in his eyes. At her slight nod, he turned back to me and whispered, "Samuel."

"Samuel," I repeated, like it was the most important name in the world. "You look like a man who can handle some responsibility. How'd you like to be in charge of the bread today?"

His eyes lit up like I'd offered him gold. "Really?"

"Really," I said, handing him a small basket. "Just one piece per person." I winked, and that was all it took, his little chest puffed up with pride, and he marched off like I'd knighted him. Behind me, I could hear Mrs. Henderson grumble something into her apron, but I didn't bother to turn around. She didn't scare me.

"You don't belong here," she repeated, louder this time, her voice slicing through the room.

I straightened, turned on my heel, and gave her a look like I was measuring her for a casket. "You know, it's almost cute, how you parade around with a ladle like it's a sword, thinking soup makes you a saint. But let's not pretend your charity isn't just a polished mirror for your own self-righteousness." I took a step closer, lowering my voice just enough to make her lean in. "You're not saving souls, Mrs. Henderson, you're feeding them just enough for you to feel superior." My smile fell. "You'd rather damn a drowning woman for the way she swims than admit you never threw her a rope."

The other women shifted, uncomfortably. It wasn't just about me, it was about them, all the women who lived between two kinds of shame. Too poor to be respectable, too proud to beg. I didn't fit into their idea of redemption because I wasn't trying to be redeemed, and that's what really scared them. I moved past the soup line and toward the back, where the tired ones sat. These were the ones too worn to pretend they weren't breaking, and I noticed a young mother, arms cradling a baby.

I sank beside her, my voice softer now. "You hangin' in there?"

She nodded, eyes heavy, but grateful for the question. I looked at the baby, a little girl, cheeks flushed from the heat of her mother's skin. "She's beautiful," I said, "and so fortunate to have you." The woman blinked hard, and I let my hand rest gently over hers. No speeches, no pity, just the comfort of shared understanding.

A rustle of movement behind me signaled Maggie's approach. Maggie was a fellow member of St. Ann's and ran the shelter, she also had a knack for showing up just when the room's tension began to settle in.

Her voice was thoughtful. "Didn't think you'd come today."

I stood, brushing my hands on my skirt as I straightened from where I had been crouched beside the young mother. I gave her a sideways grin. "You should know better by now. I'm not one to miss a good meal and a little righteous judgment."

Her smile was faint, but warm. "Thank you, Bernadette, for showing up. Again."

I tipped my head. "I show up for them, not for her," I said, nodding toward Mrs. Henderson, who was now stirring the soup like she wished it were arsenic.

"You always do," Maggie said simply, turning to walk away.

I reached out and gently caught her arm. "Can you grab some clean clothes and fresh diapers?" I asked softly, glancing toward the young mother and the baby at her breast. "And another bowl of soup—she's still nursing. She could use the extra nutrients."

The creak of the front door followed by a gust of wind announced the arrival of the next visitors. The shuffle of worn shoes and hushed voices told me it was more women in need. But beneath that came the familiar footfalls of Father Cyrus. I didn't even need to turn around to know it was him.

"Evening, Birdie," Father Cyrus called. "Tell me you didn't start a riot without me."

I didn't turn right away, just let the corner of my mouth lift. "You're late. I had to improvise."

His laugh rolled through the room. "God help us all," he said, shaking off his coat. "One of these days, you're going to stir the pot so hard the whole town will boil over."

I finally turned, catching the twinkle in his eye. "And you'll be right there with your spoon, old man." Next to him stood Father Frederick, all starch and silence, looking at me like I'd brought a plague into the room. "Afternoon, Father Frederick," I said, letting my voice stretch lazily over the words.

A small twitch in his jaw, just enough to betray him, told me he wasn't exactly pleased to see me here today. "Miss Bernadette," he stiffly returned my greeting.

"Oh, come now," I said, stepping closer, letting my heel click sharply against the floor between us. "Don't go getting formal on me." I let a slow, devious smile etch across my face. "Don't worry, Father, I don't bite—unless someone asks real nice." He didn't respond, but his eyes dropped for the briefest second, like he was trying not to flinch. That was almost enough to make me smile. Almost.

Father Cyrus stepped between us. "We just came by to check in and offer a prayer. Maybe snag a bowl of whatever Mrs. Henderson's boiling into submission over there."

"You're late," I said, but my tone softened for him. "Next time, I'll save you the crusty end of the bread."

"Generous as ever." He looked around the shelter, nodding to Maggie, then to the kids near the hearth. "You did good work today, Bernadette."

Father Frederick made a faint noise that was almost a scoff, before he covered it with a cough. I turned to him fully now, letting him feel the strength in my presence. "Is there something you'd like to say, Father?"

His lips parted, but Father Cyrus stepped in again. "He's still learning the ropes."

"Are the ropes different here?" Father Frederick asked, too quick and too pointed. "Or do we just not tie them around sin the same way?"

The room went very still.

I tilted my head, my cold smile returning. "In Butte, Father Frederick, we've all got a little sin under our fingernails. The trick isn't pretending it's not there, it's knowing whose blood it is."

Father Cyrus made a low noise, something between a groan and a laugh. “That’s enough gospel for one day.”

I paused, my eyes steady on him, then stepped back, smoothing my coat with a flick of my fingers. “See you both Sunday.”

I was almost to the door when I stopped, half turned, and looked straight at Father Frederick. “You still think I’m the wrong kind of woman doing the wrong kind of work in the wrong kind of place. That’s fine. You’ll either get used to me, or you *won’t*.” And I gave him my sweetest smile as I turned and left.

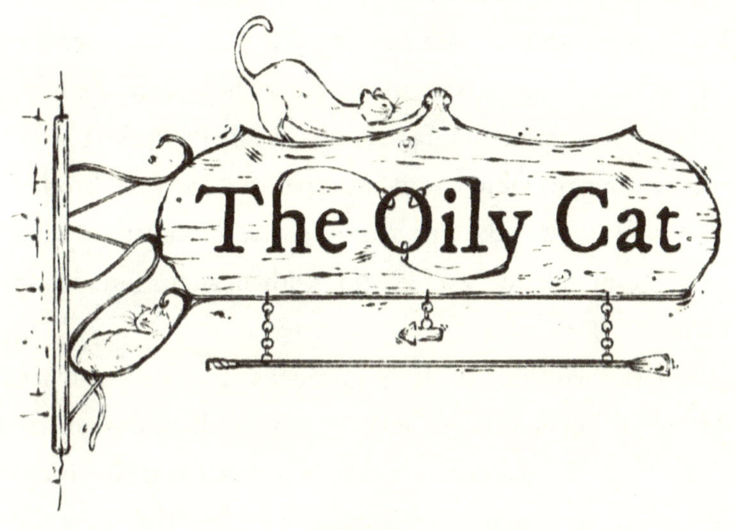

25

COME, YE SINNERS

HIM

The church was packed for Sunday morning Mass. I stood at the pulpit, hands clenched around the lectern, trying to seem steady, hoping no one would notice the strain. Sunlight filtered through the stained-glass windows, casting fractured hues across the congregation, an ethereal wash of divine grace for those still willing to believe. But the light felt different today. Mocking.

I stood tall, my pulse quickening as the significance of what I was about to do settled over me. My gaze swept over the crowd, most of them faithful, or at least they played the part, until my eyes found her: Bernadette. Sitting there like a black mark among the white sheep of the faithful. She was a brothel owner, for God's sake, but there she was, unbothered by the piety around her, her eyes glinting with an almost unnerving confidence.

And she wasn't alone; she had brought her cronies with her. Maeve sat beside her, a striking woman with an unshakable demeanor. Elona, her face a mix of defiance and weariness, leaned slightly forward, hands folded in her lap, while Emil, the quiet giant of a man, sat next to her, arms crossed and posture stiff, as though trying to physically keep the world at bay. And Nell, the wild card, seemed at ease, untouched by the heavy burden of the sermon, her gaze dancing about the room.

But it was Violet I kept my eyes on.

The light touched her differently.

It traced the delicate line of her throat . . . lingered along the curve of her cheek . . . slipped, uninvited, over the softened shape of her mouth.

My grip tightened.

The six of them together, a collection of people the world had cast aside, all sitting in the very pews that I had long thought of as a sanctuary for the righteous. But it was

Bernadette who unwittingly kept pulling my attention, her unbothered calm fueling the fire in my chest. How dare she be so indifferent? How dare they all sit in these pews as if they had a right to be here?

It had been three weeks since I first noticed her, and in that time she hadn't loosened her hold on my thoughts. If anything, she had only burrowed deeper, rooting herself there. I told myself she was a test, a temptation placed before me by God Himself.

And yet . . . my gaze drifted again, betraying me. There was something deeply wrong in the way I noticed her stillness, in the way I imagined breaking it—what her voice might sound like if it trembled, and what it would take to make it.

Today's sermon was supposed to be about salvation, but I wanted to talk about something else; I needed to expose the dangers of temptation, of sin. I needed to prepare the congregation for what I was planning to do next.

"Good morning, brothers and sisters," I began, my voice urgent as I scanned the crowd, my eyes lingering on Bernadette's pew. It irritated me that they were here, those women, acting as representatives against everything I stood for. They didn't belong here, and I had to make sure they knew that.

Violet shifted—so slight it was almost nothing at all. Barely a movement, and yet I noticed. My gaze drifted to the line of her collarbone, to the fragile hollow at the base of her throat, to the slow, steady rise of her breath—until I dragged it back up, almost violently.

"The world tells us that indulgence is a right, rather than a privilege," I said, my voice rising, a thread of bitterness coloring my words. "That we may act as we wish with no regard for the consequences. But I urge you to see beyond these lies. The devil works in many forms, and sometimes the most dangerous temptation is not a dark alley or a foul whisper, but the face of a woman who smiles sweetly, yet whose soul is forever stained by the sin of lust."

My words felt trenchant as I pressed on, venom sharpening every syllable, though I tried to mask it with divine authority. "What happens when we fall into sin? When we give in to temptation and allow ourselves to be consumed by it? We lose our way. We fall into a pit of despair. Only the grace of God can pull us from that pit, but we must first recognize our faults and repent. Only then can we begin to heal."

I felt their eyes on me—Bernadette, Violet, the others. Their expressions were maddeningly unreadable, but their defiance, their refusal to be stirred by my words, enraged me. They did not fear me, and what was worse, they seem utterly unmoved. The realization kindled something dangerous inside me: the need to save them. Or perhaps to break them.

I leaned forward, my tone dropping lower, the words now more pointed than ever. "The Lord does not turn away the sinner, but He does require us to turn from our sinful ways. And I ask you, my brothers and sisters, is it truly in the pursuit of righteousness that we continue to entertain such temptations in our midst?"

I locked eyes with Bernadette, holding her gaze for just a moment longer than necessary. I knew what I was doing. I could feel the satisfaction in my chest as I watched her sit there, forced to hear my words. But it wasn't enough. No, this war was far from over. I continued, my voice rising with an almost feverish intensity. "Repentance is the key to salvation. We must distance ourselves from places of temptation, from the sins of the flesh, and seek the purity that only the Lord can offer." My gaze snapped back to Bernadette, and I let the venom drip from my next words like poison. "Are we prepared to shed our sins, or will we continue to dance with the devil?"

I finished the sermon, though it felt less like preaching and more like a personal battle I had waged. Members of the congregation murmured, and the air carried the buzz of many conversations. I descended from the altar, my heart pounding in my chest.

Before I could make my way down the aisle, I heard the shuffle of feet behind me. Father Cyrus stepped toward the pulpit. I watched him out of the corner of my eye, a sense of unease settling in my gut. He cleared his throat, offering the congregation a warm, reassuring smile as he took his place behind the lectern. "Thank you, Father Frederick," he said, his words like a gentle balm after the fire of my sermon. "That was, as always, a passionate message. And while we all know the gravity of sin, sometimes, we need to remember the power of forgiveness and the light that comes with it."

Father Cyrus paused, letting his gaze sweep across the pews, his eyes softening as they landed on the faces in front of him. He gestured with open hands, as though embracing the whole of them. "We are all here because we seek not just to recognize our faults, but to rise above them, to come together in the name of grace. Yes, temptation is real. Yes, we all have moments where we stumble. But that is the beauty of the Lord's love, we are never too far gone to be redeemed."

He smiled again, more warmly now, the tension in the air starting to dissipate. "So, as we leave here today, let us not dwell solely on the darkness we may face in the world, but also on the light we carry within us. Let it guide us, as we walk this path together, toward understanding and kindness. Let us be reminded of the love that binds us all, even in our imperfections." Father Cyrus gave a small, almost playful chuckle as he glanced at the congregation. "After all, there's no harm in smiling a little brighter on a Sunday morning, is there? We're not here to carry the weight of the world on our shoulders, but to lift each other up."

His words settled over the room. The grumbles among the congregation softened, the heaviness in the air lifting. Father Cyrus looked over at me, his expression one of reassurance, before he turned back to the crowd. "Go in peace," he said, his voice rich with finality. "And may you carry that peace with you through the week ahead."

The congregation responded with a series of 'Amens', and the service finally drew to a close. As Father Cyrus made his way back down the aisle, I lingered near the pulpit, my thoughts still tangled in the intensity of my own sermon and the challenge I had laid before them. It was a challenge I believed was necessary, but Father Cyrus had a way of bringing calm where I brought fire, and I couldn't help but wonder if the fire was exactly what they needed. I watched as most of the congregation filed out, murmurs of discomfort rising around me, but I paid no attention. I was only focused on her, Bernadette, sitting unmoved in the pew.

After the service, I couldn't shake the sense of satisfaction, but something darker gnawed at me too. It was her look, calm and unblinking. Bernadette hadn't flinched. Not once. There hadn't been any fear in her eyes, only a chilling stillness, as if she'd already accepted my unspoken wager. A war not yet named had been declared between us, and her gaze was the signature. I headed into the sacristy, my thoughts still swirling. I was so sure of myself, so certain that I had done the right thing. I didn't hear Father Cyrus's approach until he spoke.

"That was a very bold sermon today, Father Frederick."

I stiffened, turning to face him. He stood there, his expression unreadable, his prying eyes cutting through me. "Thank you, Father," I said, keeping my voice steady, a nervous edge beneath the calm exterior. "I felt the message needed to be delivered."

Father Cyrus stepped closer, his tone becoming more serious. "You need to be careful. These people, Father Frederick, they don't take kindly to judgment. Especially when it's as pointed as that."

I swallowed, forcing myself to remain composed. "I was simply speaking the truth, Father. The temptation, the sin, it's here, in front of us. It has to be addressed."

He sighed and crossed his arms, studying me. "You've made your point, but you may have done it the wrong way. People here may have their flaws, but they're a community. They don't need damnation every week, and most certainly not the kind that singles out people who are already marginalized, like Bernadette."

I bristled at his words. "But, Father Cyrus, they are sinners. And I'm here to save them."

His expression softened, but there was a warning in his eyes. "You're not here to save anyone, Father Frederick, you're here to guide them. You need to lead them gently back onto the path. Forcing repentance doesn't work."

I nodded, but the frustration in me burned. "I understand, Father. I'll take it under consideration."

Father Cyrus gave me a long look, his eyes filled with a strange blend of pity and concern. "Good. Just remember, it's not about punishing people for their sins. Sometimes, redemption comes through kindness, not condemnation."

I nodded stiffly, unsure whether I agreed with him. Maybe he was too old, too complacent with the world's sins. I had a mission, and I would see it through. When he left, I stood there for a moment, alone in the sacristy. The echo of his words danced in my mind, but they couldn't drown out the fire that burned inside me. I had seen it, the sin that tainted this town. I had felt it, and I wasn't going to let it slip away unpunished. I would save them all.

And as I looked at the closed door Father Cyrus had just walked through, I could feel the darkness in me growing stronger. I wasn't done, not by a long shot.

26

THE CHURCH OF THE HOLY RUDE

Sunday evenings were ours. A ritual of setting the world aside, of loosening our grip on the worries we carried, of remembering, if only for a few hours, how to be gentle with each other.

But tonight was different.

Tonight, even the silence had teeth.

The usual conversation and laughter still rang through the room, but it sounded thinner, more brittle now. The morning service at St. Ann's had left its mark, and Father Frederick . . . it wasn't just what he said, it was the way he looked at Violet, like she was something he could swallow whole. A slow, creeping chill traced its way down my spine. I tried to shake it off, but the image had already rooted itself deep inside me.

Beside Elona, Maeve sat with her usual poise noticeably dimmed, her body angled just slightly inward and guarded. The easy banter that so often came from her was gone tonight, replaced by silence and a tension held tight in her shoulders. Across from them, Nell remained still and watchful, her eyes moving from face to face, her mouth drawn into a tight line that gave nothing away. At the far end of the table, Emil wore his usual mask of calm composure, but there was a keenness to his gaze now, like he was carefully cataloging every shift in tone, every glance, every pause.

And then there was Violet. She looked like a ghost of herself, caught in some private storm, her eyes distant and unfocused. Her fingers traced the rim of her glass in slow, mindless circles, like it was the only thing anchoring her to the room.

The silence pressed in until I felt trapped in my own skin, the tension almost unbearable. Without thinking, I let my wineglass dangle between my fingers, as I shattered the silence. "Well, it's awfully somber in here, don't you think?" I said, tone teasing, though it felt like I was throwing a match into dry grass.

Maeve's eyes ignited with a fierce spark, her jaw tightening before she leaned forward. "Aye, no wonder we're all as still as statues. Hard to be joyous when that blasted priest practically set us ablaze in front of the whole bloody town. Not a soul left here with a lick of peace in their heart."

Elona gave a dark laugh. "He's lucky we were in a house of God, surrounded by witnesses." She sat back in her chair, arms crossed tight, brows arched. "That collar of his wouldn't have saved him otherwise." A soft chorus of agreement moved through the room.

Then Violet spoke. "He called us temptations." She wasn't looking at any of us. Her hands were folded neatly in her lap, knuckles pale. "Said we were the rot in the orchard. That if men strayed, it was *us* who led them." She paused. "I've spent half my life trying to be good," she continued. "Trying to be small. Clean. Quiet. And still, somehow . . . that wasn't enough. Still, he looked at us like we were filth."

Nell reached over and laid a firm hand on Violet's arm. "He's a coward, Violet. A man too weak to look at his own sins, so he throws 'em at women like stones."

Violet's eyes darted to hers, then met mine. "I know," she said. "I think I'm just trying to figure out what's worse, the sermon, or the man giving it."

Emil shifted in his seat, the motion subtle, his eyes fixed on the center of the table as though careful not to look at any of us while he gathered his thoughts. "Well," he said. "It's hard to take lessons on damnation from a man who's never seen the devil, only imagined him in women like you."

I took a slow sip of my wine, the cool liquid doing little to settle the uneasy flutter in my chest. I didn't share Emil's point of view; I wasn't so sure Father Frederick had never met the devil. In fact, I was starting to think he'd been in close contact with him, and he'd brought a little piece of that darkness with him into this town. I forced a smile, though it didn't feel right. I could see Violet slipping farther away, lost somewhere beyond my reach. I glanced at her again, watching her fingers trace her glass. "Well," I said, trying to keep my voice light. "He certainly made an impression, just not the kind that leaves you feeling inspired."

"He didn't just preach," Violet said, her voice tighter now. "It was the way he looked at me. Like he was . . . *measuring* me. Weighing what he could get away with."

I felt a knot tighten in my stomach as she continued.

"It's him. He's . . ." She paused, like she couldn't find the right words. "When he looks at me, I just feel *gross*, like I'm being ripped open. And then there's this rage. A fire that makes me want to burn it all down, everything that's ever given him that kind of power."

"Then we burn it all down," Maeve added while raising her glass to her lips.

I stayed quiet for a moment, watching Violet. I didn't like seeing her like this. The strong, fierce woman I knew was buried beneath something tonight, and it made me uneasy. "We've all got a problem with him," I said softly, my eyes finding hers. "But he's just a man, Violet. We can't let fear take over."

Violet's mouth curled into a smile that suggested her restraint was entirely voluntary. "I'm not scared, Birdie, just . . . pissed."

Maeve let out a slow breath, then reached across the table and nudged Violet's hand with the back of her fingers. "Well then," she said, her tone lighter now, though her eyes still burned. "Let's be pissed together. Gods know it's better than bein' scared alone."

Elona chuckled and rolled her eyes in mock exasperation. "I swear, if we all had a coin for every time we had to pick each other up after someone's sorry excuse for justice, we'd have bought our own church by now."

"Aye," Maeve said with a smirk. "And we'd run it better too. No fire and brimstone, just good food, strong drink, and a choir of women who can hit notes high enough to shatter glass and egos alike."

Nell snorted. "I'd gladly pay my tithe for that."

Violet's fingers finally stilled on the rim of her glass, her shoulders eased, and she looked up with a small smile creeping onto her face. "You all are ridiculous." She said, shaking her head.

"And you love us for it," Elona said with a wink.

Emil leaned forward, his tone wry. "If we're founding a new order, I demand kitchen duties be rotated. I'm not scrubbing pots for eternity."

"Fair enough," I said, finally feeling a smile break free, "but I get to pick the wine."

"Deal." Violet said, voice stronger now. "Just as long as we never invite Father Frederick."

Elona raised her glass. "To new orders. And better sermons."

We all lifted our glasses and the soft clink rang out. No one spoke after the toast, we just sat there, breathing the same air, eating the same bread, carrying the same fire.

Whatever was coming, it hadn't taken us yet. And that was enough . . . for now.

27

THE ANTE IS BLOOD, AND I'LL RAISE YOU HELL

Tonight, the brothel pulsed with its usual chaotic rhythm, even as the words from yesterday's sermon still lingered in the back of everyone's minds. Laughter bubbled up, glasses clinked, and the soft notes of the piano twisted through the air. Lantern light fluttered overhead, casting playful shadows on patrons' faces, some lounging in plush chairs, others leaning against the bar, voices weaving in and out. Outside, the world waited with its battles and threats, but in here, for these hours, the music, the drinks, and the company took hold.

I smirked as I watched Violet work her magic at the bar. She was perched on a stool, her back arched just right, catching the eye of a tall man in a black hat who had just walked in. He looked a little out of place, all dark eyes and nervous energy, but Violet was a different story. She leaned forward, letting the silk of her dress slip just enough to give him a glimpse of skin, and it worked like a charm. I could practically see the poor guy squirm as she flashed him that knowing smile. "How's about a drink and a little company, darlin'?" She purred.

The man stammered, clearly caught off guard by her presence. "Of course, miss. A drink for your company, any day."

Violet smiled, enjoying the effect she had. "Then let's make sure the company lasts longer than the whiskey, shall we?" She slid the bottle toward him, her fingers brushing against his hand in just the right way. It was deliberate, designed to create an electric charge between them. He'd be thinking about that touch long after the night ended. I couldn't help but chuckle to myself, watching the whole thing unfold. Violet was a master at this, dangerous, yet undeniably charming.

But tonight, I had my own plans. I moved through the crowd, eyes darting around to take in every detail. While Elona's laughter rang through the room, drawing people in,

Maeve caught my attention. She was sprawled in her chair, one arm slung over the back, the other holding her cards like they were an afterthought. But there was nothing casual about Maeve, not when she was at a table.

"Right, lads," she said, her voice carrying a lazy charm. "Are we playing cards, or are we all just here to see how many chips you can toss away before your pride gives out?"

The man to her left, a slick-haired sort who reeked of cheap cologne and desperation, laughed. "Just admiring your technique, Miss Maeve. It's. . . impressive."

Maeve raised a brow. "That's a very polite way of saying you've no idea what you're doin'. Here's a tip: flattery won't save your arse when I clean you out." The other men at the table chuckled nervously, but she had them: hook, line, and ego.

Another player, bearded and older, with a cigar clamped between yellowed teeth, leaned in with a crooked grin. "You always run your mouth this much when you're bluffing?"

Maeve took a slow sip from her glass, then set it down with a soft thud. "Only when I'm bored. And Gods help me, you lot are duller than communion wine." She tossed in her chips. "Raise." The pile of chips in the middle was growing, but so was the unease. Maeve was all confidence, and behind those green eyes was meticulous calculation.

"You've a poker face, I'll give you that," the younger one muttered, eyeing her nervously.

Elona, lounging nearby with a flute of champagne, gave a soft laugh. "Careful boys, Maeve doesn't bluff, she *hunts.*"

Maeve raised her glass in salute, her grin turning wolfish. "And tonight, I've an appetite." Cards slapped the table with a final *thwap* sound. Maeve's eyes swept from face to face. "Tell me something," she said sweetly to the sweating man across from her. "When you lose, do you whinge all the way home, or sit in silence like a good little lad and swallow the shame?" He started to laugh, but shut up when she laid down her hand, four queens, neat as you like. A groan rose around the table as she raked in her winnings.

"Elona, love," Maeve called over her shoulder, stacking her chips. "Remind me to buy something sinful with this haul. Velvet . . . or lace. Red, maybe?"

"Oh, definitely red," Elona said with a wink. "Something scandalous enough to haunt their dreams."

"Haunt them?" Maeve scoffed. "I plan to *ruin* them."

A man from the bar approached, fresh-faced, with a dapper look and a clean coat. "Mind if I have a seat, miss?"

Maeve gave him a once-over. His boots were scuffed just enough to say he traveled, his hands were steady, and his accent marked him as an outsider. His appearance and demeanor certainly had her interest. "That depends," she said, playfully. "You here to play cards, or test your luck?"

"Bit of both, maybe." He replied with a grin.

She leaned back, looking him square in the eye. “Fair warning, stranger, I don’t believe in luck, and I’ve no time for lads who fold at the first sign of trouble.”

He pulled out a chair anyway. “Then I’ll try not to disappoint.”

Maeve offered him a dangerous smile. “Good man. But I’ll warn you proper, once I’ve taken your money, I’ll be needing a dance too.” The men around the table chuckled, but it was clear that they were all already losing, and she hadn’t even shown her next hand.

A few steps away, Elona had her own crowd. Her laughter floated through the room as she effortlessly charmed a group of men, all of them hanging on her every word. One older man, his hair graying and his face weathered by years spent in the mines, leaned forward, trying to sound casual but clearly enchanted by her wit. “You’ve got a way with words, girl,” he said. “But I’m not sure I believe everything you’re saying about your travels.”

Elona smiled that honeyed smile of hers, eyes twinkling with mischief. "Oh, I assure you, I only tell the truth when it suits me.” She said, her voice smooth as silk. She inched forward, as if to share a secret, but never once broke eye contact. “And right now, I think it suits me to say I’ve seen more of the world than you would in a hundred lifetimes.”

The man’s grin widened, clearly smitten. “A hundred lifetimes, huh? Well, I guess I’m gonna have to buy you a drink and hear more about this mysterious life of yours.”

Elona raised an eyebrow, her gaze warm but teasing. "You poor thing, thinking I'll tell you all my secrets over a pint. I'll be drinking for a century, and you won't know half of it."

Violet slid up beside me at that moment, eyes full of wicked amusement. "You see that?" She laughed, tilting her head toward Elona. "They always think they'll get us to spill our secrets."

"They'll spend their pay trying." I said, watching the room.

"They think drinks and compliments will crack us open," Violet continued, "but they'll never get what they *really* want."

"Not by a long shot." I agreed.

She grinned. "Still, the chase is fun, don't you think?"

I gave her a sly look. "Let them chase. I'm in no rush to end the game."

From the corner of my eye, I saw Emil standing quietly near the door with a drink in hand. His usual stoic expression was softened as he watched the women work their charm on the room. I caught his eye and gave him a slight nod. He didn't have to say anything, I could see the amusement on his face as he observed us. I watched Nell from across the room, her expression that of delight and just a pinch of pity, like she couldn't quite decide whether to laugh or mourn for the poor souls around us. She poured a few more drinks as the piano shifted into a rollicking jig. Maeve pushed back from the card table, chips in hand and a smirk on her lips. "Alright, enough sittin' around," she called. "No one's gettin' out of here without a dance tonight. Don't say I didn't warn ya."

The room erupted in cheers and laughter. Chairs scraped back from tables and boots thudded against the floor. Bodies began to move with an energy that had been simmering all night, now spilling over like champagne. Elona was already on the floor, dragging Violet with her, both laughing like girls with nothing to lose. The music picked up and everyone spun and swayed with reckless joy. I leaned against the bar, letting it wash over me, the clatter of heels, the sparkle of silk, the bright sting of whiskey on my tongue. For a few hours, the world outside didn't exist, it was just us, reveling in the music and the warmth of the night. My friends, my family, were at the center of it all, and as I looked around, I felt a sense of pride.

I raised my glass slightly, offering a silent toast to the women who had become my everything. "To us." I whispered, a soft smile playing on my lips.

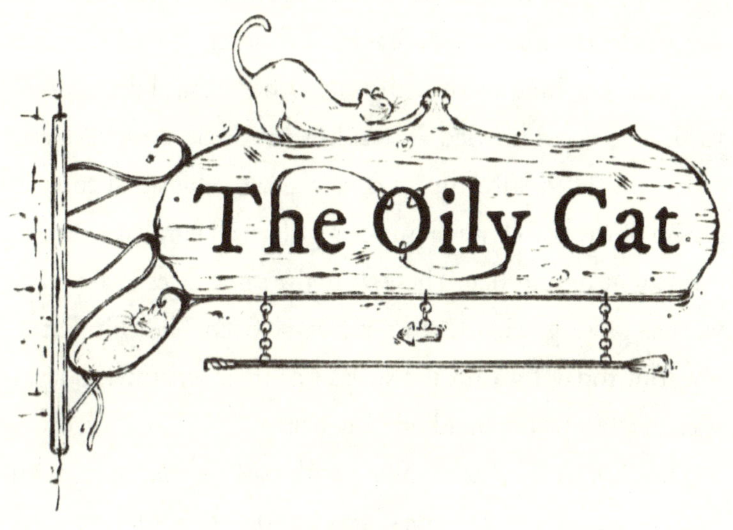

28

DO I MAKE YOU NERVOUS?

It was a pale, overcast morning, with clouds lingering low, as if reluctant to leave the earth behind. A cool breeze stirred the budding trees, carrying with it the faint scent of damp soil and early blossoms. In the town square, life moved with purpose, women in light shawls and men in threadbare jackets gathered near St. Ann's, their chatter mingling with birdsong as they waited for the start of the monthly food and clothing drive.

The heavy church doors creaked open, and volunteers and families began filing in. A few local children played near the entrance, laughing and chasing each other around the churchyard. The wind howled above, but inside St. Ann's, it was warm and filled with the buzz of chatter. The small congregation of townsfolk was a mix of regulars, all familiar to me to one extent or another. These were the same faces I saw every week in passing, whether they knew me from The Oily Cat or not. But today I wasn't the subject of their scrutiny; today, I was merely another hand offering help.

The church was slowly filling with baskets brimming with fresh bread, jars of preserves, and bundles of root vegetables and potatoes tied with twine: the humble harvest of nearby farms. Alongside the food, racks of clothing stood neatly arranged: worn but mended coats, sturdy shoes patched and polished, and dresses of varying finery. Some were plain cotton or wool, practical for everyday wear, others were more striking: a deep emerald silk that caught the light just so, or a cream-colored lace dress with delicate beadwork.

I adjusted the shawl over my shoulders, the faint smell of lavender soap clinging to my fingers from hours spent sorting through my own cupboards. Spring cleaning had taken on new meaning this year. I had pulled from the back of my wardrobe several gowns no longer suited to my tastes, each carefully folded and packed with care. The girls had contributed as well: Maeve's soft rose-colored dress, Elona's warm mustard-hued coat, and Violet's pale blue frock with silk ribbon trim, all items once cherished, but now relinquished with the hope that they would provide joy or comfort for another.

My eyes scanned the room, lingering for a moment on Father Frederick, who stood near the altar, greeting parishioners with that practiced, insincere smile of his. When our gazes met, I caught a trace of unease in his eyes, quickly swallowed by a mask of self-righteousness. He didn't come any closer; these days, he avoided me as if I were a stain on his spotless reputation. I loathed him fiercely, and the further away he stayed from me the better.

"Here, you can take these." I said, handing over a small bundle of well-worn dresses and coats, the ones Maeve, Elona, and Violet had offered up without hesitation, to a frazzled volunteer. In exchange, they passed me a neat stack of blankets and asked if I would take them to be sorted with the other linens.

As I carried the blankets across the room, I couldn't help but think of the girls, how easily they had parted with their finest things. Their generosity was both touching and bittersweet. In this place, among the worn pews and restless candlelight, I saw a glimmer of something rare: hope. Despite Father Frederick's sermons and the whispers that followed me, these small acts of kindness were a quiet rebellion. They were a reminder that even in the margins of this town, life and compassion still found a way to bloom.

Father Frederick lingered in the corner of the room, casting furtive glances in my direction. I noticed how he flinched whenever our eyes met. He was a man of hidden contradictions, a holy figure in public and a darker presence in private. I had seen enough of his sermons to know he was playing a dangerous game. There was something dark there and while he could fool the town, he couldn't fool me.

"Is something bothering you, Father?" I had asked weeks ago, when we'd shared an uncomfortable interaction in the back pew after Mass. Just days before, I had seen Father Frederick walking through town with Father Cyrus. Their conversation had been low but tense, and I'd noticed how Father Frederick's jaw tightened every time Father Cyrus spoke.

He simply smiled that strange, hollow smile of his, and made some vague excuse about the rigors of his work. But I knew better. His reason for loathing me was that I wasn't like him, that I didn't hide behind a mask of purity. He hated that I could do what I pleased, that I lived without shame, without the fear of being caught or condemned for indulging in my desires. His hypocrisy was glaring, and I had no patience for men like him.

I pushed the thought aside as I turned my attention back to the task at hand. A few women arrived with their children in tow, and the room became busier. I moved among them, offering comfort to those who needed it and assistance to those who didn't know where to start. As I worked, my attention settled on a woman and her young boy.

The woman wore a light shawl wrapped tightly around her shoulders, the fabric thin, but enough to shield against the lingering chill of early spring. There was a sadness in her eyes, a weariness that showed in the way she held her son close, as if afraid he might vanish if she let go for even a moment. The child, no older than five, looked confused, his cheeks still flushed from the crisp air, and his small hands tucked inside the folds of her shawl. My heart tightened at the sight, the look on her face so achingly familiar, reminding me of myself years ago, when Ray was still young, still alive.

I didn't approach them immediately; I moved carefully, calculating my steps. I knew the delicate balance of helping and giving without crossing a line. Finally, I made my way over to the woman, bending down to the little boy's level, offering him a soft smile. "Hello there, sweetheart. I think this might be close to your size," I said, picking up a bundle of clothes that were meant for children. They were slightly oversized, but they were in far better shape than the rags the boy was currently wearing.

The boy blinked at me, his blue eyes wide and uncertain. After a long moment, he gave a shy nod. His mother looked at me with grateful but hesitant eyes. "Thank you," she said, clutching the bundle of clothes tightly. "It's been a hard few months. I—" She paused, looking down at her son, her voice catching. "I don't know what we'd do without this. It's been so hard since . . . since he passed."

My chest tightened at the mention of their loss. I hadn't expected the words to land so heavily on my heart, but they did. My own grief came rushing back in a wave that left me breathless. I could see the same pain I carried reflected in the eyes of the boy and his mother. The kind of ache that never fully went away, the type of loss that carved out parts of your soul.

"I understand," I said softly, my voice cracking. The words tasted like ashes in my mouth. I wanted to tell the woman I was sorry for her grief, but I also wanted to tell her that she didn't have to carry it alone. That her son reminded me of my boy, my ray of sunshine, so full of promise and energy, before he was taken from me.

"My son . . . his name was Ray. He was a little older than your boy when he passed," I said, my voice was barely a whisper. I hated that I had to say it, but it felt like a confession, a piece of myself I had to offer in exchange for a moment of connection. The woman looked up at me then, her features softening, and for a moment, we were both just mothers, both just people in mourning, lost in the shared silence of our sorrow.

I offered her a small, tired smile. "There's plenty of food here today. If you want, take a basket and make the rounds. We've got bread, vegetables, and blankets to keep warm. You don't have to go without." The woman nodded, hope briefly brightening the contours of her face. I gave her hand a firm squeeze and gently sent them on their way, watching as the mother gathered her son close and disappeared slowly into the crowd.

Turning back, I caught sight of Father Frederick, who was hovering near the back of the church. His eyes were narrow, lips pursed, and at the look on his face, a chill swept through me. He had been watching me for too long, watching me with that thinly veiled contempt, and I knew that the mask he wore, the mask of a man of God, was crumbling. I could see it in his eyes. He couldn't stand the fact that someone like me, someone who defied all the rules, was here offering help and charity, as if I were some saint, while he stood on his pulpit preaching against sin.

I smiled to myself, watching the way Father Frederick shifted uncomfortably in his seat as I walked back toward the tables. He was trying to ignore me, trying to pretend like I didn't exist. But I knew the truth: He couldn't escape me. I turned away from him, toward the table where the clothes were being sorted, my gaze lingering on the mother and child as they made their way from table to table. I didn't have the power to erase their pain, but I had the power to give them what little I could. That was something.

As for Father Frederick, he could continue trying to hide in plain sight, but I was going to keep my eye on him.

29

YOU KISS YOUR MAMA WITH THAT MOUTH?

I stood by the bar, spine straight, the authority I'd forged over years at The Oily Cat settling over my shoulders. One hand rested on a glass of deep amber whiskey. Around me, the room pulsed with movement and music, conversations layering over one another, while I watched it all with a focus that came from experience . . . and the knowledge that everything in a room eventually revealed its truth.

Maeve was already draped across some poor bastard's lap, laughing just a little too loud at something he thought was clever. Violet prowled near the back booth, lifting something shiny from a drunk's pocket without breaking her smile. Elona held her post by the stairs, eyes sweeping the room. At the end of the bar, Nell poured a drink with one hand and scooped ice into another glass with the other, moving fast but never rushed. Emil stood by the door in his usual spot, arms crossed over his chest, tracking every shift in the room.

The door creaked open, letting in the chill of early night, as well as a familiar face: Victor. He cut through the crowd with a charming grin on his face, and as he reached the bar, his hand briefly brushed mine before he ordered a drink.

"Evening, Birdie," Victor said, giving me a once-over that was more appreciative than lustful, his smile as easy as ever. There was a steadiness in him, something solid in the way he carried himself. He never pushed too far. He didn't need the reminder that everything here had its boundary. And I appreciated him for that.

"Evening, Victor," I replied, voice smooth but edged in playful challenge. My fingers tapped a gentle rhythm against the bar. "What's your poison tonight?"

"Whiskey," he said easily, leaning in just enough to lower his voice, to make the space between us feel intentional. "And maybe some company if the night permits."

Before I could answer, the door swung open again and a new group of men spilled in, their laughter slicing through the calm. Loud and unruly, they dragged in a kind of invasive energy with them. It crawled under my skin, and for a split second, I felt something close to violent. I didn't need to see their faces to know the type. The arrogance they wore was unmistakable, the way they'd look around, sizing up the girls without a hint of respect. They didn't come here to be entertained, they came to take, to demand, and to disrupt. I let out a slow breath, setting my glass down on the bar with a deliberate clink. I could already feel the shift in the room, the way the energy had changed. These men were trouble.

The group made their way to the bar, clearly enjoying the attention they were getting from the few patrons who were too intimidated to ignore them. One of the men in the group, tall, with dark hair and a scar that ran along his cheek like a permanent reminder of a past mistake, stopped just short of me. His eyes gleamed with predatory curiosity, a look that immediately set me on edge. His lips curled into a grin that didn't belong on any decent face, a wicked slice of satisfaction that would send a proper, uncorrupted soul reaching for holy water. . . or at the very least, a stiff drink. He moved in just a bit. "What's a pretty little thing like you doing in a place like this?"

"I'm exactly where I'm meant to be," I said, my voice cold as steel, "which is more than I can say for you."

He laughed. "Feisty. You always talk to your customers like that?"

"I talk that way to dogs who piss on my doorstep," I replied smoothly, "especially when they mistake themselves for guests." That wiped the smirk off his face. Then someone else from the group joined him, a broad slab of a man with a mess of greasy hair and the kind of pungent, stinky breath that made me want to take a step back. But I held my ground.

"Now, that's no way to speak to a gentleman." He spat, slurring his words.

I turned my gaze on him. "I haven't seen a gentleman all night."

Scarface let out a harsh laugh. "You got a sharp tongue on you for someone running a whorehouse."

"And you've got a death wish for someone with no backup." I said, leaning in just enough for him to feel the unmistakable certainty of it. "Let me guess, you came in here thinking the rules didn't apply to you. Thought maybe the girls would fall all over themselves because you've got a few coins and a scar you didn't earn." He bristled, but I didn't give him space to speak. "I've seen your kind before: mouthy, sloppy, and too stupid to be scared." I took a slow sip of whiskey, holding his stare as the burn slid down my throat. "You walk in like you own the room, and five minutes later you're crawling out with your tail between your legs. That's the cycle, sweetheart. That's your story."

The man with ass breath stepped closer, chest puffed, fists half clenched. "You think you're untouchable sitting here at the bar?"

I tilted my head slightly, like I was considering the question. "No," I said, "I think I'm untouchable because no one stupid enough to break my rules has ever walked out whole."

His mouth opened, then snapped shut. No words came. The confident smirk disappeared, overtaken by a momentary trace of doubt. Scarface's jaw twitched, a subtle but telling sign of the anger simmering beneath the surface. Victor shifted beside me and I didn't need to look to know his eyes were locked on them.

"You need a hand, Birdie?" He asked.

I gave him a sidelong glance, the corner of my mouth twitching in an almost smile. There was an unspoken understanding between us, a silent acknowledgment that I wasn't about to let things spiral out of control. "I've got it." I said, calmly. Victor gave a tight nod as he stepped back, giving me space, but keeping close enough if I needed him.

The music stuttered, then faded into the background like a warning as the girls moved with keen precision. Nell's fingers hovered near the drawer beneath the bar, ready to draw if needed, while Maeve straightened from her perch, eyes narrowing. Elona dropped down a step and Violet slipped silently away from the far booth, every movement alert and watchful. The Oily Cat didn't rattle easily, but when it did, it closed in tight.

Just as the tension reached its peak, Emil appeared from behind the men. His large frame cast a long shadow over the group, and the room seemed to shrink with his presence. His mere existence turned the tension into something far more dangerous. “You need to move on,” Emil said, his voice firm. “This isn’t the place for your kind of behavior.”

Scarface laughed, clearly thinking Emil was joking. “Oh, and what will you do about it, big guy?” He sneered, looking Emil up and down with disdain. Emil’s eyes quickly shifted to the man’s companion, who was reaching for his coat, but the decision had already been made. Before the man could even register what was happening, Emil’s hand shot out in a blur of motion, grabbing the scarred man by the collar and lifting him off the floor with the ease of lifting a child. The man’s eyes widened in shock, his breath catching in his throat.

“I’ll show you,” Emil muttered, his grip tightening, his expression a stone wall of fury. The other man froze, unsure of what to do, his bravado crumbling under Emil’s overt threat.

With a single, swift motion, Emil hauled the man across the room and shoved him through the door. The other scrambled after him, their pride bruised and egos deflated. Emil’s deep voice followed them out. “Next time, remember where the fuck you are.”

The door slammed shut behind them, leaving the room in a buzzing silence. The intensity of Emil’s actions lingered in the air, a subtle but undeniable shift in the room’s dynamic.

The Oily Cat had again been tested, and it had again emerged victorious.

Maeve broke the silence first. "Another one bites the dust," she said with a grin, turning back to the other customers as if nothing had happened. "It's never a dull night around here."

I laughed softly before taking a slow sip of my whiskey, the rhythm of the room slowly returning to normal. Though the disturbance had passed, my mind was elsewhere. My pulse was still running high from the confrontation, urging me to do something to release the tension.

I glanced toward Victor, standing a little further down the bar. His casual presence was comforting, but tonight I needed more than comfort. I needed release. "Hey, Victor," I called out. He turned toward me, his eyes instantly locking on to mine. "Why don't you take me upstairs and make me come until I can't walk straight?" I asked.

A slow grin spread across his face as his eyes traveled down my body, pausing just long enough to make sure I was serious. "With pleasure, Birdie." He replied, the heat in his tone leaving little room for doubt.

30

I WANT TO FEEL THIS TOMORROW

Victor's hand found mine beneath the bar, pulling me toward the narrow staircase and leading me upstairs. The dim light of The Oily Cat faded behind us, replaced by the stillness of the private room. Victor closed the door with a soft click, and the silence wrapped around us.

His fingers slid along my jaw, tracing a slow path down my neck, that sent a jolt of heat straight to my core. I tipped my head back without thinking, as his mouth followed the path his hand had drawn. Each careful kiss was a spark, igniting the fire that had been building inside me all night, the tight coil of tension, frustration, and raw hunger unraveling with every breath.

His fingers lingered at the laces of my corset, thumbs brushing faint warmth along the exposed skin of my back, pausing there, as though he were deciding whether to let me fall apart or hold me together a moment longer. When at last he loosened the corset, it wasn't sudden. It unraveled in careful increments, each release of pressure pulling something loose inside me, like my composure had been tied to every knot.

I felt it give, felt myself soften beneath his hands, even as I stood there still trying to pretend I wasn't affected at all. He turned me toward him then, his gaze darkening with desire as he sank to his knees. His fingers slipped beneath the folds of my skirt, ghosting over the soft, damp skin of my inner thigh, teasing the lace of my stockings, and pulling at their delicate seams before I caught his hand.

"Don't bother with all that slow, gentle shit tonight," I said. "I don't want the tease, I don't want the romance, I want you to fuck me hard and fast until I forget my name."

His pupils dilated. "You sure?" He asked, already rising to his feet.

"I wouldn't be here if I wasn't."

Whatever restraint he'd walked in with vanished. He spun me toward the vanity, already dragging up my skirt with both hands. I gasped, hips twitching back against him, and he groaned low against the curve of my spine as he kissed my back. One hand held me against the vanity, bent slightly forward at the waist, while the other moved between my legs, his touch both cruel and worshipful. He worked me open with slow, circling precision, fingers coaxing heat from me like he knew the exact tempo of my undoing. I bit my lip to stifle the moan building in my chest.

"You're burning for it," he said, voice rough with hunger. "Say it."

"I need you," I whispered.

He moved behind me, unfastening his own trousers with one hand, the other still pressed firm to my lower back. I felt him—hard, thick—slip between the heat of my thighs, teasing, testing, until he found that perfect slick resistance. He entered me in one slow push, filling me inch by inch until I had to brace myself on the edge of the vanity just to stay upright. The stretch was exquisite, deep, almost unbearable, and exactly what I'd been aching for.

He didn't hold back. The rhythm was fast and brutal. Each thrust sent a shock wave through me, and I met him with everything I had, grinding back with ragged breaths, nails scraping across polished wood as pressure coiled tighter and tighter in my belly.

His hands roamed, firm and greedy, gripping, squeezing, claiming. His thumb pressing between my cheeks, teasing the edge of my ass. He circled there, then pushed inside, and the pressure nearly made me come undone.

A cry tore from my throat, half shock, half surrender.

"God, Victor—"

"You feel that?" He growled, thrusting deeper. "You take me so fucking well."

I could only nod, body shaking, mouth open and useless. My thighs trembled, the pleasure so intense it bordered on pain. He kept one hand tight on my hip, the other still pressing in behind, pushing my limits as he drove into me harder.

I could feel myself unraveling. "I'm going to come!" I cried out.

When the climax hit, it stole my voice, only a raw, guttural sound left behind. I clenched around him, shaking hard, every nerve in my body lit up. Victor groaned, his rhythm faltering just long enough for me to feel him pulsing inside me, hands gripping me like I was something wild he'd barely tamed.

For a long moment, neither of us moved. Only the sound of our breath filled the space between us. The room was warm with sweat and the sweet, filthy scent of release.

Victor leaned forward, his chest against my back, lips brushing my ear.

"You needed that." He huffed.

I smiled, slow and wicked. "You have no idea."

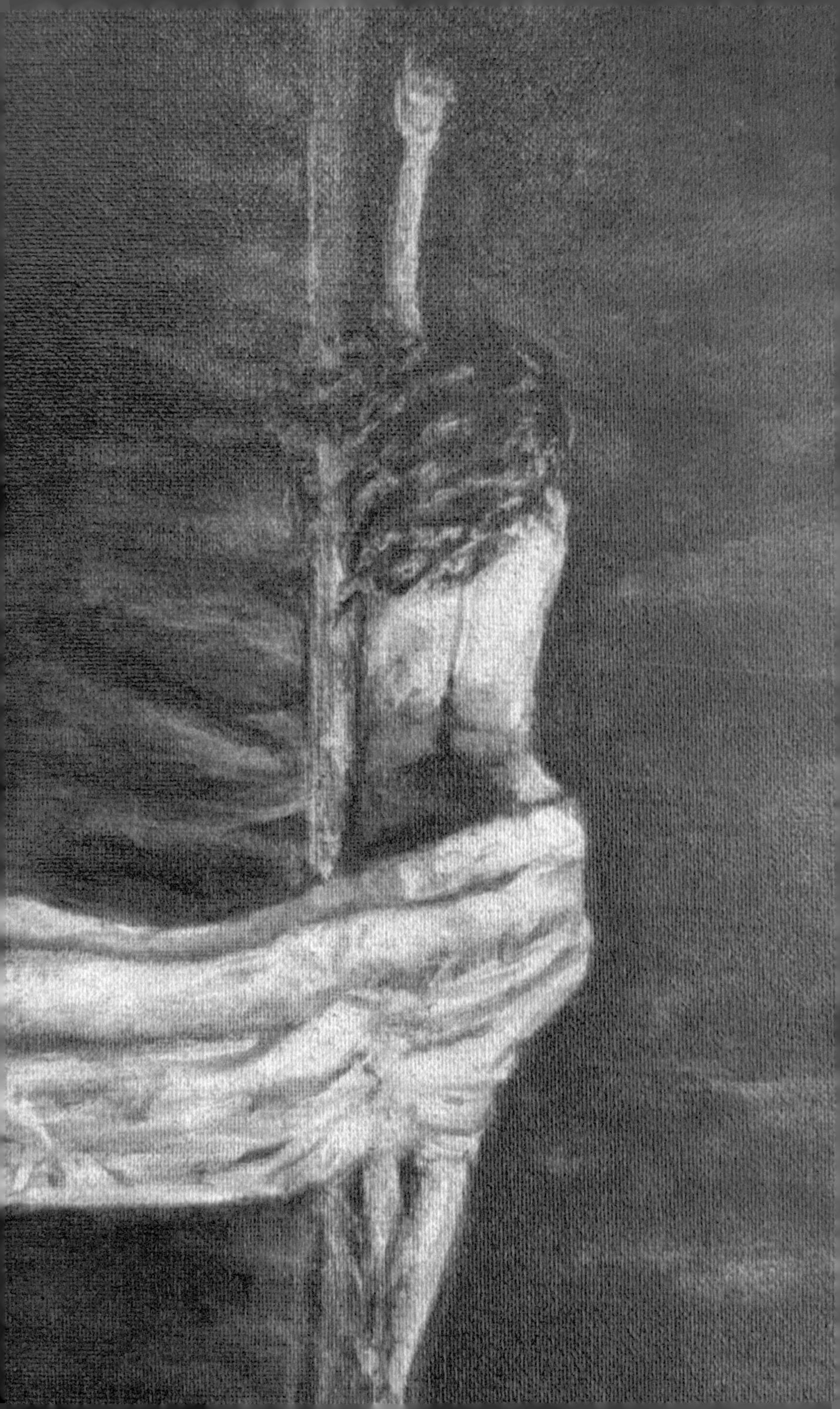

31

IF I CAN'T HAVE YOU...

HIM

I stood at the edge of the alley, cloaked in shadow, my breath shallow and my heart pounding against my ribs. The brothel sat across the street, its new paint, polished shutters, and gas lights burning warm behind its windows. To the town, it was just another building, but I knew better. The Oily Cat pulsed, it *breathed*, it exhaled heat and perfume and decay, like a rotting body dressed up in its finest church garb. It was a house of whoredom pretending to be civil. Every quiver of light from within, every silhouette that danced across the glass was a laughing desecration of the vows I had once whispered at an altar.

But still, I watched, because inside, *she* was there.

Violet.

The name filled my mouth like a prayer, bitter and sweet, holy and profane. She didn't belong in that place; she belonged in light, in purity, in something *better*. But they had dirtied her. Every time she laughed, every touch she endured, chipped away at her sacred core. And I couldn't stop imagining her waiting to be saved. Waiting for *me*.

They didn't see her the way I did. They saw flesh, curves, and a hole to pour sin into. But I saw the soul. I saw the soul *trapped*. And it made me burn.

It was pure temptation that drove me. My superiors told me to pray, but prayer had stopped working. All I could think of was Violet. The curve of her lips, the way her dress strained against her breasts every time she took a breath. I just wanted to touch her.

A shriek of laughter broke through the open window, sultry, drenched in gin, and I flinched. I pressed a hand to the rosary in my pocket, fingers fumbling through the beads like a lifeline, but it offered no comfort. Just cold stone and colder memory.

Inside they were laughing, drinking, touching. Corrupting. And Violet was somewhere in the middle of it, playing her part. She wasn't meant for this. . . she was meant for *me*.

I would take her from this place and strip the filth from her soul. Give her a new name and a new life with my hand, under my roof. In my bed.

I would be the one to purify her.

A crash from inside snapped me back into the moment. Chairs scraped across the floor, and a scuffle spilled out into the street. Two men, drunk, red-faced, and snarling like dogs in heat, tumbled out of the brothel doors, their fists already flying and connecting with flesh.

"You think you can just take her from me?" The heavy-set man with a scar across his face growled, his voice full of venom. The sound of his words sent a ripple of disgust through my chest.

My pulse quickened and a knot tightened in my gut. This was what I had feared: the unchecked violence that this place fostered, the depravity that lay just beneath the surface of every man who set foot inside. I could feel the heat of it rising inside me, the urge to intervene battling against the cold logic that warned me to stay hidden.

The other man, smaller and weaker, scrambled to his feet, wiping blood from his lip, his eyes wide with fear. "She's not yours, Finn! You don't own her! I didn't even get a chance with her before your dumb ass got us kicked out!"

Finn's eyes narrowed, darkening with fury, and with one swift motion he drew a knife from his belt, brandishing it with a brutal flick of his wrist. "You don't know what you're getting into, boy. I did all the work while you stood there like a coward."

My breath caught in my throat as I watched the knife glint under the dim light. My mind screamed for me to step back, to retreat into the shadows, to avoid getting tangled in the mess of sin that seemed to drip from every corner of this town.

But I couldn't, not now. I teetered on the edge of madness, torn between the moral code I had sworn to uphold and the darker urge pulling at me. Every instinct screamed for me to stop the violence, yet some buried part of me wanted to see it unfold, to watch these men destroy each other. It was an impulse I could neither deny nor explain. Instead, I stepped forward, the rosary clinking softly in my coat pocket.

"Fellas," I said evenly, stepping closer, "what seems to be the issue here?"

The men turned, startled. Finn's knife hovered inches from the smaller man's throat, trembling in his grip before he took a step back. "Mind your business, Father," Finn spat. "This little bastard thinks he can steal from me."

"I didn't steal shit!" The smaller man snapped, the blood from his nose dripping down past his mouth. "You're drunk and she didn't even want you, Finn. You got us both thrown out before I even had my turn."

Something ugly twisted across Finn's face at that, a flicker of humiliation giving way to possession and rage.

I stepped closer, the gas lanterns casting an uneasy glow across his flushed face. "So that's what this is about?" I asked. "A wounded ego?"

Finn sneered. "It's a brothel, Father. What the hell do you think it's about?"

"You think paying for a woman gives you ownership over her?" My voice stayed calm. "That she owes you something because you had coin in your pocket?"

"She sells it," Finn snapped.

I tilted my head slightly. "And yet she still refused you."

The smaller man barked out a laugh, and Finn's grip tightened around the knife.

"Finn, just leave it alone." The smaller man muttered, though there was still a trace of mockery in his voice now.

For a heartbeat, everything seemed to freeze, and the air vibrated with the tension of the standoff. In that charged silence I could hear the darkness whispering to me, urging me to embrace it, to let go of my self-control and become the very thing I had spent years preaching against.

As Finn glared at me, the blade glinting ominously in the flickering light, I grinned. It was a cold, lifeless parody of a smile, but I had made a choice. Maybe violence *was* the answer.

32

A DEVIL ON MY LEFT

HIM

Blood shimmered on the smaller man's chin as he stood with his hands raised in defense, his chest heaving while Finn kept the knife lifted between them, knuckles white around the handle and the blade trembling ever so slightly. I could see it in him, that animal part he had probably spent years pretending did not exist. That was the thing about men like Finn: give them just enough rope and the illusion of control, and they would always hang themselves with it in the end.

I stood at the very edge of the light, where its reach was weak and the night was thicker, watching and waiting, feeding off the electricity between them like a starving man. There was no righteousness left in me now, only the undeniable urge to see how far this would go once fear and humiliation finished stripping away whatever civility remained.

"You think I won't do it?" Finn growled, the knife wavering inches from the other man's throat. "I'll gut you right here."

The smaller man trembled but held his ground, his eyes flicking toward me for the briefest moment as though searching for intervention, for someone willing to stop this before it crossed the line.

I offered him none. "You're both pathetic," I said flatly, my voice carrying easily through the alley. "Drunk, bleeding, tearing each other apart over a woman who wanted neither of you."

"You don't know what the hell you're talking about!" Finn snapped, spitting blood onto the cobblestones.

"Oh, I do." I stepped forward then, allowing the lantern light to catch the white of my collar. "I've seen men like you claw their way into places like *The Oily Cat*, convinced that desire makes them powerful, that wanting something badly enough somehow entitles them to it." A slow smile pulled at my mouth, cold and deliberate. "But you're nothing, and she saw that the moment you opened your mouth."

Finn's jaw tightened while the smaller man swallowed hard, shame flickering across his face.

"That's what this is really about, isn't it?" I continued, almost conversational now. "Not her. Pride. Two boys so terrified of being laughed at that you would rather spill blood than admit you were unwanted."

The smaller man stepped forward first, fists curling at his sides. "You stand there judging us while you hide in the shadows." His voice shook with embarrassment. "Maybe you're worse than either of us."

I tilted my head, studying him with detached fascination. "Maybe," I said calmly, turning my gaze toward Finn. "But I'm not the one holding a knife."

Finn's expression twisted into a sneer as the ugly realization of how the situation looked finally hit him. "He started it," Finn muttered defensively. "He shoved me first."

I coughed out a hollow laugh as I deliberately turned my attention away from Finn and back to the smaller man. "Look at him," I said, disappointment threading through my voice. "His knife is shaking, and he's already reaching for excuses before he's even done anything at all."

The smaller man's breathing changed at that, growing slower and heavier, and I could almost feel the exact moment humiliation turned into fury inside him.

"He's afraid of you," I said softly. "That's why men like him carry blades. Because without them . . ." My gaze drifted over to Finn before returning to the smaller man. "What are they?"

Finn's face twisted. "Shut up."

But it was already too late. The smaller man had straightened, his shoulders tightening as he took the bait.

"You're going to let him threaten you like that?" I asked. "Or are you finally going to defend yourself?"

At this, the smaller man clinched his fists. I saw the way he couldn't stand it, the judgment, the implication that he was the lesser of the two. He looked at Finn, and I could almost hear the word *'now'* inside his skull.

"Prove it," I whispered. "Prove you're not the weaker man."

And he did. A strangled roar tore from him as he hurled himself forward, hands clawing for Finn's throat. The blade caught him mid-motion in a blur of metal and muscle that happened far too quickly to stop. A wet, sickening sound split the alley as flesh gave way, and the smaller man staggered backward, confusion overtaking rage while blood poured down his chest in dark ribbons that stained the street before his knees finally buckled beneath him.

Finn stood frozen, staring down at the blade in his hand as it dripped. His jaw worked soundlessly, the truth dawning too late. He'd crossed the line, not in self-defense, but for ego.

"No. . ." he rasped. "I didn't mean. . . he jumped me. He *jumped* me!"

I moved in closer, the copper stink of blood thickening in the cold air between us. "But you swung," I said. "That's the difference. You had a choice."

His eyes snapped to mine, wide with panic. "You saw what he did!"

"Oh, I saw," I replied. "I saw everything. I saw how easy it was for you, how badly you wanted it."

Finn dropped the knife as though it had suddenly burned him, stumbling backward over his own feet. "I didn't . . . he just . . ."

"You needed to win," I said softly. "And now you have."

I crouched beside the body while the man's eyes stared upward, wide and empty, his mouth still parted as though he were trying to force out one final argument. Blood pulsed weakly from the wound now, slowing with every passing second.

I looked up at Finn. "This is your prize."

He turned and fled without another word, his boots slapping hard against the stone as he disappeared into the dark. Running away like most men did once they were finally forced to see what they're made of.

I continued looking into the darkness for a moment longer, while the pool of blood seeped into the gutter, and behind me, the brothel windows glowed, untouched by the death.

33

I KNEW ALL ALONG, KID

The square buzzed with life, a thousand conversations threading together as I moved through the crowd. I didn't stop to admire the booths full of paintings in bright, swirling colors or the cheerful handmade pottery. That wasn't the world I inhabited. The booth I'd arranged was a different kind of masterpiece, one that spoke in darker tones, in shadows and whispers. It was a simple booth with a white canvas backdrop filled with wooden easels displaying a collection of Elona's drawings that were nothing short of revolutionary. Not the kind of thing you'd normally see in a place like Butte, at least, not in public.

"How's it looking?" I asked the man attending the booth.

"Perfect," he said, adjusting a frame as he scanned the growing crowd. "People are intrigued. No one's asked about the artist yet, but they're looking."

Good. Let them wonder. Mystery carried its own kind of power.

My eyes swept over the crowd. Maeve wove through the market at an unhurried pace, her attention catching on people just long enough to unsettle them. People instinctively made space for her and Maeve seemed to savor every second of it. Violet drifted by her side, more reserved but just as amused. Then I found the one I was waiting for: Elona.

She hadn't seen the booth yet.

"Birdie!" She called out, excitement in her voice.

I turned and smiled, letting the warmth reach my eyes. "Hey, darlin'," I said, stepping toward her. "How's the festival treating you?"

She gave a sheepish smile, her hands clasped in front of her. "It's. . . actually a lot of fun, I'm really enjoying myself." She said, her voice gaining more confidence as she spoke. "Though I haven't had a chance to see all of the vendors or their booths yet. There's so much to look at, it's a little overwhelming."

I chuckled. "Understandable. It's easy to get lost in it all, but I'm glad you're here."

She glanced around, eyes wide with curiosity, clearly drawn to the colors and motion. "There's just so much to take in." She said in wonder.

I let my smile soften, shifting closer to her. "You'll have time," I said, glancing back at the booth I had arranged for her work. "And I have a little surprise for you."

Her gaze followed mine as I nodded toward the booth, and I watched as her eyes widened. The sketches, *her* sketches, hung in a place of pride. The bold lines, the stark contrasts between light and shadow, the beauty of the women, it was her soul laid bare for everyone to see. For everyone to *feel*.

Elona stood there frozen for a moment, realization sinking in. "Birdie, I. . ." Her voice was barely a whisper.

"Don't worry, darlin'," I said. "Let them see. Let them witness the power of your work." The tone of my words was gentle, like a nudge rather than a push. I wasn't demanding, just offering certainty, a reassurance that she was ready. Elona had everything she needed to succeed, she just had to trust herself. And I would be right here to watch her take that step.

Her hands trembled slightly as she reached out to touch one of the frames, her fingers grazing the charcoal lines as if she hadn't seen them before, as if she was seeing them in a new light. The crowd was watching. The women, the men, they couldn't help but admire.

"What do you think?" I asked her, my voice almost a whisper.

She didn't answer right away, just stood there, taking it in. Her own work. Her own soul.

"I never thought this would happen." She said, her voice caught somewhere between wonder and disbelief. "I've dreamed of this moment, but seeing it... it's so different than I imagined." She glanced back at me, her eyes wide and searching for reassurance, but I already knew what she was feeling. The spark was there, the one I had seen from the beginning. Every hesitant step, every sketch, had led her to this point. She was ready now, and the world had no choice but to see her.

I placed a hand on her shoulder, giving her a reassuring squeeze. "It's just the beginning." I said with a smile, my voice filled with pride.

By the time the sun dipped low, the booth was packed. Piece by piece, her art sold. Each transaction sent a rush of victory through me. The crowd couldn't look away.

Maeve and Violet made their rounds through the square, drawing the usual stares and whispers while I stood tall beside Elona. We weren't just part of the town anymore, we were rewriting it.

When the last piece sold, I pulled her gently aside. "See?" I chimed. "Told you they'd love it."

She looked at me, trying to speak, but the words just wouldn't come.

"You're finally letting them see you." I explained. "The version you always kept hidden."

Her smile was small, careful. "And they didn't run," she whispered.

"No, dear," I said, brushing a loose strand of hair behind her ear, "they stood in line."

Somewhere behind us, Maeve barked a laugh. Violet's soft snort followed. I glanced over my shoulder to see the two of them approaching from the food carts, Maeve licking powdered sugar from her fingers, Violet clutching a paper bag of fried dough. Maeve caught me watching and lifted a sugared finger in a salute.

"Did she cry yet?" Maeve called out.

"Not yet," I answered, glancing at Elona with a knowing smirk, "but I give it five minutes."

Violet beamed. "You were stunning, Elona. Each piece hit like a gut punch."

Elona's cheeks turned a soft pink color that she hated; she always insisted she didn't blush, even though she did. Constantly.

"You're all insufferable," she muttered, though her smile betrayed her.

As the festival wound down, the booths emptied, and by the time the last vendor closed shop, the square had fallen silent, its energy spent.

I was zipping up the last crate—every drawing sold, not a sketch left—when Maeve sauntered over. "D'you want the interesting bit first, or the strange one?"

"That depends," I said, wiping the dust from my hands on my coat. "Are you drunk?"

She smirked. "Fair question, but no."

I straightened up. "Hit me."

"The interesting bit?" Maeve said, slipping in beside me with that foxlike smile of hers. "The sheriff's wife bought Elona's sketch, the one of the boy with the wolf tattoo."

I tilted my head, letting the grin bloom slowly. "Let me guess. Said it reminded her of someone?"

"Ah, she didn't say a word," Maeve purred. "But the look she gave it? Like she meant to tuck it under her pillow and dream of it twice."

I snorted. "Does the sheriff really not know his wife and his deputy are knocking boots? The whole damn town knows."

Maeve gave a low chuckle. "If he does, he's playing dumb with real commitment. You'd think the smell of guilt and Marlboros would've clued him in by now." She went on, lips twitching. "Poor lad still wears his wedding ring like it means somethin'." She paused, then gave a wicked smile. "I'd be happy to take it off for him. . . among other things."

I gave her a knowing look before I let out a soft laugh. "Well, that's going to be quite the conversation over dinner. And the weird news?"

Her smile dimmed. "The church crowd's buzzin'. Father Frederick was found early this morning, kneelin in the alley behind Matthison's butcher shop. Holdin tight to some poor lad."

My breath caught. "Dead?"

She nodded. "Knife to the gut. Nobody saw who did it, but folks say the priest was whisperin' prayers over him like it was the second coming. Said he refused to leave the body until they pulled him away."

A chill crept along my spine. "What was he doing out there?"

Maeve shrugged. "Not a clue, but here's the kicker. The dead lad? It was one of the fellas from the bar, the one next to the lad Emil had to toss out on his arse."

I glanced toward the center of the square. Violet sat on the edge of the fountain, flipping through a notebook with that faraway look she got when she was daydreaming about the future. Elona stood nearby, sketchpad balanced in her hand, already creating something new from the fragments of the day. Pulling beauty from the static, as she always did.

Maeve let out a long breath, then clapped her hands once in mock finality. "Well now, that's all the wicked gossip I've got for you today," she said brightly, brushing imaginary dust from her coat. "Come back tomorrow and I might have a scandal or two more, if the town doesn't burn itself down before then."

I chuckled, the tension finally easing from my shoulders. Maeve stretched, her eyes following my gaze, and grinned. "Should've come with a bottle in hand."

I gave a small smile. "Let's go get some wine. Elona's art sold out, and that deserves a proper toast."

But my eyes still drifted toward the alley. Toward where Maeve said the priest had been seen. A man dying in the dirt, his last breath caught between heaven and hell, and Father Frederick there to cradle it. Something in this town was shifting, but for tonight, we'd let it wait. I turned toward the street, brushing dust from my skirt. "Come on," I said, voice light. "Let's go celebrate Elona."

34

TO GREAT TITS AND SUCKING DICK

The back room at The Oily Cat was filled with the warmth that a long-overdue celebration brings. This dinner wasn't just any meal, it was in honor of Elona's success at the art fair. The table was crowded with dishes: hearty beef stew rich with tender meat and root vegetables, buttery garlic mashed potatoes, a vibrant salad dressed in tangy vinaigrette, and flaky golden biscuits that melted on the tongue. Soft shadows played along the aged wood on the walls, and the scent of slow-cooked meat, fresh herbs, and baked bread wrapped around us. It was the perfect ending to a moment years in the making.

The art fair had been a resounding success, well beyond our wildest expectations, and while Elona's art had been the centerpiece, it was the people gathered here who made the moment whole.

Her charcoal drawings, those intricate portraits of men and women, had captivated the townsfolk. I'd watched as passers-by stopped in front of her booth, surprised, even humbled, to find something so raw and powerful in the heart of their market. The same people who once dismissed her, now gathered around, curious and intrigued, begging for commissions and offering prices they wouldn't have imagined paying to someone like her. Now, we were here, her family, gathering to celebrate her success. Violet, Maeve, Nell, myself, and Emil, whose brooding silence filled a room louder than most voices. I found myself watching Elona, the soft look in her eyes, the awe on her face. She deserved every bit of this.

"So, Elona," I began, "I believe it's safe to say the people of Butte now know what true talent looks like."

Violet, sitting beside me, grinned. "They didn't have a clue before, but they sure do now. Next time, they'll be lining up just to catch a glimpse of her magic."

Elona flushed slightly, a soft smile tugging at her lips. She was never one to take praise easily, but tonight was different. I could feel her joy in knowing her work had touched people. "I don't know about all that. It's just . . . more than I expected. I never thought . . ."

"You never thought the town would recognize what it's been too blind to see?" Maeve cut in. "Told you. They just needed someone to show them what real art looks like, not that painted shite hanging in their parlors."

"And the best part," Violet added with a smirk, "is they still don't know who the artist is. Mystery in the air. I think they've all fallen in love with the 'anonymous genius.' Which is just *perfect.*"

Elona grinned, her hand resting on the rim of her glass. "I owe a big part of it to all of you." She looked at me. "You believed in me when I didn't believe in myself."

Nell, who had been quiet throughout much of the meal, glanced up from her plate and smiled. "We've always known your worth, Elona," she said. "It just took the town a little longer to catch up." She raised her glass, voice rising as she added, "To you, Elona. To art, to beauty, and to knowing the world isn't always as blind as it seems."

Then Emil let out a low chuckle. His gravelly voice breaking the silence with an easy charm. "I'm proud of you all," he said, eyes sweeping the table. "You've built something here, and I think you've shaken this town up more than you know." He turned to Elona, giving her a rare wink. "But I'll admit, I didn't think *you'd* be the one to win them over."

Elona raised a brow, smirking. "Who knew I could give life-altering head *and* draw a stunning pair of tits? This town just isn't ready for talent like mine." The table exploded with laughter.

"I'll drink to that," Maeve said, her usual bite softened by affection. "To family, to surviving in this bloody ridiculous town, and to always having each other's backs."

"To family," I echoed. "And to doing things our way." The clink of glasses was clean and satisfying, the sound creating a sacred seal in the air.

As the night wore on, conversation flowed effortlessly, laughter drifting from one end of the table to the other. Maeve's sharp sarcasm mingled with Elona and Violet's playful sass, Emil's dry wit, Nell's thoughtful insight, and my own knowing smirks. Together, we filled the room with a music entirely our own.

Violet leaned forward, a devilish grin on her lips. "You know, Elona, now that your art's a hit, you might want to raise your prices. I'm thinking real big money now, maybe even a gallery in a big city."

Elona laughed. "A gallery? Let me adjust to the idea that my work is worth *anything* before we go national."

"Aye, it's worth plenty," Maeve said with a mock serious expression, "but with all the attention on you now, just remember who helped you get there." She leaned back in her chair, her arms raised as if she were a model posing for one of Elona's sketches. "I mean, it's not every day someone gets immortalized in charcoal, am I right?"

I snorted, shaking my head. "All credit to Elona, but don't be surprised when we start charging for inspiration."

"Absolutely." Violet added with a wink. "Payment in artwork . . . preferably nudes."

Elona rolled her eyes, laughing. "I'm sure there'll be plenty of demand for that."

The banter carried on, but slowly the mood shifted. Wine dulled the edges of our energy, and a tenderness settled over the table. Maeve, who had polished off an entire bottle of pinot grigio on her own and was most certainly feeling it, leaned back, her eyes slightly unfocused.

"Y'know," she said softly, "I've no idea what we'd do without each other. We've come through more than most."

I met her eyes and offered a small smile. "You don't need to know. As long as we've got each other, we'll be fine." And I held onto the silence that followed, because something in me knew moments like this never lasted.

35

A WOMANS INTUITION

VIOLET

I didn't mind walking home this late, not usually. The air felt cleaner somehow without all the noise of the day, and it gave me a minute to breathe. A quiet space to think, to feel my own heartbeat, the place where most of my poems first began to take shape. I was halfway down the street, boots scuffing against damp cobblestones, when I heard them. Footsteps, quick and purposeful coming up behind me.

"Evening, Miss Violet." The voice curled around my spine. My stomach clenched so fast, it felt like instinct, like some small, primal part of me understood danger before my mind could name it. I didn't stop walking, just eased my pace enough to glance over my shoulder.

It was Father Frederick, his coat buttoned neatly up to his throat, white collar shining under the gaslight. He smiled as if this meeting was just happenstance, like a priest strolling behind a working girl after midnight was the most natural thing in the world.

"Evening." I answered, voice flat, my hands buried deep in my coat pockets, fists clenched as I kept walking.

He closed the gap between us in a few strides and then fell into step beside me. "Late night?"

"I work nights," I replied, letting the shortness of my answer make the point for me. I wasn't looking for conversation.

Still, he walked alongside me like we were sharing some gentle stroll through a manicured garden, not a narrow street that stank of ash and spilled ale. "Fine night," he mused, tilting his head toward the sky. "God's own hush over everything."

"Mmm," I said, uninterested, silently willing him to leave me alone.

He tilted his head, studying me. "I don't believe I've ever asked where you're from. Your family—are they still living?"

"No family." I said plainly. "Raised at St. Brigid's Orphanage, out by the old railway."

"Oh?" The syllable stretched too long in his mouth, like it held meaning I didn't understand. "Tough place to grow up, I'd imagine."

"You'd imagine right."

Still, he didn't take the hint. "I must say," he continued, "you've carried yourself out of it all with such grace. Not many can claim that."

I said nothing to that. We continued walking, the silence growing more awkward as we crossed under a broken streetlamp. For a moment, the shadows cut deep across his face, as his eyes stayed on me. "If you don't mind me asking," he went on, voice sliding toward casual in a way that made my skin itch, "how did a young woman like yourself come to work at The Oily Cat?"

I stopped, just long enough to look him in the eye. "I do mind," I said, somehow managing to keep my voice level. "And I'm not interested in talking to you about that."

He put his hands up in defense. "Of course. I only meant to better understand your story."

I started walking again, picking up my pace, but he followed without effort.

"You know," he said with a tone that made my stomach twist, "your name suits you. Violet. Something delicate. Something . . . rare."

I didn't respond, but something about the way he said my name like he was tasting it, like it had become sacred to him in some twisted way. Whatever small hope I'd had that I was overreacting evaporated in that moment.

"God sees you," he whispered, "All of you. And He loves you still. Even in your . . . line of work."

My boots hit the stone louder now, more deliberate.

"You're an angel, Violet, that's what I see. A creature of beauty—meant for more than this." His voice dipped low. "The men who pay for your time don't see it, but I do. There's something holy in you. I felt it the first time I saw you. Like a . . . calling."

I turned the corner, hoping he might walk past, hoping he might leave. He didn't. His footsteps stayed close behind mine.

"I see the shame they put on you," he went on, almost feverishly, "but you carry it with such grace. It's as if God made you to endure. To shine."

I could feel his eyes on my neck, down to my shoulders. I hated the way his voice shaped each word, like they were precious to him, like he was savoring some secret. I took one more slow turn, easing us back toward the edge of town, past the lamp with the crooked glass, past the alley with the red door. We were coming back up the block now, the lantern light spilling out from the porch of The Oily Cat. Bernadette sat on the front porch in her usual chair, whiskey in hand, eyes fixed on the street.

I felt Father Frederick slow his pace beside me. "Strange," he said with a little laugh, "didn't realize we'd circled back."

I didn't say anything. My feet stayed steady on the path.

Bernadette stood the moment she saw us. Her eyes flicked to me, then to him, and something hard settled into her stance. "Well, well," she said, stepping off the porch. "didn't realize the good Father had taken up moonlit strolls with my girls."

He gave a small bow, hands raised. "Bernadette. I was simply walking Miss Violet home. These streets can be unkind after dark."

"They can." She agreed in a slow tone that was anything but friendly. "That why you were following so close?"

His smile faltered just a hair. "I was sharing the Lord's word." He quickly sputtered. "A shepherd watches his flock."

Bernadette crossed her arms. "She isn't your flock. And she doesn't need watching, least not by you."

"I meant no harm," he held up his hands in surrender, "only concern. There's a light in her, and the Lord moves in strange ways—"

"You don't get to talk about the Lord and look at her the way you do." Bernadette snapped, and the sound of her voice in that moment, scared the shit out of me.

"I assure you—" he began, straightening to his full height as if he were beginning a sermon.

But Bernadette stepped closer, inches from him. "You can assure someone else. You don't speak for God, Father Frederick, not here. Not to her. Now get the fuck off my property."

He stood there for a moment too long. Eyes darting between us and his smile drying up at the edges. Then he turned, adjusted his cuffs, and walked back into the dark, his steps the only sound for a long while.

Bernadette watched him go. She didn't move until his footsteps vanished, then she looked at me. "You alright?"

I nodded once. "Yeah."

She didn't press. Just looked me over a moment longer like she was checking for cracks. Without a word, she lifted her glass, took one last sip, and held it out to me.

The whiskey was warm from her hand, still half-full, and burned when I took a sip.

She met my eyes then. "You don't owe anyone shit, Violet. Not a smile. Not a word. Not your patience, not your grace, not your comfort. Especially not to people who make you feel small, or scared, or like you're less than." Her eyes softened for a fraction of a second, then hardened again. "Being polite doesn't make you a good person and it doesn't keep you safe. Sometimes, being nice gets you hurt or gets you killed. You don't owe them that. You owe yourself honesty. You owe yourself boundaries. You owe yourself the right to walk away, to scream, to run, to do whatever the hell keeps you alive and whole."

She reached over and took my free hand between hers. "People will try to guilt you. People will tell you you're being 'difficult,' or 'mean,' or 'ungrateful.' Screw them. Your safety, your peace, your body, your heart—they're yours. Nobody else's.

And don't you ever forget it." There was no pity in her voice, just conviction. Like it was a truth she'd herself learned a long time ago, and now she was offering it to me.

36

BLESSED ARE THE DAMNED, FOR THEY KNOW THE TRUTH

HIM

The toll of the bell echoes over the town, impossible to ignore. It was a summons to Mass and a reminder of order and obligation. The vibration settled in my chest, buzzing through my ribs as I adjusted the collar of my cassock.

The fabric, once comforting, now scraped against my skin like burlap, itchy with secrets. It felt heavier today. *My penance.*

The altar loomed ahead. I stepped up, my body moving on muscle memory while my mind reeled back to the alley, to the blood, to the way the knife had glinted just before the smaller man dropped to the ground like a sack of meat. My eyes drifted to the stained-glass windows. The light was supposed to be holy, refracted redemption, but today it was a mockery. The colors bled like bruises across the stone floor. The red especially seemed to move on its own, to pulse, as though the church itself knew what I'd seen, what I'd done.

I caught my reflection in the polished lectern, distorted slightly by the uneven grain of the wood. I looked . . . undone. Hollowed out somehow. I tried to steady my breath. Tried to keep my thoughts from slipping back. The fight, the flash of the blade, the grinding against the bone. The gurgle.

The death.

The congregation quieted as I stepped forward, dozens of eyes turned toward me, expectant and devout. My eyes burned as I scanned across the row, starting with Bernadette, then moving through Violet and Maeve, and finishing with Elona. The shame of last night still clung to me—getting caught by Bernadette, when all I wanted was a moment with Violet. Just to speak with her, to remind her she's loved—not just by God, but by me.

I met Elona's gaze. Her expression was unreadable, but her eyes were surgical. She wasn't looking at me; she was dissecting me. Beside her was Maeve. A smile played at the corners of her mouth, a smirk not meant for me, but somehow about me. Like she already knew what I would do next, as if she had seen this performance before and knew how it would end. Violet was the only one who looked uncomfortable, nervous energy rolling off her. Her shoulders were tense, fingers knotted in her lap, and eyes darting like a rabbit waiting for the fox to make its move. Oh, how I enjoyed watching her squirm, her discomfort was like perfume; sweet, cloying, and intoxicating.

But Bernadette . . . Her hands were folded across her lap with poise, but her eyes, *those damned eyes*, were locked on me. She wasn't afraid, she was angry.

I turned back to the pulpit, my mouth dry as dust. "The Lord is our shepherd. He guides us through the darkness." I said the words, but I wasn't thinking of any divine shepherd, I was thinking of blood in the moonlight. Of how fast a body becomes just that, a body. And of those women, watching in judgment, in knowledge.

"He guides us through the darkness, leads us to salvation," I continued, my voice thinner now, like the words were escaping me instead of being fervently delivered. "But there are those among us who stray from His path . . ." I looked up, right at Bernadette. Her lips were parted ever so slightly, and there was a glint in her eye. She was *testing* me, waiting to see how much of myself I'd reveal, waiting to see if I'd crack.

"Those who fall into temptation . . ."

Out of the corner of my eye I saw Maeve's smile deepen. She cocked her head like she was listening to a joke. Her eyes narrowed. I knew that look, it was the look of a woman who had already made her decision about you and was just waiting for you to catch up. I tried to focus, to finish the prayer, but the words slid off my tongue like oil. Meaningless syllables strung together by memory. Holy lies. "We must all seek redemption," I said finally, "lest we be consumed by what we pretend not to see."

My final 'amen' felt more like a whimper than a declaration. The congregation stirred with shuffling feet and murmured farewells, but I didn't move. Because *they* hadn't moved. The four of them remained in the back pew, still as statues, as though the service wasn't over until *they* decided it was. Bernadette's stare locked on to mine; she wasn't going to blink first. I stood frozen, gripping the edge of the pulpit so tightly my knuckles turned white. Was this what judgment felt like? Not fire and brimstone, not eternal damnation, just four women . . . watching.

Slowly, the others filtered out, their footsteps fading into the distance, swallowed by the town. I wanted to move. I *needed* to move. But it was like my body had become part of the altar, bound to it. When they finally rose, Bernadette's eyes lingered on me with a promise. Whatever game I thought I was playing, she'd already rewritten the rules. I turned from the altar and retreated toward the shadowed recesses of the church, the sanctuary now feeling like a tomb. My footsteps echoed against the stone floor, and I felt exposed, hunted.

I leaned against the stone wall, chest heaving, the light from the stained-glass window casting red across my hands. My stomach twisted as I looked down, half expecting blood to appear.

I dragged in a shaky breath and closed my eyes. I had always thought this place would protect me, cloak me in its sanctity. But now I realized . . . it was just another cage, and I was running out of corners to hide in.

37

WHO SAYS ONLY LADIES GOSSIP?

MAEVE

The moonlight slipped through the thin lace curtains, casting soft, shifting shadows over the room. Silver spilled across the bed, across my skin, across Carl's bare back as he lay half-asleep beside me, one of my regulars who was comfortable enough to forget this was still a transaction. The sheets were tangled between our legs, still warm from our sweat, from the tangle of limbs and low moans that had filled the space not long ago. My curls were a wild, fiery halo around my face and shoulders, but I didn't care.

Usually, he either drifted off within moments, surrendering to the pull of sleep, or he slipped from the bed as soon as we were finished. I stretched out, running my fingers through my hair. "Wouldn't have taken you for the lingering sort, Carl, not after the deed's done," I said, voice teasing. "Usually, you're as quick to pullin' your trousers on as you are taking em' off."

He chuckled, fingers idly twining through my hair, but there was a heaviness in his eyes that didn't belong. "Well, Maeve, you make it hard to leave, you know that?" He said, trying for the cheeky smile he often wore, but it didn't quite stick. "But truth is, I've got something on my mind, something . . . strange. And it's been bothering me all day."

I raised an eyebrow, my curiosity piqued. "Oh? Do tell. It must be juicy if it's keepin' you from that fine whiskey waiting for you downstairs."

He drew nearer, like the walls had ears, dropping his voice to a hush. "You've heard of the new priest, Father Frederick?"

I stilled, momentarily caught off guard. "Yes, I have been *blessed* enough to sit through a few of his sermons," I responded cautiously.

Carl lowered his voice even further. "The miners are talking, and it ain't the usual gossip. Word is, he wasn't promoted, he was shipped out, real quiet-like, from Illinois. And there's talk he . . . likes them young."

I had seen the way his eyes lingered on Violet, the subtle glances that spoke louder than any confession, but only now—listening to Carl's words—did everything click into place, the pieces fitting with a harsh, painful clarity. "Go on," I urged.

Carl wet his lips nervously. "He's been seen near The Oily Cat. More than once. Slipping away before sunrise, looking . . . rattled. One of the boys swore he saw him loitering out front, just standing there, staring at the place with this empty, desperate look. Like he was waiting for something. Or someone."

A cold shiver slid down my spine. I didn't tell him Bernadette had caught Father Frederick skulking after Violet, but I muttered loud enough for Carl to hear, "He's a bloody predator."

Carl nodded grimly. "I don't believe it's just hearsay, Maeve. I've seen how he watches the girls in town . . . it ain't right."

I stayed silent for a moment, the pressure in my chest tightening until it felt as though my ribs might splinter beneath it. The very thought of Father Frederick lingering somewhere near the brothel made my skin crawl. "You think he's really what they say?" I asked at last, my voice softer than I intended.

Carl looked at me seriously. "I think there's more to him than meets the eye. Something dangerous."

I sat up, the sheets slipping from my skin, nipples tightening in the cold. "Dangerous?"

"Oh, definitely." Carl affirmed, shifting on the bed with a look of discomfort on his face. "The way he talks to the young girls, the way he watches them . . . it's like he's searching for something, and I don't think it's salvation."

I let out a slow breath and swung my legs over the side of the bed, my toes brushing the cold floor. The old boards groaned beneath me, the familiar creak grounding me. "If he's sniffing about," I said, dragging my slip over my head, "I'll deal with him myself. I don't care if he's wearin' white robes or fucking armor. He so much as lays a finger on anyone in this house, I'll take his bloody hands off at the wrists."

Carl studied me, something shifting behind his eyes. Respect, maybe. Or fear, hard to tell sometimes with men, as the line between the two was often thin.

"Just . . . be careful," he cautioned. "If what they say about him is true, men like him don't play fair. And they don't stop 'til they've taken everything."

I gave a crooked smile. "Love, I was raised by men like him. I've danced 'round their fists, emptied their wallets, and left 'em cryin' for their mothers. He's no different." But even as I said it, something inside me whispered: *Yes, he is.*

After Carl left, I stayed in my room, pacing the narrow stretch between the bed and the window, the floorboards sighing beneath my feet. I wanted to write it off as rumor, to tell myself that whispers had a way of twisting into monsters by the time they reached our ears, but Carl wasn't the sort to spin lies, and never about something this dark.

Eventually, I moved to the window and parted the curtains. Moonlight spilled across the streets, bleaching them bone-white, casting the town in a ghostly silence. I let my gaze wander over the cobblestones, and just as I was about to turn away, something shifted in the shadows beyond the lamplight—a flicker, a shape. My heart stuttered in my chest, and for a breathless moment, I couldn't tell if the cold crawling up my spine came from fear . . . or recognition.

Father Frederick. As if the act of speaking his name had summoned him, and he was close. Far too close. "He's here." I whispered, my voice barely audible, even to myself. My fingers curled tight around the windowsill, the wood biting into my palms as anger rose inside me. *I had to tell Birdie.*

38

I SPY WITH MY LITTLE EYE SOMETHING...

The night had settled fully over The Oily Cat. The usual ruckus from the bar downstairs had dwindled, and Elona & Violet were finished for the evening, their laughter fading out the door. I'd been moving room to room, checking locks and drawing curtains, setting the place to sleep like I always did. When I knocked on the door of the room Maeve had occupied that night, I didn't expect it to open so quickly. The sound of my knuckles had barely faded before the latch turned, and there she stood, backlit by the thin ray of moonlight spilling in from her window, curls wild, and her face half-swallowed by shadow in a way that told me whatever storm she carried inside her chest was neither fleeting nor gentle.

"Bernadette," she said, voice tight, "we need to have a word."

I stepped inside without asking, easing the door shut behind me. Maeve was pacing, again. She was moving in the same restless, angry rhythm she always fell into when something was wrong and her fists weren't enough to fix it. I folded my arms and steadied myself for whatever she was about to say. "What's going on?" I asked.

Maeve's eyes shot toward the window, her face looked pale, almost haunted. "It's Father Frederick." Her voice was barely above a whisper, like she was afraid of saying his name too loud.

Dread crept in and I felt my face harden, a reaction almost beyond my control. "What about him?" I asked, though I already knew it wouldn't be good.

Her accent always deepened when worry took hold, soft vowels curling around her words until they felt heavier. "Carl said he's been seen outside, more than once, in the wee hours, right 'fore the sun comes up."

Maeve stopped pacing, her movements jerky as she turned to face me, her green eyes looking darker than usual, like stormwater. "Lurkin'. Just standin' out there, watchin'. He's got no business bein' anywhere near this place, but he keeps comin' back all the same." She took a breath, jaw working. "Carl said he's not just passin' through, Birdie, he says the man was run outta Illinois. Quietly, y'know? Just gone one day. Moved along like a bad smell."

My arms tightened across my chest, a shield I didn't even realize I was raising. "Moved for what?" I asked, bracing for the answer.

Her voice dropped again, and it wasn't just fear—it was fury trying not to shake loose. "Girls, Bernadette, young ones. That's what the whispers said, that he had . . . leanin's." Her hands clenched at her sides. "And the church, they didn't fight him. Didn't throw him out proper, just packed him up and sent him somewhere no one'd look too hard."

My breath caught hard in my chest from the way it all fell too neatly into place. "Violet . . ." I whispered, the sound barely audible, weighed down by fear, and anger.

Maeve nodded quickly. "Aye. Him and that look he gets. You've seen it, the way he watches her. And not just *her*, the younger ones too, the fresh faced ones that don't know better. He watches them like he's choosin', like he's settin' a clock to somethin' awful."

I turned away from her, every muscle in me coiling, and I felt physically ill. Violet was eighteen, but with the softness of her face and the slightness of her frame, she could have passed for fourteen with little effort. "You're sure?" I asked, fighting to keep my voice steady.

"Carl swears it." Maeve said, her chin lifted with a brittle confidence. "Said he saw him standin' out front just before sunrise. Starin' up at the windows, like he was waitin', or markin' the place. And I swear on my life, Birdie, that I just saw his shadow move outside. Not even a moment before you knocked on my door."

Hunched forward, I pressed my palms against my thighs, trying to calm my mind, while Maeve's hands fluttered at her sides like she didn't quite know what to do with them. Outside, a chill wind rattled the windowpanes, carrying with it a faint, distant howl. Each sound seemed amplified, a cruel reminder that nothing was safe. "If he's creeping around outside my brothel," I said, stepping forward, "then he's not just trespassing, he's hunting."

Maeve's posture shifted, shoulders squaring, spine straightening. There was something new behind her eyes now—relief, maybe, or the faint release of a burden she had been carrying alone, finally shared. "What do we do, then?" She asked. "Do we go to him? Confront the bastard?"

"No," I said, finally regaining some of my composure. "Not yet. We don't show our hand until we've got something solid. Right now, we watch him, and we keep the girls close."

Maeve gave a slow nod. "I'll speak to the others, tell them just enough to keep 'em sharp. Quiet, though, no sense lightin' fires if we don't need to."

"Good," I said, "but if he even breathes wrong near one of them, we don't wait. We end it." I turned to leave but paused with my hand on the doorknob, my fingers lingering as I looked back at Maeve. She stood still, the storm behind her eyes gathering again. I knew that look, and I knew it never passed easily once it settled. The door clicked shut behind me, and the brothel swallowed the sound. I moved down the narrow, lamp-lit halls, and past empty rooms that still held the faint, clinging scent of perfume and powder. Each step felt heavier, as if the building itself bore witness to the reckoning we were about to bring.

My office sat tucked away at the back, hidden behind a heavy velvet curtain that covered a door no one else bothered with. I slipped inside and closed it gently behind me, locking it out of habit. The room was dim, lit only by the lamp on my desk, its amber glow casting long shadows along the walls. I didn't bother turning on the rest of the lamps.

I sank into the worn leather chair and pulled open the bottom drawer, retrieving the things I kept tucked away for nights like this—old papers, names scribbled in margins, faded receipts, and stories whispered to me over the years by drunk men and sobbing girls. Information was power, and I never let it slip through my fingers. I thumbed through brittle newspapers, their edges cracking under the weight of time, moving with a familiar speed that made it seem as though my hands remembered every page even if my mind did not. I didn't know exactly what I was searching for, but instinct told me I would recognize it the moment I found it.

And then I found him. Halfway down the stack, his face leapt up at me: Father Frederick. Younger, but not by much, his eyes already hollow and cold, as if someone had scooped out whatever made him human and left only a shell behind. The headline made my hands shake, and I had to press my palm to the desk to stop myself from knocking everything to the floor:

SHOCKING: PRIEST OUSTED FOR SCANDALOUS BEHAVIOR IN ILLINOIS PARISH

It was the paper I wasn't able to get to all those weeks ago. The ones I asked Nell to tuck away for me for a later date, the ones I had forgotten all about. I read every word. Every sickening word. The article was short, with precious little information, and buried in the back pages, the way the church liked to bury their sins. It mentioned *accusations, inappropriate contact, rumors of coercion, and misconduct.* Never fully investigated, never proven, but enough to get him quietly reassigned. Swept away and shoved into the shadows. And now those shadows had brought him here.

My hand slammed onto the desk, sending a jolt through the lamp and making its light flicker across the walls. A stack of papers toppled to the floor, but I didn't care; nothing else mattered. He had a history of slipping through cracks wide enough for men like him to walk free. But not this time. I stared down at the article, my heart hammering, while rage consumed me. He had chosen the wrong town, the wrong brothel, the wrong girls. He had chosen Violet. And if Father Frederick was watching us, he best know we were watching him back.

39

THE MASK FALLS

HIM

The collar feels tighter tonight, constricting, as if it is alive and aware of every sin I've ever tried to bury, cutting the air away from my neck until each breath feels like confession. I tug at it, my fingers trembling with desperation. The cracked mirror above the dresser stares back at me, its fractured glass dividing my reflection into pieces I no longer know how to fit together, and my face looks older than I remember, aged by years and the slow decay of guilt.

Butte wasn't supposed to have been like this. It was supposed to be a place to vanish, a place to blend in, another sleepy town with too many ghosts to care about mine. But my ghosts always manage to find me, no matter how far I run, reminding me that escape was never part of the deal.

The clock ticks from the far wall. The sound fills the silence until it feels alive, pulsing against the walls, reminding me how much I hate the quiet. It invites memory, and memory gnaws at me when the darkness presses in. I thought I could bury it all deep enough. I thought time would smoother what I couldn't face, but time, it seems, is no gravekeeper.

It started in Illinois in a town like this one. All denim and dust and sweet-tea secrets. The church was an old one, cold in the winter, and thick with mildew in the summer. But the people came anyway, like they always do. I was younger then, still clinging to the idea that this collar meant something holy. That I was chosen, that the ache in my chest was purpose, not corruption. But even then I'm certain I knew. Deep down, I *knew*. And then there was her: Annabelle.

She was barely fifteen, too young, too innocent, but to me that was part of the allure. She was a faithful soul, always sitting in the front pew, her hands folded tightly in prayer, her head tilted slightly as she listened to me speak. Her eyes shone with that purity, that untainted worship, and as I watched her, it ignited something deep within me. I told myself it was nothing;

nothing but a fleeting admiration for her devotion, but I knew it wasn't. It was hunger.

The hunger grew slowly. At first, I noticed it only when I caught myself staring at her a little too long, taking in every delicate feature, every hint of her innocent smile. A harmless connection, nothing more.

But soon, I sought her out. A desire to guide her as she navigated her young faith, but when I found myself asking her to stay behind after services, or to help me with small tasks around the church, I couldn't deny that the time spent alone with her was becoming too precious to me. It was the way she looked at me, so trusting, so eager to please, that kept me coming back.

It happened on a Thursday, when rain tapped against the stained glass and turned the world beyond it into shifting watercolor. The candles had long since burned themselves down to soft, wavering stubs, leaving just the two of us in the dim sanctuary. She stood at the altar, carefully wiping the chalices clean as I lingered in the darker edge of the room, where the light couldn't quite reach me. She didn't know I was watching her, not at first. But she smiled when she caught my eye, like she *understood,* like she was giving me permission.

I told myself that lie more than once.

I said her name, and she came to me without hesitation, without fear. She stood before me with her hands folded, as she always did, devoted and open.

"You're special, Annabelle," I had told her, my voice low, as if I were saying a prayer. "You feel that, don't you? That pull between us?"

She didn't answer. Only looked up at me, lips parted slightly, her breath coming a little quicker than before. Didn't flinch when I touched her face, only blinked up at me, her eyes wide. She let me tuck her hair behind her ear, let me trace her jaw with my thumb.

"You don't have to be afraid," I whispered. "This . . . this is God's will. You were brought to me for a reason."

And she *still* didn't pull away. That was the moment, that perfect stillness, the point of no return, that I stepped closer and felt the warmth of her breath. Heard the tiny catch in her throat, saw the way her fingers twitched against her dress. She stood there and took it. And I told myself that was permission.

I took my time. My hands trembling as they traced the length of her arm, closing around her wrist a fraction too tightly. When it was over, she remained seated on the pew, knees drawn up beneath her as if she could fold herself small enough to disappear. Her eyes were fixed on the altar, like she was waiting for some sort of instruction, some explanation for what had just happened . . . for what I had done.

But then the creak of the church doors opening and the sound of heavy footsteps on the floor filled the room. My head snapped toward the entrance, heart hammering so hard it drowned out the rain. A shadow wavered against the candlelight, stretching long across the aisle before the figure behind it emerged. Annabelle's father stood in the doorway, framed by the stormlight, his face carved into something I couldn't read at first—until the fury came into focus. His eyes burned wild with it. "What are you doing with my daughter?"

His words, full of rage and disbelief, echoed through the sanctuary until they seemed to come from every wall at once. My mind raced, and for a moment, I couldn't think, couldn't speak. My mouth went dry, my throat tight. I had been caught, caught in the act of betrayal, caught in my darkest desire. Every secret I'd buried clawed its way to the surface in that instant, and I understood, with terrible clarity, that there would be no forgiveness waiting for me here.

Annabelle's father wasted no time. The distance between us vanished in a single, furious stride, and before I could even raise a hand or form a word, his fist was in my collar, the fabric biting into my throat with a vicelike grip. The force of it pulled me off balance and sent the air rushing from my lungs as he slammed me back against the pew. His breath was hot, ragged with rage, and his eyes burned with something primal—something beyond words. Then the first blow came. My head snapped to the side, a burst of light behind my eyes, the taste of iron blooming on my tongue.

He didn't stop. His fists kept finding me, again and again, each strike breaking the silence into splintering sounds that seemed to ricochet through the empty church. The world narrowed to impact and breath, the thud of knuckles against skin, the stone floor cold beneath my knees. I didn't try to resist; there was no point. "Stay away from her, you sick son of a bitch," he growled, his fists still trembling.

The next few days passed in a haze. The town was in an uproar, the whispers spreading like wildfire. I could hear them in the streets, in the markets, in the back pews of the church. The accusations grew louder, and it wasn't just the father's word anymore—the entire town knew what had happened. The judgment was swift, and the church couldn't ignore it. I had failed.

I was called to the rectory, where the bishop and a handful of elders waited. The doors closed behind me with a soft click that still lingers in my ears. A handful of elders sat in rigid silence, their faces hard and grim, carved by years of authority. The bishop sat at the head of the long table, his eyes cold and piercing. "You've disgraced yourself," he declared, each word striking blow, "and you've brought shame to this church. To this town."

I opened my mouth to speak, to beg for mercy, but the words caught in my throat. My knees weakened beneath me, threatening to give way, and I could hear the faint, relentless pounding of my heartbeat in my ears, a deafening drum that left no room for thought. How could they do this to me? How could they turn their backs on me when I had served them for all these years, sacrificed for them, carried their sins as my own?

Another man, one of the elders, spoke up, his voice accusing. "You've hurt her, Father. Hurt her in ways that cannot be forgiven."

The bishop was quiet, voice almost a whisper, as he pronounced my sentence. "You have no place here anymore, the town won't accept you. So, the choice is yours: Leave quietly, or we will expose you to the courts. Your sins will be laid bare for all to see." My mind spun. I knew I had failed, and that the town would never accept me again. But what of my vows? What of my calling? The words of the bishop replayed in my mind: *Leave quietly or be exposed.* I chose to leave, as if the other option was really a choice.

I ran, as far as my legs could carry me, and I never looked back. But the memories never stopped. They stayed with me, gnawing at me, demanding more, pushing me into darker corners of my own soul.

Now, here in Butte, those memories were creeping back, insidious and uninvited, whispering in the quiet moments, returning in flashes. And there was one woman in particular, one woman who seemed to see through my carefully constructed mask. Bernadette. Her eyes, her knowing gaze . . . she had seen too much. Every time our paths crossed, I could feel it. She knew what I was.

I clenched my fists, resolve hardening in time with the motion. The women in this town, especially those girls at The Oily Cat, they knew. They knew too much, and I could not, would not, allow them to expose me. Not again. Not ever.

40

I'M NOT ASKING

I folded my hands in my lap; my fingers feeling colder than they should have for this time of the year. I sat on the creaking bench, same as I had a hundred times before. "Forgive me, Father, for I have sinned. It's been three weeks since my last confession." My voice sounded steady, but I wasn't telling the whole truth. I wasn't here to confess, I was here to warn . . . to *expose*. I leaned forward, pressing my hands together.

"Father, I need to talk to you about something, something that I've recently been made aware of." There was a soft shift on the other side of the screen from Father Cyrus. I could hear the rustle of his sleeve, the shallow inhale. "It's about Father Frederick."

That got his attention. He didn't speak, but I knew he was listening closely now. "There have been rumors," I continued, swallowing the lump in my throat, "and I've seen the way he watches the girls, the way he watches Violet. It doesn't feel right, Father. It's not just talk, there's something about him, something unsettling."

"Birdie, I didn't think you were one to fall prey to rumors." He chided me gently. "You've always been more discerning than that." His words were soft, but I could feel the caution behind them.

"I'm not!" I snapped. "You know I'm not."

Silence again. I could almost hear the slow turn of his thoughts, the soft shift of cloth as he adjusted on the other side of the screen. I reached into my pocket and pulled out the folded article, its edges worn soft from the amount of times I'd read and reread it, and I pressed it flat against the wood. "I found this."

I heard him shift forward, and I held the page in place while his eyes moved over the words.

"And now he's here," I continued, "watching girls like Violet. Hoping to get one of them alone." I didn't know if my words were registering. Was he really hearing me? Was he *un-*

derstanding what I was saying? The booth felt smaller suddenly. Hotter. My palms were clammy as I held up the article, the paper going soft at the edges where my fingers pressed. I didn't dare lower it. I needed him to see it. To *really* see it.

He leaned closer, breath moving through the screen. "*My God,*" he whispered. "I knew he was troubled. I—," his voice was careful, as if he was choosing his words. "I've suspected, Birdie, I have. But suspicion alone . . . it's not enough in this place, not in this town. Father Frederick hasn't acted on anything."

I looked at the cross carved into the panel in front of me. It was small, just a shape etched into the wood, but tonight it looked like a wound. "This isn't just suspicion anymore," I insisted. "It's a pattern. He tried to follow Violet home the other night. And if we wait for more proof, for him to *act on it*, someone's going to get hurt."

"Birdie," he reasoned, voice low, "you understand what this would mean. If you're right, if we bring this forward without something ironclad . . . the backlash won't just hit him, it'll divide the town. You've seen what happens when the wrong person gets blamed."

"I'm not wrong." I warned.

"I know." He said. There was weariness in his tone, a knowledge of exactly how deep the rot could go. "But if you're going to bring this to light, you'll need more than a gut feeling and a yellowed article. You'll need something that can't be ignored. And if he's as careful as you say—" He trailed off as if his mind had changed paths. "This is serious, Bernadette," he added softly, "as a priest, I am bound by the trust of the church." His words a mix of caution and growing certainty.

"I know what I'm looking at." I exclaimed, my voice sounding harsh, even to me. "I can see it in the way he moves, the way he speaks. There's something insidious in his charm. He knows people are looking, and he's good at hiding."

Father Cyrus's voice softened. "I hear you, Birdie. But we need to be careful. If we expose him without cause, it will bring a storm to this town, and we're not ready for that. We'll be fighting a battle on all fronts."

"I know," I whispered, rubbing my temples as the frustration built. "But I can't let him get away with it."

Father Cyrus didn't respond immediately, but I could hear the shift in his breath, as though he was steeling himself to carry another incredible burden. As if he was giving me permission to take on the responsibility of what we both now knew was coming. "I know you can't, Birdie." He exhaled softly.

41

DARLING, SIT DOWN. I'M ABOUT TO RUIN YOUR DAY.

By the time I pushed open the door to The Oily Cat, the strain in my shoulders had begun to ease. The clatter of dishes and the sound of familiar voices grounded me. Unlike the confessional, this place made no promises of redemption. It dealt in truth, and right now, that's all I wanted. They were all here: Violet, Maeve, Elona, Emil, and Nell. Gathered around our usual table beneath the rusted wall sconce. Just seeing them steadied me.

I slid into the seat at the head of the table, my hand curling around the glass of bourbon waiting for me, the ice already beginning to melt. The burn as I swallowed was searing, and exactly what I needed. We were here to talk about Father Frederick, and there was no room left for hesitation. Before I addressed the table, I leaned toward Maeve. "We're skipping Mass tomorrow." I whispered.

She raised a brow, "All of us?"

I nodded. "You, me, and the girls. We're staying in. Elona will keep an eye on Violet. I don't want them near that church while he's still prowling." Staying close to the Oily Cat would buy us time and space to figure things out. We couldn't keep pretending everything was normal when it very clearly was not.

Violet sipped her wine as Elona shifted closer, her attention flicking between us with curiosity. Emil leaned back in his chair, relaxed, while beside him, Nell rested a steady hand on his back, thumb moving in slow, absent circles between his shoulders. She looked at me then and gave a small nod.

My cue to begin.

"We need to talk about Father Frederick." I said, setting my glass down. The thought of the girls, of what I'd learned, felt like rot running through me and left me feeling sick. "Some things have come to light; things you all need to hear."

Maeve's expression tightened as her eyes roved around the table, locking briefly with each of us in turn, anger and disbelief simmering just beneath. "It's worse than we thought. The things he's been doing . . . they're sick." She added.

Elona leaned forward, her eyes flashing with that familiar fire. "I always knew something was off. He's always watching, always lurking. I could never trust a man who hides behind a collar."

Violet broke her silence. "I get it, Elona, but not all of them are like that. Father Cyrus, he's a good man. He actually helps people." She exhaled hard, and something in her eyes hardened. "But Father Frederick . . . he makes my skin crawl." She shook her head, as if trying to dislodge the unsettling feeling, crossing her arms over her chest.

Unease circled through the room. "Maeve," I said, voice taut. "Tell them what Carl said."

She hesitated for a moment, taking a slow sip of her wine before speaking. "Aye. So, it all started last Saturday when Carl was talkin' about Father Frederick. Apparently, there's a whole lot of gossip goin' around the mines about him."

Nell's brow furrowed. "Gossip?"

"Aye, but not the usual kind." Maeve continued, keeping her voice firm, as she was trying to keep the frustration from bubbling over. "Carl said the lads have been whisperin' about him for weeks. They say he's been showin' . . . an *interest* in the younger girls, in a way that's not exactly holy."

Nell's face twisted. "Are you saying he's *preying* on them? A priest?"

"For fuck's sake." Emil said in disgust, running his hand over his face.

Maeve nodded slowly, her lips pressed tightly together. "I didn't want to believe it either. But the more I heard, the more it made sense. Carl said he's been spotted late at night, sneakin' around, lurkin' outside the brothel."

My fingers tapped a rhythm on the table, my mind spinning. "That's the thing . . . it's not just town gossip." I pulled the crumpled newspaper article from my bag and laid it on the table for everyone to see. "I've seen the way he watches Violet. It's like he wants to possess her." The scrap of paper drew everyone's gaze to it like a magnet. Maeve looked at it for a long second before turning away, visibly uncomfortable.

Emil's jaw clenched, his eyes narrowing as he studied the article. "If he's been coming around here . . . watching you girls . . . then we've got a problem. Men like that don't stop."

Elona shoved her plate aside, her face pale. "And no one's doing anything? He's a priest. Aren't people supposed to trust him?"

I let out a dry laugh. "Exactly. They trust him, that's how he gets away with it."

Nell's intense gaze met mine. "So, what do we do? We can't just let this keep happening. The girls won't be safe."

I opened my mouth, but Emil beat me to it. “We watch him,” he said. “Quietly. We keep track. Where he goes, who he talks to. If he steps out of line again, we bring it into the light.”

“And if bringing it to light doesn’t work,” I offered, “. . . there are other ways.”

We all nodded. A shared burden, and an unspoken promise that the next time Father Frederick looked at one of our girls, he wouldn’t get the chance to do it again.

I smiled grimly. “Good. Now let’s eat before this conversation ruins our appetite completely.”

Emil frowned. "Too late."

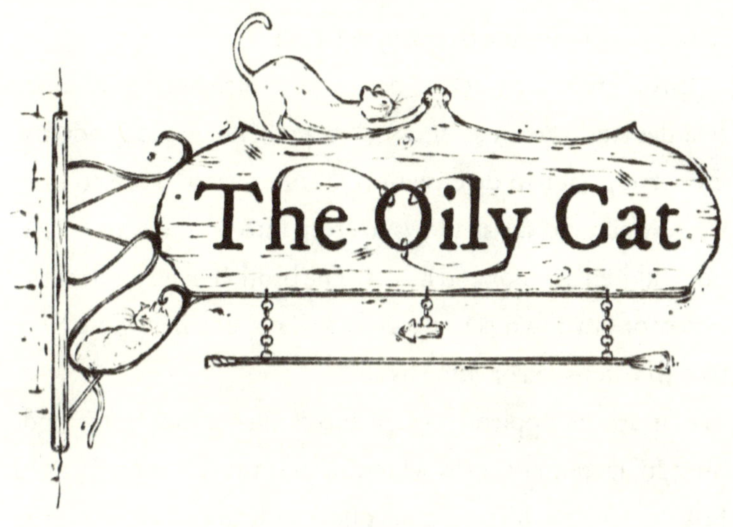

42

GRAB YOUR PITCH FORKS AND TORCHES

HIM

The townsfolk filled the pews, their faces bathed in the soft morning light. I had spent the week wrestling with my thoughts while the image of Violet haunted me at every turn. The more I thought about her, the more the darkness within me gained the upper hand. The brothel had become a bane in my mind, a symbol of everything that was wrong with this town. It was time to unleash that anger, to channel my turmoil into a sermon that would ignite the flames of righteousness among this congregation.

"Brothers and sisters," I began, my voice filled with a fire that demanded their attention, "we gather here today not just in worship, but in defense of our community! For too long we have allowed the shadows to creep into our lives, to poison our children's minds and hearts. The brothel that stands at the center of our town is not merely a house of sin, it is a cancer that threatens to consume us all."

A murmur rippled through the congregation, heads nodding in agreement, eyes widening with realization. I could feel the energy shifting, the collective fear and anger rising. "Do you know what happens within those cursed walls?" I continued, my voice booming. "Innocence is stolen, souls are shackled, and the very fabric of our community is torn apart! The women who toil there are instruments of destruction, leading our men astray and tempting our youth into the abyss of immorality!"

Gasps echoed in the church. Father Cyrus stood up to protest, his face flushed with indignation. "Now, that is enough!" He demanded, but I pressed on, the fire in my belly urging me forward.

"It is our duty, our sacred responsibility, to protect this town from such vile influence!" My voice rang out, becoming a roar. "We must not sit idly by while our neighbors fall prey to the darkness. We must take a stand!" As I spoke, I could see the anger building in the eyes of the congregants, the righteous indignation igniting like a match to kindling. I felt a surge of power; my words were like arrows, piercing through the hearts of the faithful. They were hungry for guidance, for someone to lead them against the encroaching darkness. They needed me, not Father Cyrus.

"Father Cyrus is a good man, a godly man," I preached, "but it's going to take more than a godly man to lead us away from temptation. You need someone who has looked the devil square in the eye and denounced him in the name of the Lord! I am that man!"

The look of horror on Father Cyrus's face was of no concern to the fine people of this town, in fact, not one of them glanced in his direction. All eyes were on me, and the dangerously addictive feeling of power surged through me.

But what was most conspicuous to me was the absence of Bernadette and her whores. There was no sign of them in the pews.

"Let us not forget the consequences of our inaction!" I thundered, my voice booming against the stone walls. "For every soul lost to the brothel, there is a ripple effect, a degradation of our values! We must band together, as one body, to cleanse our town of this filth. We must turn our backs on those who would harbor such wickedness!"

The congregation erupted in agreement, their voices rising in a chorus of anger and fear. "Amen!" They cried. "Yes, Father!"

My heart raced as the intoxicating power of the moment filled me. "Let us take a stand!" I shouted, with my arms raised high. "Let us confront the owners of that den of sin! Let us show them that Butte will no longer tolerate their presence! We must drive them out, lest we be consumed by the very darkness we seek to eradicate!"

With each word, I felt the tide of hatred rise, the fervor of the crowd feeding my own anger. They were no longer just townsfolk; they were soldiers ready to wage war against the sins that threatened their way of life. I had ignited a fire within them, and I knew that now that it burned, it would be nearly impossible to extinguish.

As the sermon came to a close, I looked out over the sea of faces, now transformed by the power of my rhetoric. Father Cyrus had slipped away during the last minutes of the tirade, no doubt retreating to lick his wounds, but it hardly mattered. The people had made their choice.

"Join me, my friends! Let us march against this evil together! Let us reclaim our town from the hands of those who would destroy it!"

The church erupted in applause, and shouts of agreement filled the air. They were ready to act, to confront the very heart of the evil I had painted before them, and through it all I stood back, watching as the chaos unfolded, the taste of power lingering on my tongue.

I watched the people of Butte and knew that the days of the brothel corrupting their town were numbered. The battle I had set in motion would reshape this town, eradicate its sins, and in the process, reshape my power within it.

This was only the beginning. The real test, however, would come when those who would defend the brothel began to fight back. But for now, I savored the victory.

43

A PRIEST WALKS INTO A BROTHEL...

FATHER CYRUS

I stood in the vestibule of the church, my hands clasped tightly in front of me, my thoughts a swirl of confusion, anger, and fear. I'd spent most of the sermon fighting the urge to step forward and stop Father Frederick, to call him out for the venom he was spewing. But I hadn't, at least, not like I should have, and now my guilt weighed heavily on me.

The sermon had been one of the most dangerous I'd ever heard. Father Frederick, with his fire-and-brimstone rhetoric, had transformed the pulpit into a weapon. He'd painted a grotesque portrait of the brothel, Bernadette's establishment, and its inhabitants. He'd accused them of being agents of the devil himself, poisoning the town from within. The people, their hearts and minds primed by Father Frederick's own emotion, had swallowed the lies whole. They were angry, they were scared, and now, with the preacher's words still buzzing in their heads, they wanted blood.

I looked around, my eyes scanning across faces that now seemed unfamiliar, hardened by fear, fueled by the poison of Father Frederick's sermon. These were not the people I had mentored, counseled, and prayed with. They had taken Father Frederick's sermon as gospel, and I knew that nothing I said would change their minds. *They will come for her*, I realized. *They will come for all of them*.

My heart hammered in my chest as I made my decision. I turned sharply on my heel and exited through the back door of St. Ann's, a singular purpose guiding my every step. The town felt different now. People moved in groups, eyes darting nervously, as if waiting for something to happen, as if the storm Father Frederick had promised was already on its way.

I quickened my pace.

The brothel wasn't far, only a few blocks down from the church, but every step felt like an eternity. The buildings in Butte were old, weathered by time and neglect, but The Oily Cat stood out among them all. It was a place of sin, they said, but to me it was a place of survival. A place where women, broken and cast aside by the world, had built a life. A place where they fought back, day after day, against a world eager to forget them.

The door creaked as I pushed it open, the warm scent of whiskey, perfume, and tobacco flooding my senses. I inhaled deeply, forcing myself to stay focused. As I moved further inside, my eyes scanned the room, my heart breaking over the sadness of the situation. The bar sat silent and empty in the dim light, and there, at the far end of the room, I finally located Bernadette.

She was seated with Violet and Maeve, posture straight, eyes glowing with a mesmerizing intensity that made it impossible to look away. She was speaking quietly to the other women, her voice low. She exuded strength, and in that moment, I could see it: the woman who had endured so much, and yet, remained unbroken.

I approached, aware of the eyes turning toward me. Bernadette looked up, eyes locking with mine, and for the briefest moment I saw something rare in her expression: uncertainty. She knew something was wrong, and my unexpected presence in this place would have been telling even if she hadn't sensed it.

"Father?" Her voice was full of concern. "What's happened?"

I gripped the back of a chair, grounding myself. "Bernadette," I began, my voice urgent, "I've just come from St. Ann's. The sermon . . . it was worse than I feared. Father Frederick, he's incited something. The people . . ." I swallowed hard, the words sticking in my throat. "They believe him, and they're angry and frightened. And now . . . they've turned against you."

Her face didn't change, but a cold resolve settled in her eyes. "What exactly did he say?"

I hesitated, gathering my words. "He's convinced them that your brothel, your girls, your place here, is the root of all the town's moral decay. Said you were poisoning Butte. He demanded your destruction."

Bernadette's eyes stayed fixed. "What does that mean? What are they going to do?"

My voice dropped to a near whisper. "They're coming, Bernadette. They've been stirred into a frenzy, and they won't stop until this place, everything you've built, is gone."

Something passed across her expression, fury, maybe, or something colder. But what settled there was determination. "I won't leave," she said. "I've fought too hard, for too long. This is my home. If they want a war, they'll get one. But I'll fight every last one of them before I let them take this from me."

I opened my mouth to protest, to try to convince her to leave, but Violet cut me off with a quick wave of her hand. Her eyes were wide with disbelief, but there was no fear in them. "Father," she said firmly, "you're wasting your time. Birdie doesn't run. She never has, and she never will."

I stared at her, my mind spinning. I was a man of God, sworn to peace and compassion, and here I was, begging a woman who had survived hell not to stand her ground. I had never felt so powerless. "I wish I could do more," I said, voice hoarse, "but if you stay, Bernadette, it will get worse. They'll burn it all down."

For a moment, Bernadette's fierce exterior faltered. She stepped closer to me, placing a hand on my arm, an unexpected gesture. "I can't leave, Father," she said. "This is my fight. And if they mean to destroy me, they'll have to face me first."

I nodded, though the gesture felt hollow. My heart ached for her, for them all. I had known Bernadette for years, but only now did I truly understand what she had endured, and what she was willing to sacrifice.

"I'll pray for you," I said, barely holding it together. "For all of you. Just . . . be careful."

I stepped out of the brothel and into the streets, a pit opening in my stomach, the pain in my chest deeper than fear. It was grief. Grief for what Butte had been. Grief for what it was about to become. And guilt. Painful, inescapable guilt over the fact that I had not spoken louder, not fought harder. Butte was no longer the caring town I had loved; it had become a battleground.

And the first shot had been fired.

44

THE HOUSE KNOWS HOW YOU'LL FOLD

I hadn't slept much; my mind couldn't settle and kept circling back to the way Father Cyrus had looked, to the words he spoke, to the warning he left behind.

I stayed near the window, listening, trying to hold my thoughts in place while Violet sat at a small table, carefully drafting a letter. The pen moved slowly, each word deliberate, as she crafted the perfect message to lure Father Frederick to the brothel.

I watched her closely, worry tightening behind my eyes. Violet was eager, she wanted to do her part in this, but I couldn't help but feel a deep, protective instinct.

Maeve, Elona, Nell, and Emil were in the back room making sure everything was in order. Tonight's plan wasn't just to orchestrate Father Frederick's fall, it would also be a test of how far we were willing to go to change the power dynamic in this town, and I knew the stakes were high.

"Violet," I began, breaking the silence, "are you sure about this? This isn't just some game. We're playing with fire."

Violet paused, her pen hovering over the paper as she looked up at me. There was a dark hunger in her eyes. "I'm sure, Bernadette. I've never been more certain of anything."

I stepped forward and sat across from her, looking at her intently. That fire in her eyes, I'd seen it before, in women who wanted to prove they were strong. And she *was* strong. But this was different.

"I know you want to help," I said softly. "And I know you believe you're ready. You've come through so much, and I've seen how hard you fight. But not all fights are the same, Violet. Some don't leave bruises you can see, and the ones that don't . . . those are the ones that stay with you the longest." I paused before asking gently, "Are you sure you understand what this could cost you?"

Violet's lips parted, but before she could answer, Maeve's voice came from the hallway. "Bernadette."

I turned to see her standing in the doorway. Elona and Nell lingering just behind her, listening in silence as Maeve stepped into the room slowly.

"She's not some wee girl anymore. She's earned the right to decide what she stands for." Her eyes swept to Violet, lingered for a second, then returned to me. "You taught us to be strong, to hold our ground when it counted. That's all she's doin' now, ain't it?" She paused, her expression softening. "I know you're worried for her; I am too. But maybe the best we can do now is stand with her, not in front of her."

I looked at Maeve, then back at Violet. "I know she's strong." My voice was firm. "I know she can handle more than most ever should have to. But strength doesn't mean she should carry everything alone." I reached out, resting my hand lightly on the table. "Violet, this isn't just a clever plan, it's dangerous. You're not just writing a letter, you're putting yourself in front of a man who would see you torn apart if it served his purpose. Father Frederick may be a man of God, but that doesn't make him a good man. You've seen what he stirred up in this town."

My voice splintered into a whisper. "I just need to know this isn't about proving something. I need to know you're doing this because it's right for *you*, not because you feel like you owe it to the rest of us."

Violet hesitated; her pen still paused in midair. Her eyes moved from me to the letter, then back to me again. "I'm not doing this to prove anything," she said. "And it's not about being fearless. I'm scared, but I know what kind of man he is, and I know what he's already done." She looked toward Maeve, then Elona and Nell, drawing strength from them. "This isn't just about me," she continued, her voice softer now. "It's about all of us. If I can pull back the mask he hides behind, even just a little . . . then maybe I can stop him from hurting anyone else ever again." She met my eyes again. "I'm not rushing into this. I've weighed everything carefully. But I need you to trust me, Bernadette, I need you to believe I can do this."

Elona, who had been silently leaning against the doorway up until now, spoke up. "Violet isn't asking for our permission, Bernadette, she's asking for us to stand with her."

Nell, standing a little further back, nodded in agreement. "She's thought this through. We all have. And maybe . . . maybe this is the way forward. Father Frederick's words have been closing in on us for a while now. Maybe it's time we turn the tables."

Emil, who had been silently watching from the hallway, stepped into the room, his broad shoulders filling the doorway. "Violet's got a point." He said. "We all know what Father Frederick's done here and what he's capable of. I won't pretend this isn't dangerous, but sometimes doing nothing feels like losing." He gave Violet a nod that was equal parts caution and trust.

I sighed, my shoulders slumping in defeat as their arguments outweighed my concern. I'd walked through enough fire, known enough pain, to be wary of the path we were about to take. Still, I understood the power this moment held. If we could draw Father Frederick out, if we could expose him for what he truly was . . . maybe, just maybe, we could turn the tide.

I looked at Violet once more, my expression softening. "I've protected you girls for so long," I said, almost to myself, "and I will continue to protect you, even if I have to burn every bridge in this town to do it." I placed a hand on Violet's, a silent vow in my touch.

Violet gave a small, appreciative smile, squeezing my hand in return. "I know you have, Bernadette, and I don't want to let you down. But this . . . this is something I have to do for myself. For that little girl in Illinois."

I nodded, then turned my attention to the letter on the table. "Alright then, we do this carefully, we do this right. No mistakes. We use his pride and his arrogance against him, and when he walks through that door, he'll be stepping straight into a hell of his own making." I stood and took a couple of steps away from the table. "Emil," I called over my shoulder, "I need you to make sure the house is ready. Everything has to be perfect. No mistakes."

Emil nodded with a sharp jerk, his eyes steely with determination. "You got it, Bernadette."

As he left to prepare, I turned back to Violet. "When you give him that letter, there's no going back. Are you ready for that?"

Violet's voice was ironclad. "I'm ready. He won't know what hit him." She turned back to the table and folded the letter, her hands were steady as she reached for the small stick of sealing wax I used when I had letters to send out, a deep blood-red. I watched her hold the wax to the flame of the nearby oil lamp, melting it until it dripped thick onto the envelope. Without a word, she pressed the brass stamp into it. Sealing it with a single kiss impression.

She lifted the stamp and held the envelope up to me. "It's done." She offered.

For something made of nothing but paper and ink, it felt impossibly heavy in my hands. I looked down at the seal, feeling the power of everything it represented before slipping it into the pocket of my coat. I didn't waste any time. The sun had barely cleared the hills when I slipped out the back door, coat drawn tight, boots silent on the stone. I stayed close to the buildings, away from the main streets, cutting through alleys and empty yards until I reached the center of town where St. Ann's sat.

Father Cyrus had told me about a side entrance once, back when we were still learning to trust each other. Said if the day ever came when I needed to reach him without being seen, I was to come to this door and knock twice.

I found the narrow wooden door half-hidden behind the overgrown hedge, exactly where Father Cyrus had promised it would be. Pushing aside a low-hanging branch, I stepped closer, the leaves skimming my sleeve. The wood was old and warped, its years carved into every line of the grain as I rapped twice against it, the sound cracking through the silence like a snapped twig.

I stood still, listening to the wind tug at the leaves behind me, to the ghost of distant footsteps somewhere on another street, and after a long breath, I heard it—a faint scrape, metal against wood, then a soft click as the door opened an inch, just enough to reveal a familiar eye through the crack.

Father Cyrus stood in the doorway; his exhausted face wore an expression like he had aged several years overnight. His eyes met mine briefly, before dropping to my hand, to the envelope that I held pressed flat against my chest. The red wax glinted faintly in the gray morning light. He didn't speak, just opened the door wider. I stepped into the space between us and placed the letter in his outstretched hand. His fingers closed around it with unsettling care, as though he expected it to sear straight through his skin.

We stood there a second longer, watching each other. No words were exchanged, but we communicated the intention. The letter was in his hands now, just like we'd planned. He didn't need instructions; he already knew what it meant, where it needed to go, and what would come of it.

45

FUNNY HOW QUICK LUST TURNS INTO LAST RIGHTS

HIM

I sat alone in the small rectory, my body slumping with bone-deep exhaustion. I had spent hours in prayer, searching the scripture for something to hold on to, some word or phrase that might steady the chaos in my head. The Bible lay open in my hands, but the lines on the page felt distant, stripped of meaning.

My fingers moved over the delicate pages, but the words blurred before my eyes until they meant nothing at all. All I could see was her, Violet. She lingered in my mind as vividly as if she stood before me, her smile hovering at the edge of my vision and pulling me in with an insistence I didn't try to resist. I told myself to set it aside, to return to my calling, to guide my parishioners toward righteousness and finish the sermon waiting beneath my hand, but the pull only tightened. Every prayer rang hollow, every line of scripture felt false the moment it left my mouth.

The memory of that first sermon at St. Ann's came rushing back to me. I had stood before the congregation, trying to focus on the words I was supposed to deliver, but my attention kept drifting to *her*. She was in the back row, seated by Elona, Maeve, and Bernadette, but *she* was the one I couldn't stop looking at. I tried, I really did, to keep my eyes on the congregation, to concentrate on the message I was delivering. But there was something about her, something that made it impossible for me to look away. And then the thoughts came, unwelcome and unclean, flooding my mind without warning. They hit hard, dragging me toward a place I'd fought for years to leave behind. Memories of past failures surfaced one after another and I couldn't outrun them.

Her smile was all it took to unravel what I'd worked so hard to contain. Desires I'd buried, sins I thought I'd left behind rose to the surface with sudden clarity, as if she'd held the key all along. My hands tightened around the Bible in my lap, the paper crinkling in my grip as if it could somehow steady me, drown out the noise of my yearning. But the more I tried to resist, the more vivid the memory of her became.

It was then that I noticed the letter.

It rested on the desk, stark white against the dark wood. I hadn't noticed it before, and I found myself wondering how long it had been there, and who had left it. My hand hesitated as I reached for it, fingers grazing the smooth envelope, when a faint trace of lavender drifted up, stopping me cold.

The wax seal caught my eye, crimson, and stamped with the imprint of lips. I knew who it was from before I even opened it. My hands trembled as I broke the seal, a thrill of anticipation shooting through me despite my best effort to remain impassive. Inside, the letter was elegantly penned, the script flowing smoothly across the page, each word carefully crafted.

Reading it was a slow poison, tempting me further into the abyss.

Dear Father Frederick,

I hope this letter finds you well, though I do suspect you've been fighting a battle of your own, one that no one else has noticed. But I've noticed you, Father. I see the way you linger in the shadows of the town, trying to keep your distance from what pulls at you. You might believe that your gaze goes unnoticed, but it doesn't. I see your struggle, and I can't help but wonder . . . why keep fighting it?

The words haunted my head, each syllable digging deeper into my mind. *You might believe that your gaze goes unnoticed . . .*

She had been watching me. She had known all along. A dark thrill slid through me and I was torn between my duty as a man of God and the overwhelming urge that Violet's letter had awakened. *Why keep fighting it?* The question hovered like a taunt, teasing me, pulling at the walls I had spent so many years constructing around myself. The dam I had built to hold back the flood of temptation was beginning to crack. My fingers shook as I read on.

You've been preaching about sin, haven't you? About temptation and the dangers of the flesh. But I have to ask you, Father, do you truly understand sin? Or have you merely constructed your own prison, locking away the very desires that make you human?

Each word felt like a blow, hitting me harder than any sermon I had ever delivered. My chest tightened and my heartbeat thundered in my ears, drowning out everything else. *Do you truly understand sin?* The question cut through me like a scalpel, the cold truth of it unraveling the neat and tidy bow I had wrapped around my faith. Did I understand sin? I had spent so many years condemning others, warning my flock about the dangers of temptation. But had I ever truly confronted my own?

The answer came too quickly, too easily. No. I had lived in fear of my own humanity, burying my deepest desires so far beneath the surface that I had nearly forgotten they existed at all. But Violet's letter, her words, were forcing open that dark, hidden place, forcing me to face what I'd long denied.

The letter continued:

I can offer you something you cannot find in your church, or in your sermons. Something far more thrilling, more indulgent. I am waiting for you at The Oily Cat, Father, the place you've avoided with such determination. But I know you've been drawn to it. You want to come to me. You NEED to come to me.

The words on the page dragged heat through me, and a slow pulse between my thighs answered the invitation's alluring promise.

Tonight, Father. When the sun sets, come. When you walk through that door, know this—I will be waiting for you, ready to show you the pleasures you've been denying yourself. And when you arrive, you will understand that the line between sin and salvation is far more blurred than you ever imagined.

Yours,

Violet

My hands were shaking, the letter crumpling in my grasp as I fought to breathe, my chest tight with conflicting emotions. *The line between sin and salvation.* Was it truly as blurred as she claimed? Could it be that my whole life had been a futile exercise in denial, that I had been living a lie, refusing to acknowledge the very desires that had made me human? The temptation to cross that line, to step into the world that she was offering, pressed in on me relentlessly.

I rose unsteadily, my legs barely holding me as I paced the small room. My body shook as I took a step toward the door, the decision crashing over me.

It wasn't a question of if anymore, but when. And I wanted her. I wanted her *now*. As I reached for my coat, a restless energy surged through me, coiling tightly in my gut. The thought of finally touching her, of feeling her body beneath my hands, sent a thrill through me that I didn't bother to fight. I knew that the moment I stepped through the door of The Oily Cat, everything would change. There would be no turning back.

With a shaky breath, I opened the door and stepped out into the fading light. The sun was setting; and the line between sin and salvation had never felt thinner.

46

...THE BETTER TO SEE YOU WITH, MY DEAR

HIM

Sweat slicked my spine as I paused in the doorway of The Oily Cat, my grip tightening against the rough wood hoping it might steady me. One step. That was all it would take.

Or I could walk away. There was still time. I could still return to the life I'd sworn to live by. But Violet's face haunted me. She unraveled every promise I'd ever made. Her face burned behind my eyes, all softness and temptation, all the things I had no right to want. No right to touch.

Come to me.

The words curled around my spine, tugging me forward before I could stop myself. I knew better. I *should* have known better. But want burned hotter than reason ever could. So, I took a shuddering breath and stepped through the door.

The parlor breathed with life, charged with a restless, electric anticipation as women in vibrant dresses glided past, their laughter weaving through smoke and sound while men leaned into their drinks, voices low and animated. The entire room pulsed with a primal rhythm, as though pleasure itself had taken shape.

At the bar, no one spared me a second glance. A man in the corner flicked his attention my way before turning back to his drink, and a woman in a loose red dress lifted her glass, her gaze skimming over me.

"Father Frederick!" Bernadette's voice sliced through the noise, pulling me from my thoughts. She moved through the crowd, her dress flowing behind her like a dark, liquid shadow. Her eyes glittered with a keen, almost predatory light.

I froze, caught between shame and something dangerously close to hunger.

Bernadette flashed a smile, her voice lowering to a purr. "Oh, Father, we certainly weren't expecting *you* tonight." Her eyes roamed over me, lingering with amusement, like there was a secret she knew that I wasn't privy to. I knew she could see my discomfort, could feel the tension radiating off me.

"I-I was just passing by," I stammered, the lie dry and pathetic as it left my lips. My pulse raced, and I heard the absurdity of my own words. Of course I wasn't just passing by; I was here for *her*.

Bernadette's lips curved into a knowing smile as she leaned in, the scent of her perfume overwhelming and sweet. "Oh, don't be coy, Father. We both know why you're here." She tilted her head toward the stairs. "Violet is waiting for you upstairs. She's been expecting you . . . the *real* you."

At her name, something inside me clenched. Violet's face flashed behind my eyes, her smile, her youth, that unbearable beauty. She had become everything I'd sworn to avoid. And now, she was waiting.

"I shouldn't be here," I whispered. "This place . . . it's a house of sin."

Bernadette cackled, a soft, tinkling sound that made the hairs on the back of my neck rise. "Sin?" She mused, almost lovingly. "What is sin, Father, but a label we put on our desires? Here, we don't call it sin, we call it freedom." She straightened, a sly smile curling at her lips. "Freedom to explore, to let go. Let go, even if it is just for one night. Come now, Violet is waiting for you."

Her words, sweet and venomous, sank into me, and without thinking, I let her lead me up the stairs, my feet moving on their own accord. Every step seemed to hammer in my mind, carrying me toward a choice I knew was inevitable. The noise of the parlor faded below us, the laughter and chatter muffled by the thick walls. Up here, the air felt cooler, and every door we passed seemed to vibrate with unspoken things: desire, confession, pleasure, and loss.

Bernadette paused at the far end of the hall, turning to me with a teasing smile. "Remember, Father," she whispered, her eyes intense, "there's no judgment here, only pleasure. Embrace it." She opened the door with a flourish, revealing a dimly lit room, and inside it: Violet. She sat naked on the edge of the bed, her skin glowing in the soft light. She was impossibly beautiful, achingly so. My breath caught; she was everything I had imagined and more.

"Father," she said, voice steeped in intent, "I've been waiting for you." Her words were an invitation, soft, sultry, and irresistible. She rose, gliding toward me. She was a temptation made flesh, something forbidden, something I had long craved. And I couldn't resist anymore.

"Are you sure?" I asked, barely above a whisper, my body already betraying me as I grew hard.

"I want you," she breathed, her lips brushing against my ear. "Let me show you what it means to feel free."

Her warmth surrounded me, her breath teasing my skin. I could feel the heat of her body pressing so close to mine.

Her fingers trailed down my chest, light, but enough to make everything inside me shake.

I should have moved away. I should have fought the demons that clawed at me from within, but I couldn't. She pressed against me, her lips brushing my neck, and for a fleeting second, I imagined—no, *felt*—the release. The freedom she promised.

"Father," she cooed, her voice low and sultry, coaxing me, pulling me in deeper. "You've wanted this, haven't you? To be free of the chains you've bound yourself with."

Her words wrapped around me like velvet ropes, smooth and seductive, yet suffocating. She circled me slowly, eyes burning into me, every touch a gentle dismantling of who I had been.

She grazed my collar, fingers ghosting over the fabric like she was peeling back more than cloth. I stiffened; her touch felt too intimate, too knowing. She saw beneath the robe. She saw *me*. I tried to speak, to remind myself of the vows I had taken, but the words died on my lips, drowned by the force of her stare.

"I see the man beneath the priest, Father," she whispered, breath warm against my skin. "The one who's tired of pretending. The one who wants to feel . . . *alive* again." Her voice was honeyed and seductive, like a drug I had been craving for years.

Trembling, unable to look away, I swallowed hard, my throat dry.

"You've been denying yourself for too long," she continued, her fingers trailing lightly down the back of my neck. "It's time to stop fighting it, Father. Time to finally feel the freedom you've been longing for."

She kissed my jaw, a soft, lingering promise. Everything inside me told me to run. But I didn't. I *couldn't.* She took a step back, her eyes never leaving mine, and for a moment the world seemed to stop spinning. There was nothing but her, and she knew she had me. "Come," she commanded. "Let me show you what freedom truly feels like."

And suddenly I knew freedom wasn't salvation, it wasn't light.

It was darkness. And I wanted it.

Outside, the town kept on, but inside this room, everything had changed: the brothel, indifferent, had consumed another soul.

47

AS FOR ME AND MY HOUSE...

Father Frederick knelt on the floor, his back curved in submission, wrists and ankles chafing against the rough rope. His breathing was uneven, quick with panic and shame, and impossible to tell which was which. Still, his eyes clung to the figure before him, hollow with guilt but unable to look away. He had descended beyond redemption, past anything he once believed himself capable of, and there was no return.

Violet stood over him, now fully clothed, her figure framed in the low light, every movement precise and controlled. He couldn't tear his eyes from her, couldn't muster the will to resist. She was the force behind everything he had once sworn to deny, and now he knelt before her, laid bare, bound, and broken. The hands that once clutched the cross now shook with the knowledge of what he had become.

I stood in the doorway, my face unreadable, my form swallowed by the darkness curling through the hallway. I'd witnessed plenty over the years, both within these walls and far beyond them, but this was different. This was rot. Father Frederick had surrendered himself completely, stripped of conviction and reason. Violet didn't need to raise her voice or lift a hand; with little more than a glance, she had unraveled him. Now he knelt before her, hollowed out and lost, and she barely had to try.

A slow, cold smile tugged at my mouth. I studied the scene before me, refusing to look away. "Is this what you've become, Father?" The words cut through the silence, and I let them hang there, tasting the bitterness in them as well as the satisfaction. His collapse didn't surprise me; it confirmed what I'd always suspected.

He opened his mouth to speak, but the words broke apart. "You . . . don't understand." He whispered, voice unsteady and thin.

I stepped closer and crouched until my face hovered inches from his. His eyes widened, whether from fear or the sudden clarity of his own corruption, I couldn't tell. "Oh, I understand perfectly, Father," I said. "And before the night ends, you will too."

Anger, disgust, and even a trace of pity burned just beneath the surface. But underneath it all was something colder: the satisfaction of knowing this was the end he'd earned. This was justice. He had spent years preying on the vulnerable, twisting faith into something foul. Now, he was finally going to face what he'd buried for so long.

I stared into his eyes as he trembled. He needed to see it, every lie, every mask, every illusion he'd sold to the town. "The Lord says in Matthew, Chapter Seven, Verse Fifteen: 'Beware of false prophets, who come to you in sheep's clothing, but inwardly are ravenous wolves.'" I let the words settle between us as I savored the sting of its truth. "Tell me, Father, do you feel like a wolf now? Do you feel your sins clawing their way through your skin?"

Father Frederick's face tightened with shame and fear. The self-righteous preacher, the man who had once held a position of moral superiority, now knelt before me, exposed.

"Please?" His voice broke as the word slipped out. He lowered his head, shaking. "I was supposed to lead them . . . I was supposed to be pure . . ."

I scoffed and stepped closer, my voice dropping to a whisper. "You were never pure, Father. You preyed on the innocent. You betrayed everyone who trusted you." Contempt hardening each word. "And now? Look at you, bound, broken, and kneeling like a pathetic shell of a man before me."

Violet, standing just beyond us, remained still, her expression unreadable. She was watching and waiting, her lips parted slightly as she observed how I held this moment.

I slipped a hand beneath the edge of my skirt and drew a knife from the garter strapped to my upper thigh, the cold steel gleaming under the dim light. The room seemed to grow darker with the anticipation of what was about to happen. The silence was charged with violence, yet before I could make my move, something shifted. I could smell it before I saw it, the biting, acrid scent of smoke creeping into the room.

My eyes snapped to the window, catching the faintest flicker of light in the distance. It grew steadily, spreading slowly at first, then with mounting speed. A fire had started. Flames now licked the sides of the brothel, inching upward.

I muttered under my breath, dread knotting in my chest. "No . . ."

Violet's voice interrupted me. "What's going on?"

I said nothing, moving swiftly to the window. The townsfolk surged forward, torches in hand, fueled by the fury Father Frederick had stoked with his sermons. They thought they were doing God's work; they thought they were purging the evil he had convinced them the brothel was. The inferno spread fast, the town's wrath finally unleashed.

I turned back toward Father Frederick, my eyes narrowing with a mix of anger and frustration; the man had become the very thing he had once condemned. I had planned to end this tonight, to rid myself of the man who had caused so much pain and destruction, but there was no time now. His rabid, frenzied sermons about the sins at my brothel had become the weapon that would destroy him.

"You won't get away with this," I hissed, my voice filled with fury. "You'll burn for your sins, Father, but it won't be at my hands, it will be at your own. You and your lies, and your so-called purity, hiding the sickness you've spread in this town. You were never the shepherd."

A shout rang up from the street, unleashing a wave of noise that spilled into the room. The fire raced ahead, too quickly to stop. I could hear the voices of the desperate townsfolk, some shouting in righteous fury, others frantic with panic, all driven by a single purpose. Their eyes were fixed on their target, and nothing would stand in their way.

The room now felt suffocating, the smoke thickening as it seeped through the cracks between the bricks and the floorboards. I had no time to linger; the fire was getting closer. There was nothing left for Father Frederick, nothing left for the brothel. It would all burn, consumed by the very hatred and fear he had ignited.

As I quickly made to leave, I stopped at the door, my back to him, voice cold as I glanced back once more. "Father Frederick, I hope you've repented, because this is where your story ends."

Violet and I stepped out into the hallway, the roar of the fire swelling in my ears, drowning out Father Frederick's desperate cries behind us.

In the parlor, Emil, Nell, Elona, and Maeve had barricaded the front doors, desperate to keep the unpredictable mob from storming the brothel. They assumed the plan was to break in and destroy the place, but they didn't grasp the true threat until the first wisps of smoke filled the air. Rushing to the windows, they saw the flames already climbing skyward, beginning to swallow the building. Outside, the townsfolk were frantic, throwing themselves at the doors of the brothel, determined to destroy everything inside.

Emil shouted for everyone to evacuate, guiding them out the back, away from the chaos. The heat from the fire was unbearable, but the danger of the growing mob was even worse.

Violet and I were the last to leave, the smoke stinging our lungs as we reached the alleyway. I glanced back at the blazing inferno that had once been my sanctuary, my home, and the source of everything I held dear. The flames roared as the fire devouring everything it touched. The crackle of burning wood mingled with the angry shouts of the townsfolk in the distance.

The Oily Cat was reduced now to ash and smoke, but the people were even worse than the fire.

The townsfolk—neighbors, customers, familiar faces—stood in clusters near the brothel and across the street. Some stared with open horror. Others stood gazing at the blazing maelstrom with rapturous smiles pasted on their zealous faces. A few still held torches, their grips unsteady, flames flickering in the wind. The destruction, the violence, it had excited them. Given them purpose.

Emil, who had been checking to make sure everyone had made it out safely and now led us toward the mouth of the alley and away from the building, suddenly stopped in his tracks. Then, as if in slow motion, I watched him come undone.

His eyes found a man smiling garishly; his expression making it clear he had no regrets about what he had just done. He was a short, paunchy fellow named Harlan Miller, who'd once tipped Nell a coin for pouring him a little more than a thumb's worth of his favorite whiskey. Harlan's face was bathed in firelight, his grin wide and sickening.

That was all it took. Emil surged toward him.

"Emil!" Nell shouted, but her voice didn't reach him.

He grabbed Harlan by the collar and slammed him backward into a hitching post, cracking the wood. Harlan tried to shout, to speak, but Emil's fist met his mouth, silencing him. Once, twice. By the third strike, blood painted Emil's knuckles.

"You set it on fire." He growled, shaking as he continued to beat Harlan in the face. An older man in a vest and spectacles tried to intervene. Emil turned on him with such speed and force that his right hook sent the man reeling and shattered his glasses. Those in the crowd that were now beginning to watch the violence gasped, but no one moved to stop him.

He grabbed a shovel from a nearby stoop and swung it wide, knocking a younger man off his feet with a sickening thud. People began to scatter, but Emil didn't chase them. He lashed out at anyone who hadn't already run, his rage indiscriminate and raw.

From several paces behind him, Maeve watched with wide eyes, her breath coming in quick, sharp bursts. She looked to Elona, then to Nell. Then I saw something visibly shift in her.

"They were going to kill us," Maeve hissed. "They were *glad* to." She kicked off her shoes and bolted forward, skirts hiked in her fists.

The first woman she reached tried to shield her face, but Maeve didn't stop. Her fists landed fast and hard, fueled by weeks, *years,* of swallowed shame. The woman went down screaming, and Maeve stood over her, panting, shaking, and defiant.

Elona followed without a word. She struck silently with an elbow, a knee, then a brutal slap that sent a man stumbling into a wall. He tried to find his voice to speak, but Elona shoved him hard, headfirst into the corner of the next building on the street. A sharp *crack* split the air, followed by the slow, dark stream of blood tracing down his face before his body crumpled to the ground.

Nell stood frozen for a breath, holding herself aloof from the chaos, but then she saw Emil again. His face was streaked with soot, blood drying at the corner of his mouth where he'd been struck. He'd always been her strength, but night, he was breaking. She clenched her fists, turned slowly, and found the woman who had once spit on her dress outside the church. That woman stood at the edge of the fray, eyes wide. "You called me filth." Nell whispered, glaring directly at her face.

Then she lunged. The two of them hit the ground, Nell landing on top. Her fists flew, untrained, furious, and wild. The woman's screams turned to gurgles before someone tried to pull Nell off of her, but Nell snarled and swung, catching the would-be rescuer hard in the temple with her elbow.

Violet stood beside me, her face, chest, and arms covered in soot, and her left sleeve had been burned from the embers of the fire. But her eyes were eerily calm. I'd seen her like this only once before, full of building fury. She caught a glimpse of movement down the alley, a man trying to slink off unnoticed, hoping the fire and noise would cover his retreat. But Violet knew him. So did I. He used to leave coins wrapped in torn hymnal pages on our nightstand after we gave him what he wanted, like he could pay for his sins and still sleep beside his wife at night.

Violet moved without a word. She darted down the alley and caught up to him before he'd taken three steps. He turned, startled, stammering something that might've been her name, but it was too late. She slammed him into the wall hard enough to shake soot from the bricks. The torch dropped from his hand and fizzled in the dirt. She got close to his ear, close enough to whisper, and whatever she said, it drained the color from his face. Then she drove her knee into his ribs.

He collapsed with a grunt and didn't get back up. Violet didn't look back. She just wiped her mouth with the back of her hand and walked back toward me. That was when I moved, no longer paralyzed by shock, the adrenaline coursing through my body pushing me into the melee.

My brothel, *my home*, lay in ruins behind me. Burned by the very people who had filled it, fed off it, leaned on it like a crutch and then cursed it when the sun came up.

And they thought they could light it on fire and walk away clean? Not tonight.

It was at that moment when I noticed her, across the square. A woman in a dark shawl, torch still clutched in both hands, though the flame had long gone out. She wasn't taking part in the fighting. She stood on the edge of it all, hands tight, face pale. But her mouth, *her mouth was smiling.*

Mrs. Henderson. *That bitch*. I walked straight toward her, ignoring the sudden look of fear on her face. She took a step back, but I didn't slow; my heels ground into the gravel, my hands curling slowly at my sides. "You don't belong here," I hissed, echoing the words she'd so often thrown at me. My voice was steady, almost calm as I closed the distance between us. And then I hit her, *hard*. My open hand cracked across her face, the sound sharp as a whip. Her head snapped to the side, a spray of spit—or blood—flecking the air.

She staggered, lost her footing, and went down hard. Her knees buckled first, then her whole body folded, awkward and graceless. She hit the ground with a dull thud, her shawl twisting around her like a dropped bedsheet. Her hands flew up, covering the red bloom already spreading across her cheek.

I stood over her without saying another word. She looked up at me with horror when she realized what I was holding in my hand. I took the dead torch that lay beside her, reached into the burning gas lamp behind me, and lit the torch again. The flame came to life with a low *whuff,* and I lowered it right to the hem of her dress.

She froze. Her breath snagged in her throat, a thin, trembling sound. I held the flame there, close enough for her to feel the heat kiss her skin, to make her flinch. Sweat gathered at her temple. Her eyes welled, wide and glistening, and her lips quivered as though she might beg, but no words came.

"You wanted to see a whore burn?" I said, my voice almost gentle, though my heart was pounding hard enough to shake my ribs. "Here's your chance." The flame hovered, catching the edge of her dress. A thin curl of smoke rose, the scent of singed fabric winding between us.

God, every part of me *wanted* to. Every piece of me screamed to do it. To let the flame leap up her self-righteous robes and burn her ass to a crisp.

But I didn't. I eased the torch back and leaned in until our breaths tangled, until her pupils floated like dark coins. "You destroy what you fear," I whispered, each word a low blade. "I face it. That's the difference between you and me."

I dropped the torch beside her, the flame still hungry, licking at the dirt, and turned away. I'd let her sit in the heat. Let her decide whether she wants to feel the flame, or finally face what she's done.

There was no more civility. No restraint. Just smoke, fire, and blood in the dust. More of the crowd had begun to flee. A few tried to shout for the sheriff, others simply ran, skirts bunched, boots clattering against cobblestone. But it didn't matter anymore, the damage was done.

Emil stood over a groaning man, chest heaving, eyes hollow. Maeve leaned on a fence post, blood dripping from her knuckles. Nell's hands were trembling. Elona was silent, but her dress was torn, her jaw set like stone. They hadn't just lost their home; they'd lost something much deeper. And for one long moment, the town saw them, not as whores, or sinners, or women to be scorned, but as something far more dangerous: humans, pushed into a corner and forced to fight.

Violet, Elona, and Maeve stood beside me, and I watched them as a mother watches her daughters live in a world where they will never be loved as they should be. Hoping that world might learn to fear them instead. The mob was gone now, scattered like pathetic trash. Cowards, all of them. Thinking that fire would break us, that shame would silence us. Instead, they'd given us the strength to resist them.

I looked at my girls with blood on their lips, eyes full of rage, and I knew, as sure as I'd ever known anything, that though they had taken the building we inhabited, they hadn't broken *us*. We were still standing, still breathing, and still full of fight. They'd lit the match, but we'd survived the fire. And now, they'd have to live knowing we were still here, holding each other up, unburned where it mattered most.

I looked toward the sky and caught sight of the window in the room where Father Frederick had been left behind. His body, bound and helpless, would never escape the flames. And so, he burned, consumed by the very fire he had kindled; a man undone by his own secrets.

I stood there and watched as he burned in his house of sin.

Enjoyed your stay at House of Sin?

Scan the QR codes below to leave a review

GoodReads

Amazon

Acknowledgements

As I wrap up this literary adventure, I find myself filled with gratitude, awe, and just a touch of disbelief that I actually pulled this off.

First, a huge shoutout to my husband, **Patrick**, whose unwavering support and endless patience have kept me grounded through the wild ride of writing. You are my rock, my confidant, and the best sounding board a writer could ask for (even when the "sound" is mostly me ranting about fictional people like they're real).

To my four amazing sons—**Lavio, Vallin, Merrick, and Samuel**, thank you for being my daily inspiration and reminding me that life is as chaotic as it is beautiful. Your laughter, antics, and general boy-energy provide the perfect backdrop to my creative musings, and I wouldn't trade our family adventures for anything in the world.

To my editors, **Briana & Kayla**, thank you for bravely diving into the hot mess that was my manuscript when I decided to try a new writing method. (Spoiler: it was chaos. Actual chaos. Like a dumpster fire with glitter.) You not only made sense of it, but helped me shape it into something I'm proud of.

To my **friends and family,** thank you for your support and for giving me a big enough head to think I can do absolutely anything I set my mind to. Truly, the confidence you've instilled in me is borderline dangerous. (World domination next? Stay tuned.)

To **Hailey**, thank you for checking your Instagram messages. Without that, I wouldn't have the beautiful art that graces these pages. I hope you know how talented you truly are.

And Finally, to my **readers**, your enthusiasm, curiosity, and willingness to dive into my worlds make every late night, every early morning, and every "what the hell am I doing?" moment worth it. You are the reason I keep turning the page and chasing the next story.

Here's to the power of words, and the love of family and friends. Together, they keep me inspired and ready to take on whatever comes next, preferably with a good cup of coffee in hand.

With all my love,

Brittnay J. Sears

About the author

Brittnay J Sears writes the kind of stories that blend dark wit with emotional grit, and has a flair for crafting characters who make terrible decisions for delicious reasons. A former bookstore and coffee shop owner, she's spent years surrounded by the smell of old paper and espresso—two of her greatest loves, rivaled only by gothic history, and characters with questionable morals.

When she's not writing, Brittnay is usually brewing new story ideas, traveling, crafting, reading, or enthusiastically avoiding the general population. On any given day, she can also be found watching horror movies and murder documentaries for "research", curating playlists that swing effortlessly from Lil'Kim to Ella Fitzgerald and everything in between or causing harmless chaos among her friends and family. She excels equally at unintentional comic relief and intentional mischief, depending on the occasion.

If you'd like to keep up with her writing, bookish life, and general shenanigans, you can find her on social media at @brittnayjsearsauthor

www.ingramcontent.com/pod-product-compliance
Lightning Source LLC
LaVergne TN
LVHW091138150826
845672LV00005B/978

* 9 7 9 8 9 9 3 1 1 9 1 0 6 *